Rumor's FURY

Harlow Brown

CHOSEN ONES BOOK TWO

A Note about The Chosen Series

Welcome to the second story in The Chosen series, *Rumor's Fury*
It is recommended that each book be read in order; however,
they are all standalones.

WARNING:

For Mature Audience 18+
Contains Adult Sexual Situations & Language
Most situations in this book are fictitious and are for story-
telling only. They might sound outlandish to you,
and that is okay. It is FICTION.

Dedication

This book goes out to anyone who has lost a special person who was far too young and has been left wondering what life would be like if they were still around. It goes out to anyone with a broken heart full of grief and mourning. My family experienced this unfair catastrophe, and our lives were forever changed. We will always have a hole in our souls. The one thing this kid taught me, without even knowing what he'd done, was don't look back. Never look back, because life is short. Live, laugh, love with no regrets. Eat the chips, buy the shoes, and take the trip.

Forever in our hearts and minds. We love you, Shithead.

~Don't Look Back~

Rumor's

FURY

Prologue

"Eric, I'm pregnant," Daisy said.

"What? Since when?"

"Since about six weeks ago when you knocked me up, it appears." She looked at me with those big brown eyes and that slightly pregnant glow. Or was it nausea? Whatever it was, I wanted to see it forever.

"Marry me." A simple statement blurted out instead of a sweet romantic proposal with some thought put into it.

"Yes."

"That's it?" I said with a look of shock and disbelief.

"That's it. It's that simple. This is the easiest decision I've ever made. I love you, and despite that group of thugs you hang out with, I know you're a good guy. I know you'll do right by me and our child. Your friends need help, or a boot to the head, but you're good people, Eric. You have to start seeing that you're better than what people say you are." Her eyes went soft and she looked at me like a mother would her child when she's reassuring them that everything will be all right, and that she loved them no matter what.

"I want to believe you, but I'm only as good as the company I keep. These guys have been with me through the good, bad, and the ugly. Then there's you. The crazy girl who hangs with a thug trying to make him a better person. You know some of the shit I've done. I'm no good for you, but I'm too damn selfish to let you go, and now I have you forever. Are you sure you're willing to take me on?"

"Positive, and I don't care what you've done. Living in the past and saying, 'Well, I did this and I did that so I'm worthless as tits on a boar and you don't deserve me,' isn't making this any better. Your parents taught you right from wrong, and you just need to believe in yourself that you're better than your buddies. Find new ones. Those guys are nothing but bad news."

"They're all right too, you just have to know them. They come from good people too. We just—"

"Hush. It doesn't matter. I don't care about what others think of you. I don't care who you hang around. I know you, the real you, and I know you'll take care of us."

"Until the end of time." I kissed her, infusing it with how much she and our unborn child meant to me.

I would take care of them, no matter the cost.

Chapter 1

FURY

A few months later

O N MY OWN IN a town I didn't know, I was lost in every way imaginable. The hustle and bustle of the street did nothing to drown out the noise in my head. Mind clouded with memories, I walked into a pub and ordered a Jack and Coke, easy on the Coke. Maybe I could drink myself over it. Maybe that ol' song was wrong and her memory wouldn't drown the whiskey. Maybe it'd be the other way around.

Behind me, I heard, "I know we need help, damn it. I'll find someone. I actually have a prospect in mind. A friend called in a favor, and I like to have people in my back pocket if I need them. When the time is right, I'll approach him. I'm just waiting and watching things for now. But until I find us a replacement VP, you're filling that title. I know you don't want it and don't want the weight it carries, but I don't recall asking you. Good, I thought you'd see things my way. Talk when I get back."

Not giving two shits about what I'd heard, I downed my drink and ordered another. Then another. Then another. After five or six, I paid my tab and staggered out of the pub in search of a hotel. I found one that was less than desirable, but drunk, heartbroken guys didn't really need much. I remembered free-falling onto the mattress and that was it, lights out. I had officially survived day one of my new life.

Three or four days later, I was walking the streets of Panama City Beach, Florida, strolling down memory lane, when a spunky-looking bastard walked up beside me and tried to take my backpack. I'd be damned if I let him take literally all I had left. As he tried to snag the backpack from me, I countered and took him off guard, flipping him to his back. All of my frustrations left my body via my fists. Ol' dude was tougher than I gave him credit for though. We scrapped back and forth for a while, drawing the attention of more and more people. In the distance, I could hear sirens, horns, and the words of encouragement from onlookers. He hit me with a force to be reckoned with and sent me for a loop.

Conveniently enough for me, I heard pipes from a motorcycle rumbling near. Then all at once, it cut to silence and the other dude immediately stopped his assault on me, giving me a chance to get the last blow. The man on the bike must've been some sort of god. The way the guy I was fighting stopped in his tracks at the presence of the lone biker told me something was different about this guy.

"Name's Chief. How you doin'? You lost?"

"Something like that."

"Come with me, and I'll get you some food and some coffee."

Sounded like I didn't have a choice, and I was hungry, so I obliged. It was better than my other option of walking the streets alone.

He took me to a little diner called Flap Jacks. I ordered a stack of six pancakes, a side of three fried eggs, three pieces of bacon, and a piece of toast alongside my glass of orange juice and cup of coffee.

"How long has it been since you ate a proper meal, kid?" Chief asked.

"Couple of days."

"Listen, I'm going to cut the bullshit. I've been watching you for a few days. I'll help you out. From the looks of things, you could use a little. I want nothing in return except loyalty."

"What the fuck do you mean?"

"Just exactly what I said. It ain't hard to understand. Do you want the help or not?" Annoyance seeped from his pores.

"Keep talking."

"I'll offer you a brotherhood like you've never had. No worries of being stabbed in the back."

"Wait, how does this benefit you?"

"I get someone who has my back and helps run my business."

"How do you know I won't turn on you?" I asked.

"I see it in your face. You're loyal. Seems you drew the short straw and could use the help."

"I have nothing to offer."

"Good. I don't want anything except a loyal person. I need a good brother to assist me here at the Chosen Legion. I trust you'll make the right choice."

Without thinking more of it, I decided I really had nothing else to lose and everything to gain. "I'm in."

"Come on. Let's go get you aquatinted with your new friends and discuss prospecting."

"Prospecting?"

"Well sure. You don't get to just be a part of my organization. You have to earn it. You have an upper hand though. I *want* you to be a part of the Chosen Legion. I'm on your side, kid. Remember that. Also, it'll give you a sense of belonging. It'll be good for you."

I nodded at him and finished my coffee.

"You don't have a place to stay, do you?"

"No, I don't."

"You can stay in the clubhouse. It's really nice. You'll

have your own room and can earn your keep there. Once you've been voted in, you'll start getting a cut of the profits."

I lifted my glass. "Here's to forgetting an old life."

"No," he barked at me.

"No?"

"If you forget your old life, you lose sight of who you're trying to become, and if you do that, you could fall right back into old habits. Those habits will end up getting you killed here, kid. Remember that. Don't look back. Never forget, but don't look back. You can't return to your old life, so don't spend your time in the past. Here's a card with the address to the clubhouse. You can't miss it. I'll see you when you get there. Take your time if you need to. Don't rush this. It's kind of a big decision, not one to be taken lightly. I do look forward to you being one of us though."

He got up, grabbed the ticket off the table, and paid the cashier. Heading outside, he mounted his bike and rode off back to God knew where, to do God knew what.

Seeing as my options were pretty limited, I lit a cigarette and decided to take off in search of the clubhouse.

It wasn't lost on me how odd the last hour had been. Did the biker know something about me? How did he magically appear? Why did the other guy just stop his assault on me?

Of course, I was the one trusting him, so perhaps I needed my head examined.

I don't have anything better right now, so I'm taking this.

The guy seemed legit enough. He looked me in the eye, never flinched or acted suspicious in any way, and he welcomed me to the clubhouse. Who did that for a stranger?

He had to know something more than he was telling me though. It just didn't make sense. Something wasn't adding up.

I guess my only option at this point is to watch myself and find out what exactly he knows.

Chapter 2

FURY

Upon setting my eyes on this place, my mind went into overdrive. It was huge and looked like a beach house, not a clubhouse. It was so nice that I asked myself just how lucrative his business could actually be, and if it was even legal. That was one thing I was trying to get away from, part of what cost me my life as I once knew it.

"Hey, fucker, you need to be getting out of here. We ain't buyin' anything, we don't have any use for a vacuum, we're registered to vote and our opinion isn't going to be swayed by your input, and we aren't interested in anything you have to offer unless it's thin mint Girl Scout cookies," I heard from the porch. When I looked to see who it was, I realized he had to be a member.

Damn. Do I really look like a door-to-door salesman?

"Chief told me to come here. I'm…."

"You're who? You got about ten seconds to explain yourself before I remove you."

I had to remember the name that was given to me. It was on my ID, but I hadn't looked at it nor needed it since I got here. I'd been living off of cash and hadn't driven, so there wasn't a need for my license to be pulled out.

"Five, six, seven."

"Legend. Legend Morrow."

"Come in, then, Legend. You're a shady-looking fucker, aren't you?"

"It's none of your business, partner." This dude was full-fledged asshole, which I supposed fit the typical biker persona. Once I was face-to-face with him, I realized I'd been scuffling with him just a while ago.

"You throw a good punch. You'll do fine here. I saw firsthand that you take no shit and you can hold your own. You did well against me, and I have registered hands. Welcome to the clubhouse," he said.

"You throw a mean punch yourself. I thought some of those moves were UFC style. Now, where do I stay, and how can I get started on learning this mystery business? And why did you try to steal my backpack? I ought to beat your ass now." I started to fume.

"Well, I took the bag to test you. We needed to know if you were tough enough to be one of us. And for the record, I used to cage fight. Chief told me to take you and show you around, so follow me. You can unpack your bag after we're done."

"Uh, so you got a name, or do I just say, 'Hey, you'?"

"Name is Magnum."

He took me upstairs to a nice room with a bed and a TV. Nothing fancy, but nicer than I'd ever had, with a dresser, decent-sized closet, and a queen-sized bed.

I gazed around, taking in my new space, and tried to wrap my head around what had happened to me in the last week. The longer I thought about it, I realized I'd never be able to wrap my head around it. It was a shitty situation, one I didn't see me overcoming anytime soon. It was a heartache that wouldn't stop hurting, a wound that would never heal, a memory I couldn't forget. Albeit one I had to live with.

I unpacked my things, which was a change of clothes and a couple of pictures of Daisy, no less. Not sure I could stand to see them daily, I tucked them away in a drawer. It was hard to have a lot of things when you'd had to leave it all behind.

In hopes of temporarily forgetting the events, I hurriedly put my few belongings away and went back downstairs to meet Magnum.

A couple of months passed and I did odd jobs for them, played bartender, and did anything else they asked of me. I had to prove I was one of them and not some imposter who was just going to take them down. Once I'd earned enough trust, they started taking me places and letting me in on more club stuff.

"You ready?" Magnum asked.

"As I'll ever be."

We went outside to load up. I didn't know what I thought we were riding in, but for some reason, an extended cab truck wasn't it. I was expecting more along the lines of a black utility van with only driver and passenger windows.

"You look confused."

"I just didn't expect the truck, that's all."

"Let's go. We need to hit up a couple of stores, so we fly under the radar. First things first, never buy all of your supplies at the same store or, if you can help it, on the same day. We're adding to our inventory, so you're getting in from the start, so to speak. You get to see everything from the beginning. Chief has a lot of faith in you for some reason, and he wants you to experience everything."

"He told me I was going to earn my keep around here. I guess I didn't realize I was about to learn everything so soon. I guess you guys stay pretty busy and orders are coming in steadily?"

"We've started doing business with more people, yes. One of our biggest buyers is asking for more at a time, and it's just going to be easier to own and operate three stills instead of two."

"Stills? You make moonshine?"

"Well we ain't making Kool-Aid. You okay with that? If not, you better hit the road now," Magnum snapped.

"Okay. How much does one still make?"

"One thing at a time, Legend. You'll see, but first you need to know what it takes to make a still. We're going in to buy the copper line from a home improvement store and a couple odds and ends that would make it look like we're redoing some plumbing. After that, we'll hit up another store and get the sheets of copper, plus other things that make it look like it's a home renovation project. We can get the burners and thermostats at the local department store up the road from the house, along with some oil and seasonings so it looks like we're frying a turkey or something."

"You've thought this through," I mumbled under my breath.

I thought about it for a minute and realized this was no different than what I was doing back home in Austin, only this was liquid form instead of powder. It was the same lifestyle that had ripped my world apart, and here I was in over my head again. The only two good things I could think of were that I knew how to fly under the radar and I had nothing left to lose if I went down. It was all in from here on out.

I was destined to be an outlaw. I couldn't live by the rules. I would learn to make the best whiskey around, and I'd make the most of this new life I had.

After picking up our supplies at the three different stores, we swung into a little dive and had a bite. I figured it was going to be awkward because I just knew he was going to ask questions. I didn't know him well enough to tell him anything, and I couldn't if I wanted to. Secrecy was the key to survival.

I ordered a double cheeseburger and large fries, and Magnum ordered a patty melt and order of onion rings. Both of us had a sweet tea. After the waitress took our order and brought our drinks, the inevitable happened.

"So, what's your story? Why did you end up with Chief?"

"That ain't something I can discuss, nor do I know you well enough to if I wanted to talk about it. Drop it and leave it alone. I won't tell you again," I warned, anger in my eyes.

"Legend ain't the right name for you, dude. Fury is more suiting. You always so pissy?"

"Look, I don't know you, and frankly I don't want to right now. I need some time to adjust to my new life and surroundings, and I don't want to discuss my past or open up about my feelings like some chick. I just want to know the basics of making a still and distilling some moonshine, so I can make some money. I have a point to prove to Chief, and I fully intend on making that happen. He said all things in time, and I need to accelerate that time, so I need for us to hurry up and get this production on the move. I have someone I need to see. Also, I have to prove my loyalty to you guys. I'm more than willing to do that, as I'm loyal beyond a shadow of a doubt. But I need time to think, to adjust, and to learn. I don't have time for making buddies and staying up late swapping stories about exes and painting our fingernails. If at any time you think I'm being a dick, just know that I probably am. I'll constantly and continually, no questions asked, have your back. Never doubt that. I owe you a great deal, seeing as you were a part of the reason I'm here. I didn't appreciate the brawl on the street, but now I see it was necessary. Do we understand each other?"

" I think you summed it up. You want to learn and not to make friends. I got it."

"Look, it's not that I don't want to make friends. It's difficult to explain, and I can't even if I wanted to. I want to call you and Chief friends, but I need space. I'm not some buddy-buddy guy. Just know that if I'm accepted into the Chosen Legion, every one of you will come before me. That's just how I roll. I'm loyal and I have my friends' backs when I know they have mine. Hell, even when they don't. I just don't like to talk much. I don't have a lot to say anymore." I finished my glass of sweet tea and flagged down the waitress for another.

Magnum didn't say much of anything else for the rest of the meal unless it was to answer a question I had about the still or shine. He really did know his stuff when it came to making moonshine. I had to give him that.

I wanted to feel bad for the way I was toward him, but I just couldn't make myself care enough to apologize. He knew when to stop, and I think he figured out that it wasn't that I *wouldn't* speak about things as much as I *couldn't*. I didn't question it, just let it go and appreciated the fact that he did too.

We finished our meal and headed back to the clubhouse. As we unloaded the supplies, my mind started racing, wondering what made Magnum just drop it so quickly. I figured he was entitled to his privacy just as I was asking for it. That meant no prying, and that was fine by me. I had all I could deal with already; I sure didn't need someone else's drama too.

I followed Magnum with armloads of copper and bags of supplies to the basement, where Chief was. He lifted his chin to me. The clubhouse must've cost them a fortune—no one had a basement on a beach, but it wasn't my business. I was grateful that the guys were willing to take in a stranger and show him the ropes of a lucrative business.

Magnum and Chief both got to cutting, soldering, shaping, and beating the copper pieces. The belly of the still was created with expert hands, and they polished and buffed the copper until it shone again. Once the construction was completed, we all went back upstairs to grab a beer.

"Tomorrow we'll start a batch. You'll get to experience the magic of making liquor," Chief joked.

"Sounds like a plan. Are you done with me?" I said with a yawn.

"We're good. We'll get the ingredients for the mash in the morning, we will use two vehicles and go to different stores. Be ready to go around eight, yeah?"

"Yeah, boss."

I headed up to the room that was now my new residence, stripped down to my boxers, and climbed into bed. Sleep claimed me, and the sight of my sweet Daisy filled my dreams.

Chapter 3

FURY

AFTER COFFEE, WE LOADED INTO two separate vehicles, me with Chief and Magnum solo. Inside the store, we gathered our necessary ingredients of sugar, yeast, and cheesecloth, then added TV dinners, lunch meat, bread, and cheese. Chief didn't say anything, just shook his head and grinned.

Back at the house, we got to work cracking the corn that Magnum purchased at a local feed store, putting it in buckets with water, sugar, and yeast. I hoped it tasted better than it smelled, because that smell alone was enough to steer anyone with a brain away from it. They had a batch ready that had been sitting for about a week, and it reeked of rotten corn.

"With today's technology, you'd think there'd be a way to do this that smelled better. This shit stinks."

Chief stuck his nose in the air and sniffed, then replied, "Smells like money, kid."

We got the pot cooking and ran off a batch of moonshine. Chief poured some on a piece of wood and lit it. I looked at him like he'd lost his mind, my unexperienced brain not grasping why they would waste any of the liquid gold.

"The bluer the flame is, the purer the whisky. You know you have a top-notch product if it's almost invisible." Chief demonstrated for me. "See there? Just a tinge of blue, but you can see the heat in the air. Watch this paper catch on fire," he said as he stuck the corner of a piece of paper into the clear part of the flame. I watched closely because I didn't want them pulling one over on me, but that paper never got close enough to the blue part of the flame to catch. There were actually clear flames coming from the piece of wood.

"There's a real science to this. Most people think it's a bunch of country bumpkins who look like Popcorn Sutton out in the middle of the woods cooking whiskey," Magnum piped up.

"The profit margin is huge. That's why we still do it. We sell it for $40 a quart, $80 for half a gallon, and we cut a deal for a whole gallon and sell it for $140 instead of the $160 it should be," Chief explained.

"So that's how you paid for this place?" I asked.

"Partly. It was a family home. My uncle passed it to me

because I was the only kid. But all of the upgrades came from shine profits."

I wondered to myself if any of them had gone to jail for getting caught but never asked. It wasn't the time or the place. I'd ask Chief later on when Mag wasn't around.

Drip, drip, drip, the clear liquid started filling up the catch container as it exited the worm. We were at the end of the batch. The first still, a fifty-gallon named Popcorn, ran off the biggest batch. Still two, Percolator, was our twenty-five gallon. Last but not least was our five-gallon still, Mighty Man. Our fifty-gallon still would likely produce about ten gallons of alcohol, Chief explaining that you could bank on around 20% of the vat size being actual shine. One full batch of whiskey from Popcorn alone stood to make us $1400.

Sitting in the basement with my newest allies making moonshine had me wondering how I let my life get so far out of control. How did I let drugs and bad decisions cost me my life as I knew it? How was it fair to Daisy? Why did she have to pay for my selfishness and stupidity? Now, because I was a dumbass, she was left to raise our son alone. I hoped for her sake that she found a partner who she loved as much as she did me, only I hoped he treated her better and loved my son as his own. She deserved more than I could ever have given her.

Trying to pull myself out of the funk I had fallen back into, I asked Magnum, "So when do we make a delivery? I assume you don't just stockpile the liquor."

"Sometimes we keep an extra gallon or so on hand, but to answer your question, we make a run tomorrow. One of our biggest buyers is here in town, Sully and his puppet Jay. They buy a shit ton of shine from us."

"How do you transport it?"

"Well", Chief started, "we put it in two-liter Sprite bottles, gallon jugs that water comes in, and tried and true Mason jars."

That made sense. It was clear and would look like Sprite or water, depending upon which container was being used. *Seems like they have it all thought out.* "Do they know I'm helping? I mean, are they going to freak out if they see a new guy on the scene?"

"No. They know not to question us, and I gave them a heads-up that we have a prospect. They should be fine."

After all the liquor was bottled up, I loaded it into the van, hiding several gallons out of sight under the seats. The Chosen Legion had thought of everything, getting a fabricator to make some in-floor storage compartments, which was where most of the loot was stored. No one would think to look under the seats for a hidden compartment, and if they did, it wouldn't be an easy thing to spot. The welder had done some of the best work I'd ever seen. There were no handles, so it looked like the original floor, and they stayed shut with magnets so there was no rattling. The members just used a bigger opposite-poled magnet to open the doors.

"You ready for your first run?" Chief asked me with a grin.

"Yes," I replied stoically.

"Load up. Magnum grab a couple of two-liter Cokes too, and some chips and snack cakes out of the cupboards. It'll look like a grocery run should we get stopped."

Genius. Either they'd learned from previous experience or they were just smarter than I gave a bunch of bikers credit for. It didn't matter though; these guys had street smarts I wished I would've had. Maybe then I wouldn't be here to begin with.

We pulled up outside a little shop called Sunset Tattoo. I got out and walked in, spotting a timid redhead. "Uh, is Jay around?" I asked her.

"Maybe, who are you?"

"Just tell him he has a delivery, darlin'. I'm fairly sure he's expecting it."

She walked off to the back and I heard her say, "I don't know who it is. Some dude, probably six-foot-six inches, talks with a southern drawl. He says you're expecting a delivery. Damn it, Jay, I said I don't know. Would you get off your dead ass and just go see what he wants?"

She doesn't take much shit from him.

She came back up front and resumed her place at the counter. "He'll be right out. You can look around a bit or have a seat, whatever you want."

"You do ink?"

"Yes."

"I have an idea that I want to make into a tattoo. If I explain it, do you think you can put it to skin?"

"They don't call me the best in town for no reason, mister."

"Got a pencil and a piece of paper?"

She slid it to me and I started sketching, drawing a window with the side of the wall shown too. In the window, there was a silhouette of a woman cradling her infant child facing the outside. There were some pine trees with a full moon that sat atop the tips of them. Down toward the bottom was a wolf howling at the moon. Under the sketch were the words 'Look at that moon,' something I used to tell Daisy when she was worried, upset, or just frazzled in general. It was my way of distracting her to free up her mind for a little while. It usually made her smile, which meant it worked like a charm.

When I was done, I slid it to her.

"I should be able to work with this. I can put in detail and shading to make it really stand out. It's very thought out. Who is this?"

"A special person in another time, a lifetime ago." The truth spilled out of my mouth before I could stop it. Thank God it sounded like memories of a broken heart being replayed by a love-sick fool instead of what it really was. No way could I tell her what it actually depicted. I couldn't tell anyone that.

"Let me guess, the wolf is crying out of pain and a broken heart, and the woman in the window is looking at the same moon, longing for her love to come back?"

"Something like that."

"Yes, I can do this for you. It'll take a lot of shadowing and intricate detail, so it won't be cheap. Where are you thinking you want it?"

"Name your price. I want it on the underside of my forearm."

"Seeing as it's a large tattoo and all of the detail work it's gonna take, you're looking around six hundred dollars."

"Deal. When I save the cash, I'll call you for an appointment. Do you have a card, miss?"

"Roxxi, and here you go." She slid me a card with her name and number on it.

"Who are you?" We both turned to the man coming out of the back .

"Jay, this is the man who said you had a delivery," Roxxi explained.

"What's your name, who are you with, and what do you have for me?" Jay spouted off in his best attempt at being intimidating. Truth was I towered over the guy and would snap him like a twig if he pushed me.

"I'm Legend. The Chosen Legion told me to drop by. Your delivery is outside."

"I don't know you. You new around here?"

"Look, asshole, I don't have time for meeting your

parents and all that warm and fuzzy bullshit. Either you come outside now and get your delivery, or I'm out and will resell it elsewhere. Choice is yours." I turned on a dime and walked out before I knocked the guy's block off.

"Jay, just go see what he has for you. Sully's going to be pissed if you screw up a deal. Don't be dense," Roxxi said. I could almost hear her eyes rolling.

He made the right decision and came outside to inspect his shipment. "You got yourself a real winner here, boys. He didn't take any shit I dished out at him."

"You knew who I was the whole time and still acted like that? Get your shit and give us the money. Next time don't play with me. I don't appreciate my time being wasted. I ought to tack on a twenty spot just to make up for the time I was explaining myself to you." This guy. There was something about him that I just didn't trust. He was crooked, and I'd prove it. I had a gut feeling about him.

After we unloaded, Chief stopped for gas, leaving Magnum and me in the van.

"That was good work back there. Jay's a dumb son of a bitch, and you handled him well. I have to be mean to him every time we make a deal. Just ain't got sense to poor piss out of a boot," Magnum said as he shook his head.

That warranted a chuckle out of me. I hadn't heard that saying in a long time. It took me back to a time when life was easy, back when I first met Daisy. Upon that memory, the chuckles stopped abruptly.

"Dude, you okay? Looks like you seen a ghost."

"Uh, yeah, I'm fine. Just shaking off an old memory, that's all. Not one I care to relive. Kind of hit me out of nowhere," I lied. I knew exactly where it came from. The same place all the other unwelcome memories of her came from. Deep down in my heart, in my mind. I was never free of them. The memories were both a blessing and a curse. I wouldn't trade them for the world but would love to stop remembering them for just a little while.

I felt like I needed a break. I needed to get out of my head. The more I thought and remembered, the more I thought about not thinking and remembering. It was a vicious cycle, one I didn't see breaking soon, if ever.

"You all right, man?" Magnum asked.

"Drop it. It's nothing," I barked.

"Whatever, princess. You're a moody fucker."

"What are you two bickering about?" Chief said as he got back in the van.

"Nothing important. Just that Legend don't fit him at all. He needs to be Fury for real. All of the time. Dude is moody. And it's usually pissy." Magnum said without second thought.

"Fine, then. Fury it is," Chief confirmed.

I guessed I wasn't going anywhere anytime soon, seeing as they named me and all.

Chapter 4

FURY

Present Day

"WHAT DO YOU MEAN WE'RE having a house full of girls stay here?" I asked, annoyance clear in my tone.

"Whiskey has a situation that he needs help with. His girl is in some kind of trouble. She plays for a women's softball team, and they're playing in a big tournament in Panama City Beach. He asked us for a favor, and that's what brothers do. He'd do the same for you if you needed it, no questions asked, so get over it," Magnum said with irritation. "Damnation, you're the only dude I know who would be pissed about a house full of women. You need to loosen up and get a girlfriend. Or a fuck buddy. Something, geez."

"I assume Chief knows about this?"

"Nope. We were just going to welcome trouble to our doorstep without clearing it with the president." Magnum really was a sarcastic punk; however, that time he had me dead to rights. It was a stupid thing to ask. But I was finally not thinking about Daisy every time I turned around, and now this shit.

I had been to see Daisy a handful of times in the years past, but I couldn't speak, couldn't get her attention. I couldn't go hold my newborn son, Eric. I knew his name because I saw the stork sign staked in the yard with his birth weight and length—eight pounds and ten ounces, twenty-one inches. He was an extremely hefty boy, obviously taking after me.

He was almost four now. I checked on them still from time to time, though I'd accepted the fact that the situation just was what it was.

The hardest pill for me to swallow was when I saw another man at my house, kissing my girl and holding my boy. That hit hard, and I never really recovered. It made me more bitter and angrier. Was he a good guy? Would he willingly take care of them just like I wanted from the beginning? I didn't expect it to hurt that bad when I saw it with my own eyes. It wasn't his fault though. I wasn't mad at him, or her, just still broken over the whole situation.

I'd never be whole again. My heart would always have a void in it that would never be filled. I hadn't been back to see them since the night I saw their shadows in the window about two years ago. That was my sign that she was okay and she'd moved on, just as I wanted. She'd moved on and I never would. It was my fault it was happening anyway, so it was only right that I be the one to suffer for eternity.

I'd accepted the fact that I'd be lonely all my life. That was fine. I had my brothers, my club, and my bike. I didn't need anything else. I could always find a side fling for a night or two when I need it. No strings attached—we didn't exchange numbers, and usually didn't exchange names. Unattainable and nameless. That was the way it had to be for me nowadays.

I couldn't be responsible for the downfall of another woman. Clearly I couldn't be in a regular relationship, one that had no secrets. My entire life was a secret. I couldn't undo that. I'd always be a mystery to most because I was incapable of honesty and having feelings—ones of love and acceptance, anyway. The only ones I had an abundance of were self-loathing and anger. There wasn't enough room in my cold, dead heart for love and affection for anyone other than Daisy and baby Eric, the two people who could never know how much I still loved them.

I had the brotherhood of a lifetime, the bike of my dreams, and a job making moonshine. I finally earned enough to purchase an Indian Chieftain. The guys liked to give me shit because it wasn't a Harley-Davidson, but I just took it in stride. My bike was more eye-catching than theirs ever thought about being, dark blue with black leather saddlebags and fringe. The chrome on it made the bike stand out, the darkness of the blue against the crisp clean shine. It was sleek and smooth and not as deafening as a hog. Most bikes turned heads, but mine stopped people in their tracks, and made them back up to inspect it. There was something to be said for the first American-made bike on the road. Harley has that title but if one does the homework, it was Indian that started it all. After I put all the guys in their place with their motorcycle facts, they shut up and left me alone. I pulled out all the stops. Google, encyclopedias, library books—you name it, I used it to prove my point.

I didn't need the distraction of a house full of women. My life had finally found its new normal, and I for sure didn't want to have that slight bit of normalcy varied in any way.

"You know I don't like change."

"Fury, look, if it were you in this situation, we'd help you and your girl too. Deal with it," Magnum clipped.

"Fine, I get it. I just don't like it."

"Who knows? Maybe you'll find your forever girl."

"Not fuckin' likely. My forever girl is gone, and I won't ever see her again." I surprised myself when I said it aloud.

Apparently I looked like someone had kicked my puppy because Magnum asked, "Man, are you okay? I'm not one for sharing secrets and having heart-to-hearts, but you look like something inside is eating you alive. You need anything?"

"No. That ship's sailed."

"Whatever, dude. It's written all over your face that whatever happened to mystery girl isn't out of your head yet."

"No. And it never will be." I turned and walked away before I said or did something I'd regret. Anger lit me up inside as I walked away, my secret weighing heavy on my chest at the moment.

I needed an out. A ride would clear my mind, and I could sort through my thoughts and rein in my frustrations.

I shut my eyes and took a deep breath before I started up my bike, and took off. When I got in these funks, the only thing that helped was riding. There was something about going fast on two wheels with the wind in my face and the humming of the tires against the pavement that was so relaxing and tranquil. All of the thoughts running rampant in my head were silenced and hushed, buried deep in my psyche until the next time they returned unannounced.

I found myself riding westbound on I-10 at speeds fast enough to outrun my memories and thoughts of times past, never hearing the wind, pipes, or sounds of traffic flying by as I breezed past them.

I was on a mission. I wasn't sure it was a smart one, but one I had to do. I couldn't go on like I had been for the past two years. I had to see her again. See for myself once and for all that she'd moved on and was living her life, as if the last time wasn't enough. I would see her this time and wouldn't return to the likes of Austin again. This was my farewell. My 'till we meet again.' My one last time, for real this go-round.

About twelve hours later, after a couple of gas stops and bathroom breaks, I pulled up in front of the house I used to occupy. She'd done work to the yard, giving it curb appeal that was lacking when I lived there. Pretty magnolia trees perfectly lined the driveway; azaleas and hibiscus, her favorite, filled the flower beds to either side of the front porch. Bright pinks and reds popped out against the house's new paint color—gray. I never liked it and would always tell her no when she talked about it. I guess she finally got her way.

I saw movement in the window, so I started moving slowly until I noticed a small boy. I couldn't stop staring at him. He looked like the man in my mirror with his red-brown hair, hazel eyes, and freckles. I had freckles as a kid, though I seemed to have outgrown them.

To my surprise, he waved at me. I didn't realize he saw me, so I waved back as my heart swelled. I'd just made contact with my child, the one I would never speak to or hug. The one who better off without me in his life.

While caught up in my temporary mental lapse, I saw Daisy come to the window. I was stuck, frozen in place.

The window was open, and I heard her say, "Eric, who are you waving at?" Her voice was the same as it always was, able to hold me in a trance and make me give in to whatever she wanted. That voice could reason with me when no one else could.

He replied in his innocent young voice, "I don't know, Momma. Some man on a motocycle."

She looked out the window and stared at me just as I stared at her. Though I knew who she was, she didn't recognize me. My hair was much longer now, I'd been working out so I was muscled up, and I had tattoos that I didn't have then. She'd changed too, but she was still as gorgeous as ever. She waved at me and nudged our son away from the window.

And just like that, I knew I was done. If she didn't recognize me, even with my changed appearance, she was over me. But why would she have even *thought* it was me? I was dead to her. She buried me, as did the whole damn town.

I had to move on now. I had no more business moping around. I had to start living again. She had, and our son was clearly doing well. Life turned out just like I'd wished for them.

Better off without me.

As hard as it was to accept that, there was a novel feeling of closure.

With one last look around the place that used to be

home, I revved up the bike and headed back east. Twelve hours of riding for a five-minute stop wasn't a fair trade, but it was what it was.

I decided for everyone on the road's sake and safety that I should probably get a room for the night. I needed a beer anyway, so I pulled off at a gas station about three hours east to get more gas, a six-pack of Sam Adams, and smoke a cigarette. I needed something stout tonight.

Before I drank myself into a somber state of being, I decided to text Chief.

Me: Had to get out of town for a bit. I'm fine. Staying in hotel tonight. Be back tomorrow sometime.

Chief: You sure?

Me: Yeah, I'm good now. Just needed a breather. Clear my head.

Chief: You didn't do anything stupid, did you?

He knew me better than most and knew roundabout what I was doing. I'd never come right out and said what I was doing when I left on my solo tangents, though I wouldn't lie to him. He just didn't know who or what I was trying to get out of my head.

Me: Not too stupid. I'm done now. I won't be coming back. Saw what I had to see and accomplished what I came to accomplish. I'll be back tomorrow sometime.

I hit Send, then popped open a beer. My phone rang and I checked the caller ID, seeing it was Chief. I decided I didn't really want to talk to anyone and just let it ring.

He was a relentless bastard though and kept calling until I answered.

"Yeah?" I said with no hint of emotion in my voice.

"Next time you feel like going off and getting your feelings in check, you might want to clue someone in first."

"Didn't know I needed a keeper. Sorry. Don't worry though. Like I said, I won't be leaving to come back here again."

"You all right?"

He knew I was vulnerable and unstable at the moment, but he also knew I wasn't going to do anything extreme. I had a club to help run, so I had to be coming back with my head on straight.

While I waited on his wise words of wisdom, I drank my second beer.

"Fury, I won't ever understand why you do what you do. Nor would I want to understand you. Your head has got to be a scary place sometimes, battling the person you used to be before the club and the person you are now. I think you're a moron for not at least telling us where you were going, and you need your jaw jacked for leaving without telling anyone, but if it gave you what you needed to finally move on with whatever the hell you need to move on from, then great. We need you here. You're an integral part of our family and a huge part of how our system works, and it would seriously suck if you weren't here with us. I gave you a chance four years ago for a reason. I need you. So get your feelings sorted out, and I'll see you tomorrow."

"Chief, I meant it. I won't be coming back here. I got the closure I've needed for so long now. I'll be home tomorrow sometime. Tonight I'm going to finish a sixer of beer and close this chapter of my life."

"Kid, you can't just turn it off like a damn light. You might be able to move on now, but it'll still take some time to get over. You're tough but you're still human. Whatever you're trying to drink away won't be fixed by a six-pack and a smoke. Everything happens for a reason. Just be careful and don't do anything stupid." He paused, then said, "Fury, once in, always first. Remember that."

He ended the phone call with a statement that I couldn't have needed to hear more. He always had a way of making me see what was truly important.

I finished my beers and said out loud as I laid my head down, "I will always love you, Daisy. You'll always have a piece of me. I just wish things were different and I could share that piece with you. Take care of our son."

Chapter 5

FURY

DAISY IS STILL ON MY MIND, probably always will be. Now I have a whole house full of rowdy excited women that just conquered a huge feat by winning the World Series in women's softball. There is one in particular that has a certain something about her that I can't describe. Rumor. Never have I seen such a mysterious girl in all my life. Her demeanor is fun and bold, as she celebrated the win. She has the prettiest golden hair I have ever laid my eyes on. The beachy waves that hung mid-back bounced with every move she made. Her eyes are an icy blue color, almost clear. She was tall and thin, not stick thin, but not full figured either.

It took some guts for me to even get the nerve up to say hello. I felt like a teenager asking a girl on a date for the first time. I hadn't had to initiate much since Daisy was no longer a part of my life. All of the club whores always initiated, so I was terribly out of practice. I wasn't entirely sure I even wanted to pursue her. I realize that women are not something that I can, or ever will have a meaningful relationship with again, but there is something about those clear-blue eyes that I can't stop staring at. She grins and blushes every time our eyes meet. She turns her head away from me so that I can't see her face, and goes back to talking with her teammates.

"Fury, just go say hi to her for fuck's sake. She won't bite…..too hard." Magnum rattled off as he walked past. "I have been watching you make goo-goo eyes at her since you got back."

"It's not that easy."

"Sure it is. Watch."

I knew where this was going and it was like a train wreck I couldn't stop.

"Hey, you there. Yeah, you with the blonde hair and red cheeks. Come here a sec."

"Fuckin' A man did you really have to do that? Look the poor girl is totally humiliated." I walked over to her to hopefully end some of her embarrassment and take some of the pressure and looks of others off her.

"Uhh, sorry about that. He is a first-class idiot, and top-notch asshole." Trying to find words instead of grunts and stutters was proving to be a little more difficult than I remembered, but I finally found some, "So, congratulations are in order. You did amazing out there."

"Thank you."

"You want a beer or something?"

"Only if you have any Michelob Ultra Light." she said and then winked at me.

"That is a good question. Would you like to come to the kitchen and look? Maybe people would stop looking at you, no thanks to Mag, and go back to minding their own business."

"No, thank you."

"Okay, I will be back in a minute."

I looked around and found a stash of all kinds of beer. I grabbed her a Michelob Ultra Light and walked back out to the crowd. I saw her and took in the sight. All of the girls there and the only one that caught my eye was Rumor. I had to get out of here and get a handle on myself. Maybe I just needed a fling. That would explain this weird state of chaos my mind was in.

"Here you go. There are more in the fridge, if you want them. Help yourself. "

She took it from my hands, and her fingers grazed mine as she took it out of my hand. Upon contact, our eyes met, albeit brief, there was a set of clear eyes looking back at me.

"Thank you."

I just nodded my head in content. She tried to open it

but it was a twist top and was unsuccessful. She started to use her shirt and I stopped her.

"Give it here."

She handed it back to me, I opened it for her, and returned it. The fog from the beer swirled out of the top of the bottle like a genie. Rumor watched it for a few seconds then took a sip.

"Sugar, don't need to sip your beer. Drink that shit. It gets too hot too quick if you don't."

"I'll remember that. Thank you again." She said as she turned her body away from me and headed back to join her team.

I watched her for a minute. Laughing, smiling, and not a care in the world.

Not able to put her or the situation to rest, I walked up to the group and listened in on the conversation, against my better judgement.

"That is a feeling that I can never have again. Winning the World Series was a once in a lifetime thing and I am so glad I got to do that with you girls." Charlie declared with so much truth and emotion behind her words that you could almost *feel* her feelings.

"It was a rather kick ass game if I do say so myself," Whiskey gloated.

"The fact that you were the winning run, and the way that it went down made it perfect. Your dad would've been proud." Jazz chimed in.

I knew because of recent events, that Charlie had a shitty go of things. So for her, I bet this was a monumental event.

I decided that I was going to go downstairs and fiddle around with the still. It was about time to run off a batch again, anyhow. I had a couple of buyers in line . Everything started playing in my head, Rumor, the Regulators, Charlie and the issues she had that we helped eliminate just a short time ago, the next run of shine, even keeping some kind of order in the house until these ladies left and went back to Rudy.

While I was in the basement, Chief came to check on me and see what I was up to. I decided to run a big batch instead of a little one, that way we have a backup supply.

"Alright, Fury, talk. What is on your mind?"

"Rumor, the chaos upstairs, Rumor."

"Ahh. I see. Why is she so heavy on your mind?"

"I don't know, that's the fucking problem. I can't shake her out of my head. I keep telling myself that I need to leave it alone, and not get involved in any way with anyone *ever*, but I'll be damned if she won't get out of my head. Her hair, her physique, those lips, and not to mention those clear eyes of hers won't leave my mind. Plus, she has a certain mystery to her."

"You think it is just that you find her attractive?"

"I already told you, I don't know."

"Look, you are over thinking this. You barely even

know her. You don't know if anything will come out of this, or even if she wants a *this*, so calm down. She may not want anything to do with you. Just feel her out. Don't rush anything. Hell, she is only here for about a week anyhow. I doubt that you will find the one you want to marry this week."

"You're right. I am just so damn rusty at this. I don't know where to start."

"You will figure it out. You got a buyer for this moonshine, or are you just letting off steam and getting your wits about you?"

"Both." I said honestly.

"It will all work out. Who is buying this round?"

"Jay. Something is weird with him lately. I am almost having second thoughts about selling to him."

"How so?"

"He's s just acting funny since Whiskey put a beat down on Sully and Charlie beat his ass when she helped Whiskey with that run a week or so ago. Sully may have some sort of revenge plotted that we aren't privy to. He's just acting shady."

"Cut ties. No more business with him. I don't care if he is one of our biggest customers. There are more, and we can't afford to have him snitch on us."

"Chief, that is dumb. He can't snitch on us. We have him on video buying it and he knows it. Let us at least make this money off of him and then be done. I will tell him when I deliver it that we are no longer business partners. I just get a really bad vibe from him, so I will be happy to deliver that news. Magnum already told him that we don't do business with idiots, so he has to know it is coming."

"Don't fuck this up."

With those last words he left me to my shine and my thoughts. Did I really want to talk to her? Did I really want to attempt to come out of my shell and go for something? Time would tell.

After I ran a batch off, I shut the still down and made my way back up the stairs, and was shocked that Whiskey, Charlie, and Rumor were still up. I had clearly interrupted something, because everyone silenced as I approached the top of the stairs.

"So, Rumor, what did you want to do while you are in PCB?" Charlie asked.

"Oh you know, just hang out on the beach and maybe go shopping or something. Nothing spectacular. I kind of just want to relax and soak up some sun. What about you? Seems as if you would be the one that would need relaxation more than anyone."

"Oh girl, I want to soak up all the sun, and go get a massage for sure. Then I don't care what I do. I just know that drinks are going to be involved." She giggled out.

"Charlie, let's go to bed, yeah?" Whiskey suggested, and she nodded at Rumor as they exited to their room.

There we were, the two of us, standing there staring at each other so confused and clueless. Oddly enough, she asked if I wanted a beer.

"So, umm, since you got my beer earlier, I could be nice and offer to go get you one." She said, making eye contact with me with those clear eyes.

"Sure. I'll drink one with you. No one likes drinking alone. If you don't want a beer then we can have something else."

"I'll be back with drinks then." She turned quickly and scurried out of the room.

"Here you go." She handed me a Samuel Adams Summer Ale. It wasn't my favorite, but I wasn't about to tell her that. I decided I'd just go get the next round.

"Thanks."

Awkward silence surrounded us, and we both looked around the room like idiots. She finally broke the silence with, "So, how long you been in the club?"

A question that I could answer and not be nervous about.

"About four years."

"What brought you to it? I mean, how does one just become a member? Was it a lifelong dream? Did you luck into it? Did you research which club to join?"

"Darlin', you are full of questions. Why couldn't we talk like this earlier?"

"I was nervous."

"You aren't now?"

"You intimidated me, and I didn't know how to handle that."

"Well, shit. I didn't mean to. What can I say, I just have a naturally cheery disposition that radiates off me." This was seemingly easier than earlier today. I didn't want to totally ignore her questions, so I replied, "I lucked into the club. Chief needed a loyal person, and I needed a new place to channel my energies. How about you? How long have you been with the Regulators?"

"Now who is the one with all the questions?" She smirked, still not looking me in the eye. "I've played most of my life actually, since I was about six. I have been with the Regulators for about three years. Best decision I have ever made was to try out for this team. My best friends are on that ball diamond with me."

"You want to go outside to the deck? It would probably beat standing in the middle of the living room, Just saying."

She nodded and we headed out to the back deck. The sun had set and the sky was a nice shade of blue-grey. Since the tide retreated, the beach looked larger, and the moon shone on the water, and the ripples and waves from the ocean made the moon appear to move around on top of the water.

"So are you from Rudy, too?" I asked.

"Not originally. I am from a little town outside of Little Rock. I'm a transplant to the country life."

"I bet it was a culture shock going from big city to a nothing town."

She thought about something and just simply stated, "You could say that."

This girl was not giving away anything freely. It was clear that I had to earn her trust. I just wasn't sure I really wanted to. She would be returning to Rudy and I would be staying here. There was no point, but damn it, there was something inside me that kept me talking to her.

I reached inside the door and flipped a light on. I wanted to see her icy blue eyes and beautiful features. Her blonde hair was up in a ponytail and she was totally makeup free. Natural beauty was the best kind, and she had it in spades. I had never really considered anyone to be as beautiful as Daisy, but Rumor was just as beautiful, only in a different way. Daisy was native, dark skinned, dark hair, and green eyed. Rumor was the opposite of Daisy. Polar opposites, actually. She was tan skinned, blonde hair, with those clear, icy blue eyes. Blonde girls were never my thing, but Rumor was different.

"What are you staring at?" She interrupted my inner warring with myself on who was the more beautiful woman. Clearly, I was comparing with my eyes locked on her.

"You." I said before I thought.

"Oh. Why?"

"You are mysterious, and honestly, your eyes are pretty fuckin' awesome to look at."

"I'm not looking for any kind of relationship, so you should stop there if that is your plan.

"Fine by me. I'm not looking either. I don't want to ever be in another relationship. It would have to be one of those that snuck up out of the blue and smacked me in the damn head."

"Why are you against them?"

"I was just burned by the last one, and I can't and won't repeat that ever again." I wasn't lying. The last one singed my heart and seared itself into my psyche, so there's no way it could never be forgotten.

"Were you serious?"

This is getting too close. Time to shut her down.

"I don't like to talk about the past. There is a reason it's called the past and it's not meant to be brought back to life. How about you?"

"I just seem to have bad luck with guys. They always leave me, and I get tired of saying goodbye. If you don't want to talk about the past then that is fine by me. I don't like rehashing it either. I actually try to forget it every chance I get."

Honest, beautiful, and real. How could someone ever let her go? Her exes had to idiots.

"So, what do you do for a living?", I asked her as I attempted to change the obviously uncomfortable subject.

"I am a waitress. You?"

"I'm in sales." That was as vague as I could get.

"What do you sell?"

"Alcohol."

"Like a distributor or something? Or more from more like a marketing stand point?"

How the hell was I going to answer this?

"All of the above, I suppose you could say. How about another drink?"

"You know, you are kind of mysterious yourself, Fury. Why do they call you that?"

"Because I am usually pissed off, and I am generally a dick to everyone. Not on purpose, but, again, my natural sunny disposition beams bright." Sarcasm dripped off those words. "Why are you called Rumor?"

"God-given name. My parents weren't married when I was conceived, so it was rumored that I was a thing. They thought that it would be cute to name me Rumor seeing as that is how I started life. What is your real name, Fury?"

Shit. Here we go. This is why I didn't want to start talking to anyone. It starts with a lie and keeps building. Oh well, I already started this and now I have to finish it.

"Legend." I left it at that, hoping she wouldn't keep digging.

"Well, that is a different name. I like it."

"I prefer Fury. I never liked Legend."

"Okay then. Fury it is. So, where did you get your tattoo?"

"Sunset Tattoo. A girl named Roxxi was the artist."

"What does it mean?"

"Remember when I said I don't like to relive the past? This is one of those things that I don't talk about."

I had to put a stop to this. There was no way that this could end well. Time to live up to my name. As bad as I wanted to just change the subject and continue conversation in the company of this hot girl, I decided to end the discussion all together.

"Look, I don't know why I thought talking was a good idea. Turns out I don't like it any more than I used to," I said as I entered the house and started to turn the corner. I realized, even for me, that was a dick thing to do. I turned around and went back to her and said, "Feel free to make yourself at home. If you are hungry there is food in the kitchen, and you know where the drinks are." She didn't say anything in return. She just stood there and waited for me to leave again.

Anger and confusion tormented her face. I don't blame her. I would be pissed as well if I was treated the way I had just treated her. I needed to go to bed to escape this shit storm that I brought on myself. It's best that this day ended.

I then realized that she was going to be here for a week, and that I should try to make amends and make stay here pleasant. Hopefully, we can both make the most of this week. Maybe tomorrow would be better. Maybe she would forgive me. Only one way to find out, but that had to wait until tomorrow.

Chapter 6

RUMOR

WELL, HE SURE DID HIS NAME justice. That was a shitty thing to do. I asked a simple question and he completely shut me down. I get that he didn't talk about his past, but he didn't have to be a dick about it. So much for finding a friend outside of the norm. I don't care if I ever talk to that bastard again. I could play his game. Turnabout's fair play, buddy.

Who does he think he is dealing with? Some timid wallflower? I'm no doormat. He would hear about it tomorrow. I had a couple of words to say to him, and for his sake, hopefully, no one else would be around to witness it. I don't like looking like a bitch, but damn, he was out of line.

I walked around on the deck for a while, trying to cool

down and corral my feelings. Why did I let him bother me this much? How does this matter in the grand scheme of things? I'm only here a week then I can go home and forget his name. Hell, it ain't like we are sleeping together. I was just trying to get to know him. Prick.

My thoughts drift, and I wonder why he is the way that he is. What happened to him in his past to make him shut completely down on me like that? Nothing could be *that* terrible. Everyone has a past, and skeletons in their closet. Hell, he just needs to make friends with them and visit them occasionally, so they don't come looking for him. He'd run if he knew mine. No one should get close to me. Hindsight is pretty clear. It might be for the best if he and I didn't talk. He might've actually done us both a favor and not have even known it.

I was destined to be alone. That's fine. I function better that way. When I'm alone, the cops tend to not show up as much. I mean, don't get me wrong, they still do, asking their questions over and over, threatening me with so called "new evidence" against me. I have nothing to hide. They can try all the scare tactics they want. It just sucks when they do their theatrics and try to bring in someone that I am talking to. I wish that the past could actually be the past and the sorry sons of bitches would let it go, so I could. It is hard to bury the past when they keep dragging it up.

The last time I dealt with them, I was pulled over

and I had the guy I was sort of talking to in the car. I had done so well at keeping everything a secret, and not letting my past into the relationship and then *bam* there it was with a vengeance. Instead of explaining everything, I told him a lie that he eventually busted me on that ended our relationship. I don't blame him, I couldn't be with a liar either. I wasn't ready to delve that deep into my past and take the proverbial band-aid off the wounds.

After my temper simmered down, I decided to go and fix myself a drink and a sandwich. As I made my way into the kitchen, I saw Chief sitting at the bar. It appeared that he was on his phone. I edged past him, as to not disturb him. I gave a small wave and quickly turned around and opened the fridge. A turkey sandwich and a Coke sounded good. Simple pleasures.

I was lost in delicatessen mode when I hear, "Give him some time. He will come around."

What the hell? Had he been eavesdropping on us? How did he know that shit went south?

"How did you know that we weren't exactly on speaking terms?", I asked as I shied away and retreated to the farthest cabinet.

"Mainly because I know him. I knew he would fuck this up."

"*This*? What *this*? There isn't a *this*. I just thought it would be cool to have a friend other than my girls."

"Come on, I ain't blind. I see the way you blush when

you are around him. I'm just saying that if you would still like to talk to him and have a friendship, be patient. He was burned before, so he says, and he hasn't quite gotten over it."

"Why was he such a dick to me? I didn't light the match that burned him. Why couldn't he have said he would rather not talk about it, then change the subject to the freaking weather or something? He was totally out of line."

"Look, Rumor, I don't disagree with you, but, dear, have you thought about how he got his name? He has it for a reason and he usually fits the part. It's part of who he is, and who he has had to become."

"What do you mean, who he has had to become?"

"I told you he was burned. It made him have a hard soul, a black scorched heart, and a calloused mind towards love."

"Love? Slow down. I don't even like him right now, so I damn sure don't want to talk about love. Besides, I don't know that *I* will ever be ready to love again."

"You get burned too?"

"I just", I stopped to figure out how I was going to say this without sounding like a total nut job, and without spilling the things that I try to keep hidden away from everyone. "I just don't like seeing people get hurt. When relationships or friendships end, it is always hard. I hate to see people that I care about hurting because of me. Shit always happens too. Don't try to tell me that it won't. I promise you that it will go south. It is best that I don't get involved in any way." I paused. "Every once in a while, it would just be nice to talk to someone different though."

"Look, I just want to tell you that he is a good person. He drew the short stick in life and he is a little bitter about it. He would enjoy your company. He has talked more since you have been here than he has in a long time. Just think about it."

With that, he turned and exited the room. There I was, my head spinning. Thoughts everywhere. I just don't know about this dude. He is sexy, no doubt, but I just wasn't sure that looks were enough to make me put up with the piss poor attitude when I didn't deserve it. Not only that, but I wasn't really in the market for a man. Opportunity just brought a really hot one that seems to like me, or so I thought.

I finished my sandwich, put my plate in the sink and headed to bed. There was too much to sort through at the moment, and I was tired. Besides, I was still pissed at him for acting the way he did. I went upstairs, changed my clothes, and crawled into bed. Haze slept soundly in the bed across the room. She must have had a couple of drinks tonight judging by her snoring. Raige was shaking her head as she looked up from her book in the other twin bed beside the one that Haze slept in.

"She's such a lightweight." Raige said with annoyance in her voice.

"What are you reading?", I asked.

"*The Spark Ignites*, by Kathleen Kelly. I figure that if I am going to stay with some bikers, I should read about a biker!"

"You know that is fiction and that most MC romances are fairytale, right? Most of them are not even close to how life in a MC actually is."

She flipped me off and went back to reading.

Everything started to slow down in my mind as I began to wonder what it would be like to date or marry a MC president. I thought about all of the different things that might happen, or that I imagined could happen. I daydreamed about my favorite biker show and imagined myself as the wife of an outlaw as I felt myself lose grip with reality and slip into slumber.

Crosby! Crosby! What are you doing? Don't leave me! You can't leave me. You're my other half, my reason for living. I would be so lost without you by my side. You're all I have ever known, all I ever care to know. How am I supposed to go on without you? I can't do this life alone." I stared at the gun he had pressed to his head.

"Shhh. Hush now, Rumor. You will do just fine. You are a tough girl and will find someone who is more of a man than I ever was. You need someone stronger than me to stay with you. This is just high school puppy love and you have your whole life ahead of you. I am not what you need, I can never be what you need. My time here is done and I need for you to

do me a favor and promise me that you will move on and not mourn me. I was never right for you, sweet girl."

"What on Earth are you talking about? You are my everything. My life line, my one saving grace. You are the only one that gets me and knows me and my struggles. You have been my rock, even when I didn't deserve you. Crosby, you are the love of my life, and I can't do this without you. Please don't do this. Put the gun down. You've been drinking again. Let's stop and talk about this. Let's talk in the morning when we both have a fresh outlook on the day. Now isn't the time to discuss it. Please. I'm begging you. Don't do this. I need you."

"Goodbye, my sweet Rumor. I will always love you and will never be enough for you."

BANG

I sat straight up in bed with a gasp. Panic, fear, and uncertainty ran rampant through my body. My mind raced trying to catch up, trying to make sense of what I just witnessed. I couldn't distinguish whether or not it was real, or make believe, as it was all an identical replay of the day my world changed. I looked around the room in a frantic manor and saw Raige and Haze sleeping peacefully in their beds. At that moment, I realized I was dreaming. My heart was still racing, and I knew that I had the nightmare again. The nightmare of the last time I saw and spoke to my fiancé. We had been high school sweethearts, and everything was perfect. That is, until it wasn't. He started acting out of the ordinary and detached. His best friend, Creed, tried to tell me that something was off with him, but he couldn't put a finger on it either. Creed was the first person that I called after witnessing the tragedy. I should have called the cops and I knew that, but Creed was his best friend. Besides, I had just watched my fiancé take his own life after I begged and pleaded with him to just talk to me. I needed someone that I could connect with, and someone that I knew loved him too. The cops would come regardless, and I needed comfort right then.

Creed and I were a thing in junior high. He was so cute and popular, and I was the quintessential straight-A student and all-around athlete. We were voted cutest couple and most likely to get married. Then we drifted apart, for no real reason that I can recall, over the summer between ninth and tenth grade. I was busy playing softball with my summer league and he was off to football camps at different colleges. Neither of us were distraught about the break up. It was the most comfortable breakup in the history of breakups. We remained friends and still hung out. We simply just weren't meant to be. Who finds their soul mate in junior high anyway, right?

Then my world was turned on its side by a blonde headed, blue eyed, six feet tall, ripped package of muscle, Crosby. My whole universe revolved around him and his revolved around me. We were inseparable. So much so, that we were engaged by the time we graduated high school, before if you want the truth of it. Our parents would have flipped out, so we just didn't tell anyone 'til the night of graduation. On graduation night, he made it official with the proposal and the ring. After the last name was called at graduation, Rebecca Zimmerman, he ran back up on stage and took the microphone from a school board member whose name I can't recall. He said, "Rumor, it's time that we made it small-town official. Most everyone is here tonight watching us graduate." He then hit his knee in his cap and gown and said, "Marry me, Rumor. Let me take care of you for the rest of our lives." What was a love-struck teenager supposed to say? I ran up on stage and said yes. Upon the word yes, he shouted and embraced me and spun me around. He threw his graduation cap in the air, and the rest of the small-town class of 2014 threw theirs, too.

Creed picked up pieces of me all while trying to hold his own pieces together. I knew that Crosby was his best friend, but I was the one in love with him. I was the one that was supposed to live happily ever after with him, bare his children, and take his name. My world was thrown off its axis and I wasn't sure how I was going to make it right.

Creed did. Time went on and I slowly began to heal. Creed and I talked daily and saw each other every other day. He did his best to make sure I coped, and after about a year, our old flame started to flicker back to life. It was almost like someone above was rubbing the both of us together like a couple of sticks and blowing on us to catch fire again. We always assumed it was Crosby. He would have wanted us to be happy. Crosby knew that Creed would take care of me and would have been alright with the idea of the two of us together.

Alas, I was yet again robbed of a happily ever after. Creed disappeared with no trace, not a phone call, not a letter, not even a goodbye. I am still not convinced that he isn't around somewhere. I was left with nothing again and this time, there is no one to heal my wounds, no one to take the pain away, and no one to help dry my tears. Only the love of my sisters. It's a lonely life, and I miss a male companion.

The law suspects me of foul play or something of the like because of the inexplicable nature of the disappearance case and the fact that my previous boyfriend was also gone. They tried to tie the two together, but they can't. They still give it hell though. I would never hurt Creed. I am just as dumbfounded as everyone else is.

So, now I try to not have much to do with men. Everyone I get close to leaves me, family included. At least my grandfather had a reason to go. Cancer. I watched him suffer and was greatly saddened by his loss, but so relieved that he was out of pain. My father was another good example of the bad juju that followed me like some black cloud of demise. He left without a trace when I was a small child. My mother and my step dad raised me. My step dad was the only one that I was sort of close to that is still around. We aren't as close as we once were because I have shut myself off from him. It is really for his own good.

My girls on the softball team are the glue that hold me together now. I depend on them. That is part of the reason I was so pissed at Charlie when I found out what that asshole, Hensley, had been doing to her. She never let on that anything was wrong. I found out later that it was to protect all of her teammates, but it still shouldn't have gone on as long as it did. When I found out, I hurt for her. I wish she would have let us in and let us help her.

Once my wits were about me, and I realized the dream was indeed just a bad dream, I calmed down and laid my head back down. I attempted to go back to sleep, but there was no hope. There never is when I have the nightmare, so I got up and went to make coffee.

Fury was already up and was making breakfast. "Mornin'. You want some eggs?"

"No." I clipped and went to the coffee pot. I had no real intention of giving him a chance to apologize.

"Okay, do you want anything else?"

I looked at him for a minute, my eyes set on him, glaring, daring him to say another word.

"I guess that's a no. Okay then. Have it your way." He turned around and tended to his breakfast.

I had an internal battle with myself about whether or not to confront him on his jackass attitude, or to just let it slide. If I let it slide, then he would think it is okay to treat people like that and imply that I am some push over. On the other hand, I usually say just exactly what I feel when I am mad, and right now I am beyond pissed.

"I don't know who in the hell you think you are biting my head off and then just walking out last night. I didn't take too kindly to it. I don't appreciate being treated like that. I am still not sure what I even did. You made it very clear to me that you didn't enjoy my company, but I don't know why. I would still like to be clued in as to what I did that offended you so badly. You know, on second thought, it really doesn't matter. I don't care to discuss anything further with you. I will be polite and civil because I am staying in your home, and that is the respectful thing to do, but don't bother talking to me." I got my coffee and went to the deck. I would give anything for Charlie girl to come out here. Maybe that would steer him away from me. I was certain that he would come and try to say he is sorry. Any decent person would.

Much to my surprise, he didn't. I was relieved to be honest. I didn't want to face him and have to confront him more. I drank my coffee in peace as I listened to the waves crash against the sand. Lost in my thoughts of nothing and everything, I stared at the beautiful scenery in front of me. The waves were calm and relaxing, the birds were starting to chirp and fly around looking for their morning meal, and the sun started to cast its warmth on me. A school of dolphins proceeded to jump out of the water and were making quite a scene playing around with one another, speaking to each other in their dolphin chatter. I caught myself smiling and thoroughly enjoying the sight. All previous stresses and woes were pushed away.

"That's a good sight to see. I'm glad my asshole ways didn't completely take away your smile."

The calm, serene setting that I was in turned tense. "I thought I said I wasn't talking to you."

"You did, and that's why I came out here. If you aren't talking to me then you won't interrupt me as I apologize. So, I am sorry. I don't talk about certain things, and the meaning in this tattoo is something only I know about and that is how it's going to stay. I could have been nicer about it, and for that I'm sorry. I would appreciate it if you would accept my apology. I would like for your remaining time here to not be tense."

"Well, for an asshole, you give a pretty good apology. I accept." I replied as I stood and walked past him back into the kitchen. Just because I accepted didn't mean I was just going to be hunky dory with everything and move on. I was still pissed. My feelings were hurt, and my pride was bruised. I still felt rejected. As I refilled my cup, I heard rustling around. Whiskey had gotten up and stumbled into the kitchen.

"Mornin'. How are you this morning?"

"Mornin' to you, too. Charlie is still sleeping I suppose?" I asked.

"Of course. She isn't rolling out of bed till at least nine o'clock. You hungry?"

"Not right now. Maybe in a little bit." I said as I made my way past him. "I think I'm going to go watch tv for a while."

"You're at the beach, and you want to watch the tube? Are you alright?"

"I'm good. Just not feeling the beach at the moment." I lied. I would love nothing more than to be on the beach right now, but I didn't want to see or be around Fury. I would just wait til the others got up.

I heard the patio door slide open and knew that Whiskey had gone out on the deck. I purposely didn't turn the volume up on the tv, because I knew that I would be able to overhear their conversation through the window.

"Why are you out here by yourself?" Fury asked his brother.

"Charlie is still sleeping and I didn't want to wake her, you?"

"Oh, you know, I came to apologize for being a dick and she still left me out here. I don't blame her. I don't deserve her, or for her to want anything to do with me. That's fine. It's for the best. Knowing my luck, we would hit it off really well and then she would have to go home to Rudy. I just can't help looking at her. She is.."

"I know man. I have one too. Only mine isn't pissed off at me. Give her time. Try again later if you want to talk to her. I must say though, I have never seen you this disappointed by rejection."

"Maybe it's because she isn't a whore that is just looking for a man to take care of her. She doesn't hop from bed to bed looking to be the next old lady." I overheard him say to Whiskey.

Well, it was the truth. I hadn't been with anyone since Creed. I don't know that I am all that interested. I mean, yeah, he is sexy, but he is here, and I live hours and hundreds of miles away. That isn't something I want to take on. He and his life, are just something else for the law to meddle in.

I finally decided to quit listening to them talk and turn up the tv. I found HGTV and turned on my favorite fixer upper show. I loved how the couple on screen made love and marriage look so real and fun. It was just fantasy for me though, I'd never be able to find my soul mate. I've had two and they both disappeared on me. It is nice to daydream though. Everyone should dream of having a happily ever after.

Lost in renovations and demolitions I hear, "Look, I deserve your silent treatment. I get it. Apologizing is new for me, so I'm fairly sure I still suck at it. I just wanted you to know that," followed by footsteps headed in the opposite direction.

"It's fine. It doesn't matter anyway. No big deal."

His steps halted and were followed by, "Don't. I was a

jerk to you and I owe you that. Accept it and go on." Then the footsteps continued, getting softer and softer.

The thoughts inside my head knew that he was right. The second half of his apology did suck and was almost as rude as his comments. Then, the sound of feet hitting the floor evading the immediate area stopped and what followed was the sound of a deep breath and then, "Please."

"A for effort, buddy. You did manage to get a please in there, but it's just not enough. When you apologize it's supposed to be nice and sincere, and you barked out an order. While I appreciate the thought of your apology, your delivery sucks. Just forget it okay? Forget it and go about your cranky ways and I'll act like this whole shitty thing never happened," I turned and saw something in his eyes. Remorse, regret, maybe it was uncertainty. Great, now I feel like the jerk in this equation.

"Look, Fury, I accept your apology, and thank you for being a big enough man to initiate it and realize that you did owe one."

He was in an internal war with himself and I saw it, plain as day. I wondered what he had to worry about.

"Rumor."

"Shut your mouth and listen to me. There is some kind of weird chemistry here and I think it would be cool to hang out or whatever. We don't have to jump right into bed or anything like that. I don't want anything from you. What is so wrong with just talking and enjoying someone else's company? Is your life really so miserable that you don't want that?"

He continued to look at me with that foreign stare. "It's complicated and I haven't had to deal with any of this in a very long time. I would like to have a friend, of course, but I know that I am just going to fuck this up. I'm not a nice person. Honest to God, I haven't talked this much to anyone else, not even the guys, nor have I wanted to try. I'm not real sure why I kind of want to talk to you."

He stopped talking and let the words sink in. "See? I can even manage to screw up something that simple. You should just go and find someone else to talk to."

He stared at me like I was some kind of mermaid or something, as if he was waiting for me to just scamper off and do as he said.

"Look, no one tells me what is good for me and what isn't. I make that call. Frankly, I'm old enough to dial that number on my own. I don't need a man to tell me that I do, or don't deserve something. I am quite aware of how that works. I will get out of it what I put into it. As far as fucking this up, there is nothing to fuck up. There is no *this*. I am a big girl and can handle getting my feelings hurt, or late-night chats, or whatever else you throw at me. Bring it on. But do not tell me what I should and shouldn't do."

His lips and eyes turned hard, but they were quickly replaced with softer eyes and a small crows foot wrinkle in the corner of his eyes, and a gentle upward curve to his lips. I feel like perhaps a brick in his wall had been pecked out. It was a start.

"Now, if you will excuse me, I was watching a pretty awesome beach house renovation and I'd like to get back to it." I said as I turned back towards the tv.

"What the hell just happened?" I heard him mumble as he walked away.

Instead of saying, *oh that was you being served some of what you dish out to others. It doesn't taste too good, now does it?* I just let it be and gave him his moment. I had hands down taken that argument for the win. He knew I was right, and he now knows that I am no one's puppet.

Another couple of episodes play and Charlie finally brought herself downstairs. "What the actual fuck did you do to him?" she asked me.

"Oh, I slept fine and had a peaceful night's rest, thanks for asking."

"I expect that attitude from Raige. Spill it sister."

"I told him I wasn't going to put up with his shit, pretty much. Why?"

"Because, he is in his room talking to himself and hitting shit. That's why I am wide awake and chipper this morning." she said as she rolled her eyes.

"Good grief."

"Go talk to him, would you?"

"Nope, let the big bastard stew on his actions for a

while. I am now on a mission to see how long it takes to tame the beast. If nothing else comes from this trip, other than a championship, I will break down his walls. What a sad miserable life it must be for him." I replied as the truth of the matter escaped my mouth. I said out loud.

"You like him, don't you?"

"He is attractive, but you know I don't date anymore, not since Creed." I snapped and glared at her, daring her to keep on.

She knew she struck a nerve and decided to go get her coffee. Banging and clanging around made watching tv hard, so I decided to go get my swim suit, head to the beach, and walk this last hour off. I had to clear my head, rid my mind of all of the comments and thoughts over what happened.

While walking the shoreline, I took in the salty air, the birds, the dolphins, and some kind of small jumping fish. A mile or so must have passed, so I turned and headed back. Only, this time, I was looking for sea shells and sand dollars. With my head in the sand, I trekked on until I saw feet other than my own. Startled, I gasped.

"Sorry, didn't mean to interrupt your thoughts." Chief said as he took a step back. "Calm down, and for the love of God, let your fist relax."

I had my arm reared back and ready for action and didn't realize it.

"Well, damn, you scared me."

"Sorry. What are you doing alone anyhow?"

"Clearing my mind."

"I heard. Just have patience with him. He wants to open up to you a little. He just doesn't know how."

"Why is it so hard for him to talk to anyone? Let alone me. And why is it that you know all about his feelings and are the one that is telling me this instead of him? Is he incapable of speaking his feelings to me?"

"He doesn't deal well since he got burned the last time. He has this screwed up notion that if he treats people like shit then they will leave him alone and not meddle in his life. He honestly thinks he is better off alone, outside of his brothers. You are the only person I have ever seen him apologize to since I met him. There is something there that you shouldn't over look, and frankly, he *is* incapable of talking about his feelings, as feminine as that sounds. I guess I never thought of it like that."

"Chief, I came out here to rid my head of crap like this, not to have it filled with more of it."

"Look, Rumor, I'm telling you that you have something special that he likes, or better yet, needs in his life. He connects with you for some reason. Please don't give up on him. Don't take his shit, but don't give up on him."

"You act like I have done something huge and amazing. I told him I wasn't putting up with his attitude, pretty much."

"He needed that. He didn't much like hearing it, but it did him good. Just think about it, yeah?"

"Not right now. I'm trying to find sand dollars. I don't want to think about him."

I start looking down at the ground and he reaches out his hand. There lies a sand dollar in his palm.

"Are you freaking kidding me right now? I can't get away from you people," I sighed. "Fine. I won't give up. I had already made it a mission to break down some of his walls and make him realize that life is more fun with people in it. There, are you happy? Damn, all I wanted was a little time alone on the beach to find shells and sand dollars and I can't even manage that." I said as I walked away again.

"Thanks, Rumor. You will be glad you stuck this out."

I turned around and glared at him, while seriously thinking about flipping him the bird.

How does he know? Was he some matchmaker? Well, joke's on him.

Once I was back on the beach in front of the house, I saw Charlie and Whiskey all cozy on the deck with Jazz and Briar. Those couples were almost sickening, but deep down, I did envy them. The end of the Gun's and Roses song *November Rain* started playing in my mind over and over.

Don't ya think that you need somebody?
Don't ya think that you need someone?
Everybody needs somebody
You're not the only one, you're not the only one

Axel had a point, but my somebody had come and gone, twice. What if I could help Fury? What if I could make him see that he doesn't have to be an ass to people? Was it possible to soften the hardness that encased his very being? Time would tell. I had a little less than a week to see what kind of magic I could work.

Chapter 7

FURY

Down in the basement, I was running off a batch of moonshine to deliver to Jay. He would soon find out that this is his last load from us. I'm fairly sure that it is going to piss him off and cause him to fly off the handle, but that is the price he pays for being stupid.

There were other buyers for our shine. Something is just not right with him and Sully. There were just little things he had said and done that pissed me off. He crossed the line when he went after Charlie when she was delivering his shine. I can't have, nor will Whiskey put up with, Jay thinking about, or actually crossing that line again.

After I bottled up the booze got it ready to leave, I let Chief know where I was going. I ran into Rumor in the hall and nerves shot through me.

"Hey, you, where you headed?" she asked.

"Uhh. I have some errands to run."

"You want some company?"

Well, I did, but she was not going with me on a run. I wouldn't put her at risk. We are dealing with Jay, and he was liable to get pissed and crazy.

"Thanks, but no thanks," was all that I said to her in hopes of her dropping it.

Much to my surprise she did. "Fine, suit yourself. I'm going to swim then."

Away she went, dressed in her bathing suit and cover up. Barefoot and ready for the sun, she momentarily took my attention away.

"Either go after her or leave and go do your thing, but don't mix the two. If you are going to run the liquor, you need to do it without her on your mind. If you can't do that, then call Jay and postpone the meeting and go talk to her. Fury, it's written all over your face that you want to. Go do it."

"I'll go run this and get it over with. If she is still around when I get back, I will consider it. I make no promises."

"You big, dumb son of a bitch. I suppose you will learn one way or the other. Looks like you are going to choose the hard way."

"Learn what?"

"To listen to either your gut, or your president. Damn it boy, we are both trying to tell you the same damn thing. It isn't going to hurt you to talk to the girl."

He walked away and mumbled something about being a hard-headed idiot that wouldn't know a good thing if it hit him upside his head with a few expletives thrown in for emphasis, I'm sure. Internally I reassured myself. *My first priority is this club. I have a run to do, and making money comes first.*

I loaded up the truck and got out on the highway. Jay and Sully were in route to the tattoo shop where we always did business, but something just felt wrong with this run. I drove on with caution to see if it was a fluke feeling or if there were flames close to the smoke. When I arrived, there was nothing too out of the ordinary. Sully's car was where it usually was. Roxxi's car, too. Jay's motorcycle was there instead of his car. *How in the hell is he going to haul the loot on his bike?* Nah. This isn't happening, not today, not on my watch. From the get-go they have known that things stay the same and nothing changes on delivery days.

I picked up the phone and called him.

"Jay, hey man. Are you around? I have someone interested in some ink." *Code for I have your shit and I'm close.*

"Yeah, I'm real close. Go ahead and pull on in. I'll be right there."

"Nah, man. It's cool. I'll wait on you to get there, but hurry. I have things to do and I'm tired of driving around."

"I am five minutes away. Go ahead and stop in at the shop. Sully is there and will help you."

"You know what Jay? I am driving by now and see your bike, not your car. Tell me, how the blue bloody fuck you going to… never mind. Something is wrong here. I smell a snitch. We are done. Don't call me, don't speak my name, or my clubs name." I hung up and headed back to the clubhouse. I took a back road and didn't leave the way I came in. I had to throw the cops off if there were any around. That deal had gone south and was shady as fuck, I wasn't taking chances. I actually went several different ways and took many different, unnecessary turns and side streets to throw off anyone who might be tailing me.

I only passed two cop cars and they were at the local diner. I made it back home safely and unscathed.

I went to find Chief, Whiskey, Magnum, Shooter and Briar. They all needed to be up to speed with the situation. We all gathered in the kitchen, after I got Chief updated.

"So, we are down a buyer and I have a feeling that we are being watched heavily at the moment. No runs till further notice. Jay and Sully were setting us up. It's a good thing that Fury didn't blow his gut off this time," Chief said to me as he grinned my way.

I knew what he was referring to. The blonde bombshell, and how I had purposely put her off and ignored her to make the run.

"What do you want us to do now?" Mag asked with concern etched on his face.

"We wait. That's all there is to do. Take a couple of

days off and don't worry about anything." Chief tried to settle him down a little. "Think of it as a vacation and think of the girls that are here to spend it with you."

He knew that was the soft spot for him. Girls were a weakness for Magnum. Calling him a man whore was an understatement. He changes women like a teenage girl changes her mind.

"We need to notify our other buyers that we are taking a little break and are out of commission for a while. I'll get Riddick to do that." Briar chimed in as he stood up to leave.

"Where are you going?" I asked a little more hateful than intended.

"To be with my girl, not that it's any business of yours." he said without anything further.

"I'm going to have a drink and mull over the situation and try to figure out how to get Sully and Jay back. No one fucks with my club and gets away with it," I said as I smacked my hand down on the table and scooted the chair away hastily, causing it to make screeching noises on the floor.

"Do not do something stupid. I mean it Fury. Tame it." ordered Chief.

"Yeah." I said as I went to find a beer in hopes that it would help calm my nerves.

Those two have messed with the wrong club, and they will pay for this. I have to be smart. I set out to let my thoughts run rampant, just me, my beer, and the sand. I need to be all alone where I can get some peace. No giggling girls, no obnoxious Magnum, no clear-blue eyes just asking for me to come talk.

I was trying to justify the thoughts in my head. The part of me that wanted to speak with Rumor and the part that was telling me to run battled with one another. I wanted to listen to Chief, but there is the whole *I'm dead thing* that won't go away. Eventually it will come out, and I don't want anyone getting caught in that. It isn't fair for me to keep my life a secret from her. I don't feel like she would keep hers a secret from me. *Hey moron, you aren't even talking to her. You can stop with the endless scenarios of what-ifs.* The more logical part of my inner self chimed in.

Throwing back the last of the beer, I saw her walking down the beach with Riddick. She was staying an arm's length away, and her smile didn't look like it had lately. Upon looking closer, she looked irritated.

I acted like I had been on a stroll and was headed back in the direction of the house, I purposely stopped in front of them. She glanced at me, then back to him and her eyes got big. She nonchalantly tilted her head to him. I read between the lines.

"Riddick." I nodded to him.

"What are you doing out here by yourself, dude? There is a whole house full of girls and you are walking on the beach alone."

"Clearing my mind, that's all. Why would I go in there with all those girls when you have delivered the only one that I care about talking to? Thanks, now go back to the house and find someone else to woo." I turned to Rumor and her face softened some.

"Really, dude. You seriously just stepped right in on what I was trying to do!"

"Oh, honey. I don't know what kind of delusional bullshit you are feeding yourself. You ain't my type and the only reason I was even walking with you was because you didn't take a hint to fuck off. I think you are an arrogant asshat, and you need to work on your courting skills. Don't even think I would humor the idea of anything involving you." Rumor let her real feelings fly.

"Whatever, bitch." he said as he walked away.

"What the fuck did you just say to her?"

"You heard me, and so did she."

"Fury, I don't give a damn if he calls me a bitch. So, what if I am? My feelings aren't hurt because I don't give a good hot damn if he likes me or not. Take me to find sand dollars."

Stunned, I stood stark still and stared at her. Did she just tell me to do something? Did she just totally put Riddick in his place and not care what the repercussions were?

"Uh, let's go then." I obliged so the awkward situation would end.

"Thank God I ran into you. I can't stand that jerk."

"Don't worry about him. I will handle him later. He won't disrespect you and get away with it. Since when do you get to boss me around?"

"I don't, but it worked. Fucker is gone, isn't he?"

Yes, yes, he was. No fists were used or blood shed, and the end result is still the same.

"Well played, Rumor. Well played."

"Thanks. I do what I can, and Fury?"

"Yeah?"

"I honestly couldn't care less what he thinks of me. If he doesn't like me, then that is just one less person to say goodbye to."

"Valid point."

"Now, about these sand dollars. Was that just a ploy to get me away from him?"

"Both."

"Let's go find some, shall we?"

We walked down the beach a way before she asked me anything. We took in the peace that was surrounding us. Then it hit me that I was at peace with *her*. Not that it means anything big, but I wasn't rushing to get away from her. It was the opposite.

"How long until you start talking to me? This is a bit on the boring side, and I don't know where to look for these sand dollars."

"Look, I don't have a lot to say. How's the weather and

are you liking your time here seem to be all I can come up with."

"You haven't talked to anyone in a while huh?"

"Correct. So, I don't really know what to do or what to say. I find it is easier to just stay to myself."

"How about you just ask me whatever it is you want to know. I will do the same."

I didn't give her a chance to say anything else, just butted in and said, "There are things I don't talk about. Just remember that."

"Well, rude ass, I won't know what those things are unless you tell me, so just don't be a dick when I ask you something you don't want to answer. I am a big girl and can handle the words *I don't want to talk about that.* My feelings won't be hurt a bit."

"How long have you been single?" I asked her.

"This time, a couple of years."

"This time?"

"I've had two serious relationships and they both ended abruptly. The last one was a couple years ago, and the other was a year prior to that, you?"

"Four years, or so." That's as much as I've ever told anyone. "Abruptly too. Let's not stay in our pasts. It's my fault for asking."

"Look, I don't want you to tell me anything you aren't ready to tell. I don't care about your past. I don't really care about your distant future. I don't aim to be a part of it, but

I do care about the here and now. I want you to tell me whatever it is that you want me to know."

"You don't hold back, much do you?"

"What purpose would that serve? Tell me when we could, or would, talk to or see each other? There's hundreds of miles and several states separating us."

"Right again."

An awkward silence found its way to our moment. We quit walking down the white sand beach and sat in the sand where the water meets the shore. She made foot prints over and over as the waves gently washed them away.

"My first real relationship was my high school sweetheart. He was my everything. I loved him with every ounce of my being. He had flaws but, what new high school grad didn't? His one vice was drinking. He wasn't of age, and his older buddies supplied it to him. He was drunk the night he told me that he would never be good enough, and shot himself in the head, all while I was begging him to stop."

"Damn." I thought out loud.

"Then I ended up with his best friend."

"And?"

"He disappeared. No note, no body, no call. Nothing. I'm not convinced he isn't around somewhere."

"Double damn."

"What about you?"

"I don't want to discuss it."

"Alright. Fair enough."

She turned her head from me to the ocean, trying to get a grip on the night's revelations.

"I've not told many people about Creed's disappearance. Sorry it slipped out."

"No worries. I won't tell anyone."

I thought long and hard about what I was about to offer her. If I did it then it would ensure I have contact with her after she leaves, but it might backfire on me. With worry and concern in my voice I asked, "Would you be interested in investigating it further?"

What did I have to lose? If we found out that he really was gone, then that meant we could still have an open connection. If not, it just means I'm simply not meant to have any kind of relationship with this woman, although I'm not sure that is even what I want. I could see if Chief can get in touch with his connections and pull a favor.

"Chief is in good with some people in law enforcement. I can see if he would mind looking around in this."

"I'm not sure I want to know. If he turns out to be alive, then I'm just going to be pissed off and hurt that he couldn't, or didn't, tell me goodbye, this ain't working, fuck off, or something. I got nothing. And if he turns out to be dead, well, that's two that have gotten away. I can't deal with any more heartbreak. I lost my soulmate and then fell in love with his best friend, and lost him, too. I like being in the dark. It means I don't have to face reality.

However, the cops might finally leave me alone if the truth was revealed."

"Cops?"

"Well, it looks suspicious because Crosby committed suicide, and then Creed just disappeared. In their eyes, two people close to me have ended up dead or missing, so I must be the culprit, or I know more than I'm telling." She stopped and took a breath and realized she left the conversation open to speculation. "Which clearly I'm not. I have nothing to hide. They have searched my house, my car, my parents' house, everywhere, and have come up short every time. Why would I purposely do something to ensure that I am lonely forever?"

"It doesn't make sense. Just let me know what you decide, and I'll see if Chief will pull some strings."

She nodded her head and said, "Let's head back. I'm all talked out. You can take me sand dollar hunting later."

We got up and walked back to the house, neither of us saying a word. It was mutually understood that we both needed the silence. As we walked back towards the house, our hands innocently touched, and we both looked down at them. Our eyes caught the sight of them hanging so closely together. It was as if she knew I was too scared or nervous to do anything, she took my hand in hers. She gave it a gentle squeeze and smiled at me. With her clear eyes looking at me, I stopped our trek and stood in front of her. I bent down to kiss her but hesitated. She noticed the hesitation, and lifted herself up on her tip toes and closed the space between us. When we kissed, time stood still. My nerves were temporarily gone. It wasn't a deep dueling tongues kiss, but a sweet one. One that I hadn't experienced since Daisy. I pulled away and took in a deep breath. She smiled at me and tugged on our connected hands and urged me to lead the way back to the house.

Chapter 8

RUMOR

Word vomit poured out of my mouth, spilling the truths that cluttered my reality. I didn't even care that I poured my shit storm of a life out for a biker to sort through, especially one that doesn't talk much. The kiss we shared last night had woken a part of me that I hadn't seen in a long time.

"Fury, why have you opened up to me? You've made it *very* clear that you don't talk to people."

"I like you. You don't annoy me, and I feel like you will understand me more than anyone. Everyone else just wants to get to the bottom of who I am or solve my problems. You said you didn't care, and that's a relief because I don't want to drudge up my past. In the beginning, I'm not going to lie, it was because you are fine, and I couldn't stop looking at you. Then you spoke and put me in my place, and just didn't take my shit. I respect that."

Alright then, the biker is not as harsh and crass as he portrays. This man clearly has layers as well as mystery. How many would he reveal? How many would he pull back so that I might get to know him better? These are the questions plaguing my mind. I also question, do I want to peel them back? He seems deep, dark, and intense and I am not sure I want that in my life. I have enough dark, deep shit in my own life, and I know I am not hanging around here long.

We continued walking in a quiet.

"A penny for your thoughts?" He interrupted the tranquility.

"My thoughts are worth more than that."

It was true. I have never liked that saying. Of course, my thoughts are worth more than a freaking penny.

Once we were back at the house, we made our way through the kitchen and stopped by the fridge for a cold one. He handed me a Michelob Ultra Light and grabbed a Busch Light for himself as we made our way out to the deck with the rest of the crowd.

The summer sun was setting and casting beautiful hues of orange, pinks, and reds across the sky. I sat and stared at the oceanic view as long as possible in solace. I wasn't bothered by the chatter of Haze and the rest of the girls and the few guys who were also there. I proceeded to tip my beer back and enjoy the view in front of me. I suppose it is just against some unwritten rule to be happy alone, because Haze be-bopped over to me and asked me how I was doing and if I was sure I wanted to be left alone.

"Yes, Haze I am fine. No, I'm not upset. Yes, I'm sure. No, I don't want to talk about it. There is nothing to talk about. Go on and have a good time. I was thoroughly enjoying my quiet time. It's totally okay to not talk or be in the center of the crowd all of the time. Now go. Please, have a good time. I swear I am okay. I was taking in the breathtaking sunset against the ocean." I rambled in almost a run-on sentence, so that she didn't have time to ask me the questions that I knew were soon to follow.

"Fine, drink alone. They say that's the first step to becoming an alcoholic though." She winked at me and grinned big.

I shook my head and tipped up my bottle again, remembering all of the day's events. How much Fury opened up to me. I realized I still knew next to nothing about him, but it's more than anyone else knows, apparently. I'm just unsure of how I feel about it.

I felt a hand bump my shoulder, which pulled me from my internal debate of whether I wanted to embrace this or run for the hills of Rudy. I turned to see who it was, and an upright hand was stretched out to me with a one-dollar bill in it. I looked up wondering why in the hell someone was handing me money, and realized it was Fury standing at my side.

"How about a dollar for your thoughts?"

"Nope. They are worth more to me than that, too. Good try though." I smiled at him. Something strange happened, and I thought I heard a brick in that wall of his fall to the ground. So much so that Whiskey took notice and nudged Magnum. Fury smiled back at me. It was almost as if the smile was slowly breaking through to the hardened parts of him. Until Magnum chimed in.

"Well now, the cranky bastard does smile. Quick, someone grab a camera."

That was the end of the smile, and the last of the bricks to fall. One down, a whole wall left to go. It was a start though.

"You want to go talk somewhere that isn't surrounded by idiots?" I asked him.

He stared at me, and I saw the battle within. His lips got thinner as he pressed them together in contemplation as he balled his fists then relaxed them. His eyes searched mine. For what, I'll never know.

"It is a simple question. Either you do, or you don't. You are going to give yourself an ulcer if you think about shit too much."

Still nothing. I waited and stared right back at him, trying to figure out why he was so conflicted. Finally, I helped him out and grabbed his hand. He looked down at our joined hands and stepped back. I felt like perhaps he needed to know that I was there for him, or was trying to be at the very least, the way he was for me a bit ago when I spewed my past at him.

"I can't. I just…"

"It's fine. At least now I have an answer and can go back to enjoying my sunset. I'll be here if you want to talk, but I'm not going to miss this breathtaking view to play stare out with you."

With that, I turned my attention back to the ocean and finished off my beer. I heard Magnum yell out after a loud thump met the back of his head.

"Asshole. You just couldn't let it be, could you? You had to try to call him out and couldn't let him have a minute of happiness." Whiskey said through somewhat clenched teeth.

"Hey, I was just acknowledging the fact that the moody fucker can smile. It really wasn't a dick move on purpose. I just wanted documentation of the monumental event."

I turned to see the commotion and caught a glance of the Fury's back as he exited the patio. Charlie came over and sat with me on the lounge chair.

"So, I see you two have managed to talk some."

"If that's what you call it."

"It might not seem like much, but I promise, according to what Whiskey has told me, that is huge for him. Do you want something with him? I'm just not sure I understand this budding relationship."

I sighed. *Did I?* The thought was so tempting, but the reality was this was a bad idea. Meddling cops, unsolved missing persons case, distance, fear of heartbreak all told me no.

"I don't think so. I don't think I can handle anything serious, nor do I think that's what he wants. Charlie, we just click. It's easy to talk to him and I think if he ever did open up to me there could be something, if it weren't for the distance. Don't get me wrong, he is the poster child for sex appeal, and I'm not saying a romp in the sheets wouldn't be fun, but you know me, I'm not one for casual sex."

"You are stronger than you give yourself credit for. I think you would benefit from a guy friend. You don't have any."

"That's because any guy I get close to disappears on me. I don't want to have to say goodbye again, Charlie. I just don't think I can go through that for the third time. That's another reason I don't particularly want to get close to Fury. I'm just not willing to risk the heartbreak of ending another relationship, be it platonic or romantic. My wounds are still fresh from Creed."

"Still no word from him?"

"No, and at this point I don't expect there to be. I just wish it was over without having answers, if that makes sense. I enjoy not knowing because I fear the worst, and I don't want to face that reality."

"Honey, it won't be until you let it be. Think about that. Go get yourself another beer."

She got up and went back to her man. I did sort of envy her just a little. I didn't mention that to her though.

That was a discussion I wasn't ready to have with anyone, especially her being on a love high right now.

The beer was going down smoothly. I decided I wasn't going to join the crowd again. I needed some me time. Time to sort through this mess in my head. Charlie had a point. I won't heal if I don't let myself. How do I just get over two broken hearts though? Is there a how-to book on self-healing? Why was this my life? Why couldn't I have been the lucky one that found and got to keep her forever person? Was I so delusional to think that was a reasonable request?

Lost in my thoughts, my body led me on a walk at the beach again. I listened to the waves crash on the shore then recede back into the vastness. I stopped and stared at the water. Why couldn't my life resemble the ocean? Full of life, powerful, and mostly routine? The tide comes in and goes back out, night after night and day after day, only causing hate and discontent when a storm is brewing. A storm every once in a while was okay, but damn, Hurricane Rumor was getting old. I was tired of weathering it. Acting like I am always okay starts to get old. I would give my right arm to be able to cry on my man's shoulder while he told me everything was going to be alright.

Lost in my fantasy, I hear, "How about two?"

I turned to look at the gravelly voice behind me that had become familiar, I gave him a sad grin.

"Oh, you look upset. I don't do feelings well. I don't

know what to say. You want me to go? I can leave you alone." Fury said with empathy and as fast as he could. It was like he was trying to be nice because it was the right thing to do, but he had no idea how to accomplish the feat.

"You don't have to, I'm not good company right now. Kind of in a funk at the moment."

He thought and grimaced a little, then shut his eyes and said, "I listen well."

"I don't know. Yes, no, maybe." I let out a big sigh as I kicked some sand into the water. "I would love nothing more than to talk to someone, but I don't know that I want it to be you. No offense."

All I got in return was a blank stare and confused look.

"Okay, that came out wrong. I mean, I would love to talk to you, I feel like you get me. I am just not ready, and I don't think you are either. You don't talk to anyone, and I can't be the only one communicating. I feel some sort of weird connection with you, but it's best if I steer clear, for your sake."

"Look Rumor, I promise you that there isn't anything you can say that would floor me to the point of not wanting to talk to you. I have been through a lot of shit and your story is cake compared to...uh, a lot of others". He stammered like he was hiding something.

"You won't scare me off, but I'll not force myself on you either. I feel about the same way as you. I dig you. You are easy to talk to, easy on the eyes, and you don't ask a ton of questions that I don't want to answer."

"At some point I would hope you felt comfortable enough to talk, but that is between you and your demons."

He looked at me with a serious look on his face. I could tell he was warring with himself on what or what not to say. It was almost as if he wanted to talk about something but didn't know how. He opened his lips to speak and closed them right back.

"What Fury? I see you struggling."

"It's just, I get it okay? I understand and even sometimes wonder what it would be like to have someone to talk to." He replied quickly, as if he was trying to say it before he chickened out.

"Look at us. A couple of strangers out here on the beach talking about something that we probably won't ever have again. What do you say we agree to keep each other company while I'm here? No strings attached, no expectations, just a boy and a girl that have some things in common and could use some company in our lonely lives."

"Rumor, I would like that, but it isn't a good idea."

"Why? Huh? What do we have to lose? I say we can make anything happen for a week. And that kiss earlier agrees, too."

"I don't know, what if we piss each other off and find ourselves let down again?"

"What if we don't? It's not like I am asking to commit your life to me and hold only me in your arms forever and ever. I am asking you to drink beer with me and have a conversation as adults. If we do piss each other off then you didn't need me, and I didn't need you all of this time. I'm placing odds we will recover just fine. We've made it how long without each other?"

We stared at each other for a few seconds, and I decided that I would try to get at him, or at least make him smile and break the tension.

"I'll make it easier for you. If you let Riddick get me alone again, I will find you, and bust a beer bottle over your head in while you sleep. Does my offer look good yet?"

Chapter 9

FURY

WELL, DAMN. THIS GIRL HAD made me smile for the second time in an hour. Her seriousness about our situation had me laughing. Although, I had no doubt that she probably meant it.

"Fine. You win. A week don't seem so bad. At least you are pretty. You could look like Chief or Mag."

"Here's to a week of friendship, one that no one else understands."

"No makeup parties, or hours spent gossiping about your best friend's ex though. I have to draw the line somewhere." I was only partly kidding.

"Deal."

"Let's head back, yeah?" I suddenly got an eerie feeling. It was hard to describe. A little caught off guard, a little heightened awareness, a lot of uneasy in my gut, it made me want to get Rumor out of there. I looked around and saw a car taking off in the distance.

I was going to be on alert. I usually don't get these gut feelings, but when I do, I know I'd better listen to them. Not listening to my instincts landed me where I am today. I had a bad feeling about the Ray brothers. I knew that they were bad news from the start and I just kept giving them the benefit of the doubt, like some naïve fool. And now I'm *dead* because of it. Now, because I did something, I knew better than to do, my son had to grow up without a dad and Daisy had to raise him without me to help her. It didn't take long to remove Rumor from that situation. I wasn't about to let something happen to her, too. I'd never forgive myself.

The car resembled Jay's. I made a mental note to investigate him a little further. I had a sneaking suspicion that he was up to no good. I could almost feel the proverbial knife twist in my back. I will kill him if he tried anything stupid. I knew good and well he was pissed because I cut him off. After all, we were his bread and butter. He made his money off running the booze we made that he re-sold for profit. Better yet, I bet Sully put him up to this. Sully is the one that really is feeling the sting of us not doing business anymore. He fed Jay enough to keep him loyal. Sully is the mastermind behind everything that involves Jay. From what Sax says, he's too dumb to think for himself. I believed deep down that is who was lurking around tonight. I had to tell the guys.

Back at the house Rumor went to be with the girls, and I found Magnum and Chief.

"Guys, let's go somewhere and talk. I have business to discuss. Where is Whiskey?"

"With Charlie. Where else would he be?" Magnum said as he rolled his eyes.

We meandered up to my room where we shut the door and had no girls around to distract us.

"Jay is up to something. I think I saw him creeping around outside earlier when Rumor and I were on the beach. He, or Sully, are pissed because I cut him off. It's one of the two. I know good and well that he set me up. I just caught on and avoided that shitty situation."

"What do you want to do, Chief?" Mag said in all seriousness.

"Nothing. Give him the rope and he will hang himself. He isn't smart enough to know where to draw the line. Sully uses him as some little puppet, and he will do whatever he tells him to. I actually think you should invite him over. Say for a poker game? Kill him with kindness and let him be his own demise."

"What? Are you serious right now? He is trying to sabotage us, and you are going to let him away?" I yelled at him.

"Look, Fury, I get that you are pissed. You always are

quick to jump into things without totally thinking them through. If he was setting us up, he must have already gone to the cops. We are on their radar, and they are just looking for a reason to get us. A first-degree battery charge is not going to help our case. Instead, we go legal and stop production. Our customers will have to understand. We will put the stills in the room where Hensley was being kept, seeing as it is inconspicuous. Then you are going to call him up and ask him if he wants to come play poker."

"You got to be fucking kidding me." I growled as I turned away from him. I paced the floor, and tried to find some composure, I spewed, "and just what is that going to do?"

Magnum chimed in, "Wait. He has a plan I can already tell. What's up your sleeve boss?"

"He will hang himself, I promise. Trust me. I have seen his kind too many times. He will get on a power trip and think he can pull one over on us. He is going to try to *get us back* for taking away his main income source and it's going to backfire on him. Wait and see," he replied a little too happy and cheery for my liking. "Now, are we done?" Chief asked.

"You're the boss, remember?" I snapped at him.

"Tame it, Fury."

"Fury, let's go grab a sandwich or something." Magnum was trying to make the situation less tense, but right now I just needed to be alone.

"Nah man, I'm alright. I just need...", I paused. What did I need? Revenge on him? A punching bag to let my frustrations on? A drive to clear my head? Yes, that is what I need. "to ride for a while."

"Man, don't do anything dumb. I ain't bailing your cranky ass out of jail. You'll sit there." Mag said as he walked past me.

As I walked down stairs, I saw Whiskey and Charlie curled up on the couch together watching TV. Unwelcome jealousy temporarily found a spot in my mind. I did miss the affection of a woman. I missed feeling soft skin, playing with long hair, and smelling shampoo. It was all of the little things that I got to see Whiskey getting to do that I was missing out on. I stormed out of the house right past Rumor, who was sitting outside on the porch alone.

"You okay? You look pissed, more than usual."

"Fine." I barked as I walked hurriedly past.

"Well, I'd love to sit around and chat with you, but it looks like you are too busy being a dick, and I just ain't got time for that. Later." She sassed as she spun and left the porch.

Great, now I have pissed her off, too. It wasn't my intent, seeing as we just shared a moment on the beach, and decided that we could do this friend thing. I just didn't want to involve her in any way. She doesn't need this shit on top of all of her personal issues. She deserved a break from life, not to have more shit dumped on her during vacation. I debated on whether or not to go tell her I was sorry but decided that I just wanted out. As I tore out of the driveway, the engine and road noise started to drown out the noise in my head. It's amazing how hearing nothing but the rumble of the motor, and the wind whipping by my head calmed me. After an hour or so, I decided it was time to head back.

I drove by Sunset Tattoo to see what I could see, and lo and behold, Jay's car was outside. Since I was told to invite him to a poker game, I decided to whip in and just do it, man to man. Let's see if he squirms under pressure.

"Jay," I deadpan.

"Fury. Didn't expect to see you here."

"Yeah, I bet you didn't. Listen, the guys and I are having a poker game tomorrow. You want to come?"

"You made it clear you didn't want anything to do with me. Why would I come to your house?"

"I got spooked. We can discuss future endeavors over some beer and cards. There's no good reason we can't figure something out."

I was giving it my all, trying to act like I cared and genuinely wanted him at the house. Much to my surprise, I was succeeding.

He thought for a second and replied, "I think it would be fun to hang out with the guys. What do you want me to bring?"

"Look dude, it isn't a sleepover where we are going to

paint our nails and do our hair. Just bring some beer and money to play with." I said in a put-out tone.

"You going to be in a better mood tomorrow?"

Not even giving him the satisfaction of responding to that, I replied, "Just be there at six o'clock with your money."

I got back on the bike and headed to the house. I had an apology to give…again. The entire way home, I ran through so many thoughts and ideas of what I *could* say, but I knew in the end that I wouldn't.

ON A MISSION TO find Rumor, I ignored everyone else in my path. The first place I looked was on the deck. I had a gut feeling she was out listening to the waves crash on the shore. Sure enough, there she was. Stretched out on a lounge chair lost in the sounds of the ocean. I had some making up to do, so I figured I would try to break the ice with money. I stretched out my hand, sat it on her shoulder, and inside it was a twenty-dollar bill.

"How about twenty?"

Nothing.

"Rumor?"

"I heard you." She snapped and snatched the bill out of my hand and turned right back around to the ocean.

"Well, that wasn't exactly how I thought this would go."

"Wait, you *thought*? Clearly, your idea of thinking and

mine are *not* the same. If you were, in fact, thinking, you wouldn't have stormed out earlier and snapped at me. If you were thinking, you would have stayed away from me tonight and tried your luck in the morning. So, think about this. I am going in for a beer, alone, and when I get back, I hope I don't see you."

"Harsh words for such a minor flub up, don't you think?"

"No. You want my thoughts, and you are willing to pay for them, so here they are. You, Sir, are a first-class horse's ass. I am so mad at you in this moment that I don't know if I want to talk to you for the rest of the time that I'm here. It isn't only about this time, it's the fact that you are so wishy washy, and I can't keep up. I really wanted to hang out, talk, and do stuff with you while I'm here, but I am beginning to think it isn't worth the back and forth of your fucking mood swings. You need to make up your mind. Either you are okay talking to me or you aren't. I won't allow both. You… Uggh. You need to work out whatever it is that has your panties in a twist. Here's a newsflash, I didn't do it. I am not the one holding the proverbial wedgie in your britches. Find someone else to be a jerk to. And I'm keeping the money. I hope you think my thoughts are worth the twenty. Come back tomorrow and I bet I can rustle up some more thoughts for you to buy, but you better have a better fuckin' attitude or this arrangement is off. I won't deal with this shit." She seethed as she stormed off.

One thing was for sure, I never had to wonder where I stood with her. I didn't know how to respond, so I didn't say a thing and let her storm off. Seems that might the smartest thing I could've done.

I milled around the kitchen wasting time. I wanted to give her plenty of time to get where she was going without seeing me. Finally, it felt like it had been long enough, so I headed upstairs for bed. When I passed her room, I overheard her talking to Raige and Haze.

"He is so moody, like, worse than a girl. I realize he has a good reason, or so he says. I am beginning to think he wasn't burned, and he is just an asshole by nature. Gah, why can't I find a normal guy to talk to? Is that too much to ask?"

"Rumor, why are you wanting to talk to him anyway? You know how he is. Honey, I love you, with all my heart, but if you keep going back after he treats you like shit, baby, that's on you. People get away with what you let them get away with."

"I never thought I would say this, but Haze is right. He has shown you who he really is, and he isn't worth your time. I mean, why are you tore up about him in the first place? You don't even know him." Raige mentioned.

On a long sigh out, "I don't know. It's hard to explain. When he isn't captain cranky pants, he is really cool to talk to. I like him when he is normal. It is proving to be a chore to figure out when CCP is going to make a surprise return."

They had gotten out of her what I hoped I would and would never hear all at the same time. I liked her too, but I really felt this was dangerous for us both. Neither of us were capable of any kind of relationship. The thought of this made me nauseous and made my head spin. I turned and headed to my room. As I was about to reach for the light switch, I heard, "What is your problem?" from across the hall.

I looked at Chief and rolled my eyes. He knew good and well my problem was Rumor.

"So, you still haven't let shit go and just talked to her, I see."

"You know it ain't that easy." I say as I walk into his room instead of mine.

"Why isn't it? Huh? You say that you've already lost everything, so what do you have to lose? Nothing."

I looked at him and let his words sink in for a minute, but I still wasn't having any part of it.

"I have my sanity and past to lose."

"Lose your past huh? Explain that to me, would you? I'm intrigued to find out how the hell that is possible. As for your sanity, Fury, you haven't been sane since I met you. You have always been somewhat off. I can't tell you what exactly isn't quite right, but you ain't like the rest of us. We love you all the same, but you are definitely different."

"I have to be closed off and you know that."

"Yes, you're right. However, you are using that as a

crutch. Damn it Legend, that girl likes you, and I can tell you like her. You're going to fuck up and run her off if you aren't careful. Pull your head out of your ass." He roared.

He called me Legend. He never calls me Legend. It's as if I am an errant child that is being scolded.

"Chief, I don't know what to do or how to do it. I'm not ready to face this shit yet, and I don't know if I ever want to be. I do know that I am drawn to Rumor, and I enjoy her company. I know I can't stop thinking about her, and it makes me crazy. This can't happen."

"Fury," he sighed, "If you let yourself, you might just have a good time, that's if she lets you talk to her again. It sounds like you really pissed her off this time. Here's to hoping you haven't screwed up to the point that you are nothing to her."

Nothing to her. Could I handle being someone else's nothing? I am nothing to Daisy, nothing more than a memory and a sperm donor. There was no question, Rumor would never be put in that position. I would see to that. Rumor needed to stay away from me, and I had to prove my asshole ways, or go away for a week. With the poker game coming up and Jay coming over, getting away was nixed.

"Chief, I have made up my mind. It's best for everyone if this doesn't get any farther. It wouldn't be fair to her. I can't give her what she deserves."

"Fury, you're so goddamned dense sometimes, you

make me want to throat punch you. Aren't you forgetting that there isn't a relationship? There is nothing between you two. You think she is hot, and she seems to like you for whatever unknown reason. There are no vows being said, no mortgages to pay, no parents to meet. You are a guy she seems to have something in common with, and she is a girl that has caught your eye. Stop thinking about the future that doesn't exist. Why can't you just take the girl to dinner and talk, or walk down the beach, or take her on a ride? None of those things I just mentioned involved vows, mortgages, or parents."

He had a point. I feel sure that if I did that, Rumor would be that much harder to let go at the end of the week. I would still feel like I was deceiving her. The way I am drawn to her is so strong that it scares me. I can easily see myself falling for her, but I can't let that happen. I needed to be alone. There was so much in my head that I had to sort, and clearly Chief didn't see things the way I did.

"Night Chief." I got up and stormed out of the room only to pop back in and tell him we are hosting a poker game tomorrow night, so he needed to have Riddick stock up.

I reached my room, the room that has been my home since I started over. Maybe it would give me a good quiet place to think. I slammed my door like it was the door's fault that I was in this predicament. I ripped off my shirt and flung my old, faded, holy jeans across the room. That didn't help my mood either. I did the same thing with my socks. I stood in my boxers and breathed heavily and angrily. I'm not sure who I am mad at. Not Rumor. She didn't do anything wrong. I suppose I was mad at myself. I was pissed off that I wanted to talk to her, but I couldn't. No one deserves what I potentially bring to the table. I couldn't afford for any information about me to be leaked. I hated not being able to talk about it. I often wondered if I ever did find another person, what harm would come of telling her about my past. If I was with someone and trusted them enough to commit to them and them to me, I could trust them with everything, right? I felt the need to talk to someone about it. Not my brothers. I still am not sure about a couple of them. I might tell Magnum and Whiskey someday, but that is it, and even that is very doubtful. Briar, I don't know that well, and Riddick pisses me off by just looking at him. I just wasn't risking it.

It was time that I stopped the spinning in my head, the back and forth of wanting to talk to her, and then being pissed off because she tried to talk to me. The constant tugging of the yes and no was exhausting. I climbed into bed and shut my eyes. Still unable to calm down, I decided I needed to smoke. I put on pants and went outside on the deck and sat in the chair that Rumor usually occupied. I was lost in thought as I puffed on my smoke. I laid back and relaxed a bit after I snuffed it out, and just listened to the sounds of the night. Before I drifted off, I saw Daisy and Rumor vividly in my mind. Daisy was with the kid and her new man, and Rumor was alone. Daisy didn't have a care in the world, and Rumor held the world on her shoulders. Was it a sign? Or was I wanting it to be a sign? Was it just a crazy story I saw play out in that crazy place when you are stuck between sleep and consciousness? Only time would tell.

Chapter 10

RUMOR

I HATED THAT I WAS the early riser. I stirred around and felt for my slippers, so I could head out to the deck. Peace and quiet awaited me there. I gently moved about, got to the door, softly opened it, and slipped out, careful not to wake the other girls.

Once I made it down stairs, I headed straight for the coffee. I was trying to be quiet, so I opened the cupboards to find a big mug, then went to the fridge for the half and half. I made my coffee and headed out to the deck. I was headed to the same chair I had been in yesterday, and I stopped and took in the sunrise. It really was gorgeous. The displays of different shades of oranges and yellows were a sight to see. The sunrises on the beach were far different from the mountainous ones we have back home.

I walked over to the chair and found a sleeping Fury. The thought crossed my mind to dump my coffee on him, but I refrained. I went to another chair and refused to let that cranky bastard ruin my sunrise. Last night I did some soul searching, thanks to Haze, and decided that I wasn't going to get myself in a tizzy and get my feelings hurt over him. He didn't get to have that kind of power over me. I was here to enjoy the beach and the company of my girls, and that was what I would do. It was a shame, too. I think we could have been good friends. I guess the part of me that isn't pissed off at him still wishes that we could be friends. I think he could be really fun, just not at the expense of my sanity.

I wiped my mind clean and forced myself to stop thinking about him. I found peace within myself, as I enjoyed the sights in front of me, as the colors of the morning became more vivid. Rolling with situations as they came has begun to be my new strong suit.

I sipped from my cup and relished in the serenity of the morning. I was completely in another world, when I was brought back by Fury getting my attention. Nerves started to buzz about, but I didn't let him know it.

"Rumor, I…", he paused and hung his head. Clearly the battle wasn't an easy one to fight.

"Don't. Just don't, okay? This is what it is, you are who you are, and I won't be here long anyhow, yeah?" I cut him off and stood to walk back into the house for a refill.

"I don't know how to do this."

I froze dead in my tracks. After the shock of what he said wore off slightly, I turned around with a fed-up tone said, "Do what, Fury? Huh? You can't talk? You can't figure out how to not be an asshole? What can't you do?"

"Look, I like hanging out with you. You're fun to be with and I think we could really be good friends, but no one deserves the kind of baggage that I carry. I don't want that on you."

"Huh, last time I checked, I was a big girl, remember? And could decide what I could and couldn't handle. I don't recall having a man make that decision for me, but thanks for having faith in me. It means a lot." I spun around and stormed off to the kitchen.

Only, little did I know, he followed me. He didn't even give me a chance to stop his words. He just lit right in with, "Oddly enough, I have all the faith in the world that you don't need a guy. There are just certain things that I can't discuss, and it's not fair to you for me not be honest, especially when you have shared so much with me. Had I known ahead of time that we were going to fight or bicker or whatever the hell this is, I would have gladly left and stayed at a hotel while y'all were here."

"You don't get to judge what is fair for me, so stop. You don't get to decide what I *think* is fair. Here is what I think. I think you are a coward and are scared of the unknown. You are afraid of risks, and you are afraid of feeling something. Fury, whatever happened in your past, you are using as a crutch, a cop-out. You could care about someone and not give your heart to them, you know? I would love to have a friend to talk to or hang out with that had something in common with me. Why couldn't that be us, huh? I don't need protecting from whatever it is you think you are protecting me from. It is going to be a lonely life for you if you don't open up to someone and get over yourself. Whatever happened to you is in your past, so fuckin' leave it there. You aren't that person anymore. None of that matters now. You have yourself a pretty decent thing going on here in PCB and there is no reason for you to be such an asshole to everyone. No one here deserves the way you treat them. You, sir, need to get some shit worked out in your head. I can promise you that I am done making the effort to reach out to you. Whatever you choose to do is fine by me, but you are done treating me the way you have. If having me here is such a big deal for you and ruining your life, I will gladly leave and go to a hotel. Just say the word and I'm out."

I was proud of the way I stood up for myself and put the ball back in his court. I wanted to be friends, but it was truly up to him. I wasn't going to beg to be a part of his life. I am better than that.

"You're right, okay? There are so many things going on in my head, and it's just hard."

"It's *hard?* Newsflash, life is hard. Life isn't fair, and

it isn't easy. You, Fury, ain't special. Seriously, get over yourself." I stopped long enough to breathe and fix more coffee, and then I started heading back outside.

"I have never had someone stand up to me like you do. I don't really know how to act. You call me out and it pisses me off. You don't understand what I have been through, so you don't know why it's so difficult for me to make friends."

"Right, I understand. The reason I don't get it is because you won't tell me. Maybe, one day you will. I am not asking you to right now. I'm only stating a fact and making a point that this is still all on you. You are the reason your life is the way it is. If you want it different, then change it. *You* are the only one that can. Now, I want peace and quiet. Is that something you can handle, or do I need to go for a walk?"

He looked at me as if he wanted to say something, but he didn't say a word. He sat down in the chair that I was in last night. His silence gave me a chance to let my mind catch up from the conversation we just had. It's a waiting game now. Does he stop being a childish asshole, or do I forget this crazy notion that the fucker has the capability to have a real friend?

As I watched the sun rise over the horizon, my brain took over and I reached a place of contentment. I realized, and came to terms with the fact that, he might not be capable of any of this. Not everyone is cut out for human interaction, clearly, he was one of those types.

I looked over at him and he gazed at the same sky with a different scowl on his face. I could almost hear the words he was tossing around in his head. He scrunched his nose up, squeezed his eyes shut, and pinched the bridge of his nose.

"I'm sorry. I was wrong, and I have no right treating you like I have. You've done nothing wrong. Will you forgive me? Can we start over…again?"

I turned and looked back at him with my mouth gaped open. I searched his face and could see the worry etched in his profile. Did I want to forget and forgive? Or did I want to just be done and go my own way and enjoy the beach? Either were fine with me honestly.

"That is up to you. It seems as if we are getting good at starting over. If you can be a decent human, then yes I would love to."

"I mean, all the way over?"

"What are you talking about, Fury?"

"I mean, you have made it clear that you like me, and I have told you that I like you, too. I don't kiss just anyone, and I don't keep putting myself through this mental clusterfuck for anyone, either. Why don't we go out for breakfast and coffee, yeah?" He swallowed. "Chief better be right about this." I heard him mumble under his breath.

"Are you asking me out on a date?"

"I think that's what this is. It's been so long since I have done it though, so I'm not sure I did it right." He only half joked.

"I am kind of hungry, and a breakfast date sounds nice. I will go get dressed. Be back in a few minutes."

"I'll change myself and be ready when you are."

I walked to the top of the stairs and looked back down. I saw Fury taking in a big sigh of relief. For a moment, all of my worry and nervousness washed away.

I changed my clothes, brushed my teeth, and put my hair in a top knot. When I got to the top of the stairs, I overheard Chief and Fury talking.

"Yeah, we are going out for breakfast and coffee."

"Don't screw this up. You have a tendency to sabotage yourself."

Thoughts of this intense man flew through my head. What is he hiding? Or was that what he was protecting me from? Whatever it is, I wanted to know. I was intrigued by this man, and the life he had prior to the one here after hearing that statement. I know that I can't know, as he shared with me several times before. However, the interest is still there. I will be good and not hound him for info, like I said I wouldn't.

I made my way down stairs and stared out at the ocean. The seagulls swooped down for breakfast and entertained me until Fury came back.

"You ready?"

"I think so."

"Not dressed like that, you ain't."

"What's wrong with how I'm dressed?"

"Nothing, if we were taking a car."

"You want to take the bike?"

He looked at me long and hard, "I don't often ride in cars if I can avoid it. Hence, biker." He pointed to himself and to the bike.

"I deserved that. I will go throw on some pants."

"And tennis shoes or boots. No flip flops or sandals."

"Is there anything else I should know about the dress attire? Perhaps when I come back down, I will meet your criteria?" I said with a grin and a wink as I went back up stairs.

We took a short drive to a local diner and sat in a booth at the back. He took one side and I took the other. He strategically sat in the seat that faced the door so he could see everyone that came in. It seems as if he has trust issues with the world.

"My name is Pearl, and I will be taking care of you this morning. What can I get you to drink?"

"Water and black coffee for me. Rumor, what do you want?"

"I'll have coffee with half and half, and a water too, please."

"I'll be right back."

We both scoured the menu, trying to find something to fill our bellies. He stopped looking at the menu and started looking at me. I could tell he wanted to say something but he was unsure of what actually came next.

"So, do you have plans when you get back to Rudy?"

"Depends on what you mean."

"I mean, do you just work at the resturaunt or do you attend school? Do you just work and play ball?"

"Honestly, I am very exciting. I work the same shift from eight to six Monday through Friday, and on weekends when they need me. I play ball and read in my spare time."

"Sarcasm much?"

"Clearly. Doesn't that sound like an exciting life? I'm seriously one of the oldest young people you will ever meet."

"Not boring, just simple."

He had a point. I did like the simple things in life. Simple car, simple house. I appreciate the simple joys in life, like sunrises and sunsets.

"I would say that simplicity is easier to live with than excitement all the time. I for one get tired of all the hoopla."

"What do you mean?"

"When one has Magnum in their life, things are never boring. Let's just leave it at that."

I could see that. He is very loud, and attention driven. He seemed like a nice enough guy, but one that a little bit of goes a long way.

Pearl came back to the table and took our order. I had eggs benedict and he had waffles.

The meal went smoothly. I did enjoy this lighter, nicer side of him. I wonder why he couldn't have been more like this in the beginning. It didn't cost him a thing to be nice to me. Perhaps he sees that now.

"What do you do other than your sales?"

"Ride my bike."

"You are as exciting as I am."

"Simple."

Truth. I couldn't argue with him there. I did at least read, and I like HGTV shows. I giggled out loud at the thought that crossed my mind.

"You care to share what is so funny?"

I didn't realize I had giggled out loud. I felt the blush that was covering my cheeks.

"Uh, just thinking about the oldest young person that I am. I was thinking that at least I liked to read and watch HGTV. Then it hit me that your life may, in fact, be more exciting than mine."

"Who knows, maybe all of that HGTV will come in handy one day. Were your eggs benedict good?"

"Yes. Thank you." I looked at him and gave an appreciative nod. "Why could this not have been how we started things?"

"Because I'm kind of an asshole."

I wasn't going to argue with him on that. He most certainly had been, though he has shown a softer side to me now.

"This has been nice. Thank you."

I meant it. Talking with him was easier than I thought

it would be. He didn't say much, but he wasn't totally mute. He had a nervous demeanor about him.

"You're welcome. So, what now? If this is a date, then I don't know what is next. I have never had a breakfast date. What happens at 9 a.m.?"

"First for me, too. What do you want to do? This is your town, I don't know what there is to do."

"We could go on a ride, and I could show you Front Beach Road."

I stared blankly at him.

"It's the highway along the coast. Miles and miles of beaches. Sound okay to you, or is there something else you would rather do?"

I could stand to take in the white sands, salty air, and ocean view. I nodded my head in agreement. We gathered our things, left a tip and headed out to see the scenery. He started up his bike and I hopped on with more grace than I figured I would have.

"Hang on," he said as he slowly eased onto the road. Between the blue sky hitting the crystal-clear water, the white sand, and the sound of his pipes, I completely lost myself. I thought about everything and nothing all at the same time. It was so therapeutic. It gave me a reprieve from ball, Crosby, Creed, and even Fury, as odd as that sounds. I didn't have to think about whatever this is or isn't. I was just riding.

Chapter 11

FURY

RIDING WITH HER felt good. I felt like I could do this Rumor thing. She wasn't so bad and this wasn't the worst thing I could be doing at the moment. I took a minute to give myself a pat on the back for not making her hate me again.

LATER THAT MORNING when we were back at the house, I mentioned there was going to be a poker game tonight, and the girls were welcome to come. I assumed that they would say no, because poker is a guy thing, but I was wrong. I got confirmation from Rumor, Charlie, and Haze that they wanted to attend. I assumed that Raige would come, too.

I looked around to make sure we were stocked with booze and snack food. Riddick had everything ready for, hopefully, the demise of our business dealings with Jay, and ultimately, Sully. I hated doing business with them, knowing that he tried to set up the club. He had fucked with the wrong club. No one screws over the Chosen Legion and stays in our good graces. What kind of message would that send to potential business partners?

The ball team was out at the beach and there was Magnum as well with his tongue hanging out. Charlie and Haze were waist deep in the water while Rumor was laid out reading a book. Raige was walking around talking on her phone. She had a bit of mystery about her and is also the one Magnum thinks is his next notch on his bedpost. She looks wild and reckless, just like him. She looks tough as nails, but I can't help but wonder if its all a façade. Either way, he wants her, and I have no doubt he will try to have her.

"Mag, roll up your tongue so you don't trip over it, and come here."

"They are so hot. Look at them in their bikinis. Especially that red head."

"Yeah dude, it's a good view for sure. Now, business. Jay is coming over tonight. I hope he tries something, so we can officially end business with him. I hope Chief is right and he hangs himself." I tried to get Mag's head in the game.

"Jay is a dumbass. You know this. Stop worrying about it." He said as he gawked at the ladies nonchalantly.

"He almost trapped me, and I don't take kindly to being fucked over."

"Almost only counts in horseshoes and hand grenades," he said with a satisfying smile, like he was proud to say something worth hearing. His head just couldn't focus on our conversation, because he constantly turned his head back and forth to Raige.

"Hey dumb shit, pay attention. I need your head in this tonight. The girls are coming, too."

"What?" That got his attention.

"Well, I ain't going to kick them out in a town they don't know, for hours on end."

"What? Did I just hear that right?"

"Hear what?"

"You're worried about the girls? Since when?"

"Look, we offered, or better yet, y'all offered, them accommodations. It would be real shitty to kick them out for a night and leave them to fend for themselves."

"She's getting to you, isn't she? You are getting soft on us aren't you?" he gouged, obviously trying to get a rise out of me.

"No, I'm not getting soft on you. No one is getting to me. We did go to breakfast today, and for a ride up the beach. It's not going to amount to much."

I didn't know if that last statement was true or not.

I hoped not, and I hoped so all at the same time, but hopefully that would shut him up. I do want something with her. I just haven't figured out how far I am willing to take it. There are things that have to be settled, and things that she must never know about, and that still haunted me.

The day rocked on as we watched the girls and discussed the evening's plan. As day turned to night, the girls decided to come in and get ready for the night's game.

"HEY, HOW'S IT going?" Jay said as he shook hands with Chief and Shooter, careful to avoid Whiskey and Charlie. He hadn't forgotten what she did to him. I must admit, when I heard the story, I laughed so hard at his expense.

It's not lost on me that feelings are being brought to surface since the girls arrived. I hadn't been this relaxed and, dare I say, happy, in a good while. I'd been so busy being pissed off at the world that I had forgotten how it felt to laugh, and it all started with Charlie. Without her situation with her ex, none of this would have happened.

"Good, grab a seat and let's get to betting. You're the guest, you pick your game." Chief stated with no trace of suspiciousness in his voice.

"Five card stud then, fellas. Are the ladies staying, too? Sure would be fun to look at that all night."

"You so much as breathe in the direction of that blonde," Whiskey tossed his head in the general direction of Charlie, "and I'll make sure you never see again. Do we have an understanding? She isn't over here right now to beat me to the punch this time. Although, it was worth it to see her kick your ass," he seethed as he leaned over the table. His hands were gripping the sides so hard his knuckles were turning white.

"Man, I said I was sorry. I didn't know she was your girl."

"I know you are. Now apologize." Whiskey snapped back.

"Guys, enough. Let's try to have a civil game of poker, drink, and gamble. How 'bout it?" Shooter suggested sternly.

An hour or so into the games, Rumor came around and played hostess and asked if she could grab a beer for anyone. When she gets to me, I smiled at her briefly, and after she brought us a round of beer, she sat beside me and asked if she could watch.

"And who do we have here?" Jay asked. He was starting to slur his words.

"Name is Rumor. Nice to meet you."

"For sure." He said, as he eyed her like an object, he could get his hands on.

I wanted so badly to tell Rumor that he was a worthless piece of shit, and she shouldn't waste her time being polite to him, but I also needed him to fuck up, so we could have a reason to cut ties. I sat idly and waited for him to make his mistakes.

I shot a glance over to Chief, and he winked one eye at me and grinned, pretty much telling me *I told you so.* I flipped him off and looked at the hand I was dealt.

"I'll take three," I said as I gave back an eight of hearts, four of spades, and a two of clubs. This was clearly not the best hand, but I felt like I should see what everyone else had, and as it turns out, I have a pretty good poker face.

I held a six of diamonds and a ten of hearts. The dealer handed me three more cards. I kept my face stoic, and I held the bottom of the cards on the table. I peeked at the corner of the new cards and revealed a seven of hearts. Better than I expected. I looked at the next card and saw a nine of diamonds. What are the odds? Feeling sure that lady luck was not on my side, as she really hadn't been in years, I fully expected my final draw to be a wild, random card like a four of clubs. Instead, I was surprised at what I held. I was holding a small straight. Six, seven, eight, nine, and ten. Not in the same suit, but still enough to raise the bet on.

"Raise fifty bucks." I said with confidence. Of course, I knew that they thought I was bluffing, and they would all call my bet or raise it. Not one of the guys folded, but instead, tossed out money, which is exactly what I wanted.

"Show 'em boys," Chief shouted.

We all flipped over our cards. Whiskey had a pair of aces, Chief had two pairs, Jay had a straight as well, but mine was better. He revealed a five, six, seven, eight, nine.

The ten high wins. Serves the bastard right to get beat by one number. Shooter had a hand full of junk and should have folded.

"Boys, this one belongs to Fury." Chief said as everyone discarded their cards.

I dragged my pot from the center of the table and grinned at Rumor. Perhaps, lady luck is on my side tonight. We would see. The night was still young.

"Charlie girl, get me a beer, yeah?" I heard Whiskey call out.

She came over and I watched as the love birds exchanged a look of lust before she got up and went to the kitchen. It was only a few minutes before I heard the top pop on a can. "Thanks wife."

"Welcome. Now win me some money. Fury has taken enough from you," she said with a wink.

"I'll try, Babes. Fucker has a poker face that gives nothing away. I never can tell what he is up to."

"Hey, you there." Jay said loudly.

No one paid him any mind.

"I said, 'hey, you there', blondie."

Heads turned now.

"Get me a beer, would ya?"

"I know you ain't talkin to me." Snapped Charlie. "I sure would hate to whip your ass again, but this time in front of a bunch of dudes."

"Nah, I'm talkin' to this one here," he said as he nudged his head at Rumor.

"Me?" she asked, shock evident in her voice.

"Yeah, you. You sat there and looked pretty long enough. You need to do something more productive."

I can't believe this jack ass has the balls to talk to her like that. Anger consumed me, and I felt heat rise from my toes all the way to my ears. Just as I stood up, Rumor made her way to me, put her hand on my shoulder, and pushed me back down. She got really close to him and said, "And what kind could I get for you, Sir?" She asked with a straight face. Now who was the one with a poker face? She sashayed her way to the kitchen and fetched the slime bag a beer.

I was trying to wrap my head around what was going on but kept coming up short. I started to get up to make my way over to him, and Chief shook his head one time, and cut his eyes at Rumor, then back to Jay. I knew he was telling me to see what played out. Clearly, I wasn't going to let anything escalate too much, so I let it unfold in front of me, and it was quite a show.

She sashayed back from the kitchen with Jay's beer.

"Do I need to open it for you too, Sir?"

"Nah I will…"

"Oh no, I insist. After all, I need to quit looking pretty and be more productive. What better way to be productive than to open the beer for Sir?" She took the can and popped the top on it and then poured the ice-cold Busch into his lap and said, "Oh, I am so sorry Master. I feel like I have disappointed you."

"You bitch!" He started to get up and go after her.

"You lay a finger on me, and I will end your reproduction capabilities. Be careful what you wish for. You just might get what you desire. Now, Jay, if you ever talk to me like that again, I will personally see to it that you don't walk for a few hours."

"Oh, this ain't over. I will get you back for this."

"I think he is threatening your girl, yo." Magnum piped up. He had been sitting quietly trying to make conversation with Raige.

My girl? No. She isn't my girl.

"Jay, meet me outside. Now." I demanded.

Chief nodded his head, as he knew that I was about to end things with Jay and that there would likely be a punch… or seven thrown.

Alas, he couldn't take his drunk ass away from the table, so what's a guy to do? I helped him…forcefully. I gripped the back of his shirt and drug the punk outside. I contemplated beating him to a pulp but realized that wouldn't be fair. What kind of man takes advantage of someone in this state? That didn't stop me from getting a few licks in and blacking his eyes. I did let him walk away, so that's a plus, right?

"Get your sorry ass out of here, so I don't pulverize you. Find someone else to get your liquor from. The next time you think about setting us up, you should remember who you're dealing with. What are you snitching for anyhow? You know what? It don't matter. Get the fuck off this property and don't come back. If I see you around again, you won't be walking. You'll be lucky to be breathin', and that is a fuckin' promise."

I turned around and left him there on the ground so that I didn't beat him into an oblivion. I needed a breather, a timeout, so that I could gain my composure again and sort through why I was feeling this pissed. Sure, I had had a few drinks and felt alright, but I think this was more than a pissed drunk thing. But what was it? I walked around to the back deck and lit a smoke and enjoyed the cool night air. Thoughts of what had transpired were circulating in my head, crowding each other and causing confusion and chaos. As I was sitting out on the deck, with the cool ocean breeze blowing, all I could think about was Rumor. My thoughts were so loud, I never heard her come out, until she said my name. I shot up from my seat on the lounge, startled and frustrated. I snapped, "What?"

"Fuck you too, grumpy ass."

"Shit, I'm sorry, you caught me off guard."

"Ah, so the fearless biker can be shaken."

I looked over and saw that cute little smirk. I couldn't help but grin back with a little laugh, "Smart ass."

Now the smirk is a full blown smile, "Momma always said 'I'd rather be a smart ass than a dumb ass.'"

"Well... she kinda has a point, don't ya think?"

"Why yes, yes she does." she responded with a giggle.

As I stare back into those icy blue eyes, all I can think is how beautiful she is. Before I knew it, I blurted, "You're beautiful."

"I know."

My jaw pops open, and she laughs again. That sound, it's almost magical. Then I do the unthinkable. Before I even realize it, I've moved. I'm in her space, leaning in, and, to my surprise, she closes the distance and our lips meet in a gentle, hesitant kiss. I pull back almost instantly with an apology on my lips, "Damn I…"

"What? You're sorry, you didn't mean to? You tripped? What the fuck? You're drunk? What excuse are you going to use? I mean, am I not good enough? Hell we're adults, we've had a few drinks, what the fuck's wron…"

Before she could finish I kissed her again, this time letting myself go, my hands went into her long blonde hair, fingers tangled, I pulled back slightly, silently asking for permission, and when she didn't say anything, I pushed forward. She opened her mouth just enough for my tongue to enter and intertwine with hers. When the kiss ended, breathing heavily, I stared into those icy blue eyes, and I leaned in to kiss her again. This time slower, gentler, but with a sense of urgency she seemed to recognize and accept. I slid my hands to her lower back, pulled her closer, and depend the kiss. Her soft moan of approval urged me forward, so my hands started to travel under her shirt and up her soft curves, as her hands were making a descent of their own under my shirt, up my stomach then up to my chest. I broke the kiss long enough to tug her shirt over her head, as I leaned back and mumbled, "Son of a bitch, woman."

Once again, I closed the distance and began a new assault on her lips, jaw, and neck, then I continued my descent to her perfect tits. Gently I eased her down onto the lounge chair. Not ideal, but at this point there was no going back, and it was gonna have to work. She made quick work of my shirt and took a second to admire my in. I didn't give her long, because I knew we could be busted at any time. I didn't want her to change her mind, so I kneeled beside her and went to work on her pants, gently pulling them down those fine as fuck legs that I wanted wrapped around me. It was like she could read my mind. She pulled me closer and wrapped them around my waist as I began kissing her again. I reached behind her and unclasped her bra, letting those perfect tits fall. I could feel her nipples harden as they rubbed against my chest.

She began working on my pants as I put her nipple in my mouth and sucked, which was rewarded with a soft moan. Damn, this woman was sexy. As I caught her mouth again, she finally got my pants undone. I eased her panties down her legs, kissing here and there on my way to her feet, and as I pulled my boxers down I couldn't help but take a second to be in awe of the beautiful woman lying in front of me. Slowly I climbed on top of her and started kissing her, my hands going everywhere and nowhere all at the same time. I put my hand on her hip and entered her. Slowly I seated myself inside her, and once in, I glanced up at her, kissed her and began slowly pulling out and thrusting back in. She moaned softly and ran her fingernails down my chest, which earned a moan from me. I began to pick up the pace, faster and a little harder, and as I began to build my climax, she dug her nails in as she came close to hitting her climax as well. "Damn baby, hold on," I moaned as I was about to come. Then she moaned, "Fury" in a hoarse whisper, and with that I let go of pent up frustrations and other thoughts that weighted me down. We lay there for a few minutes trying to gather ourselves and our thoughts. I pulled my boxers and jeans on and handed her clothes to her as I lit a cigarette. I walked to the edge of the deck, leaned on the railing, and tried to figure out what the fuck just happened.

What had I just done? What was I thinking? This shouldn't have ever happened. I couldn't let her think that this was something that I always did, or that I wanted all the time. I turned to find her and that's when I noticed that she wasn't there. I snuffed out my cigarette, took the butt, and threw it in the trash. Lost in my whirlwind mind, I hadn't even realized that she left. I literally ran into her coming out of the bathroom.

"Hi." was all she said.

"Shit, I thought you ran away from me."

"Nope, just had to pee. Why are you looking at me like that?

"I just haven't done that in a long time, and I didn't want you to think that's what I am after, and I didn't plan it, and I'm sorry for everything that happ.."

Before I could finish, she raised up on her toes and kissed me. "I willingly participated in that. I know you didn't plan it, so shut up. Now, I want another beer and I would like to go back outside. You coming with me, or am I going alone?"

I nodded and let her lead the way to the table. She sat on one chair and I stood beside her, both of us clearly trying to make sense of what just transpired. I had thoughts of regret, joy, hope, and heartache running rampant through my mind. I regret that I did it, I'm overjoyed that I did it, and I am heartbroken that I did it. It did, however, give me a sense of hope that I could eventually move on someday. That I was capable of having a relationship with someone else.

She stared at the ocean as I stared at her. No amount of alcohol would justify what we had just done. I wonder what she is thinking? Was she battling some of the same feelings I was? She even said that she didn't do this kind of thing and yet here I am making her do something out of the ordinary. Was she comparing me to the other two idiots in her life? Why are all these questions in my head right now? Was this some way that people dealt with the walk of shame? Wait, was she going to walk the walk of shame? Good god, what have I done?

"Rumor," I started to say.

"Just don't, okay? Clearly, you are not comfortable with things, and come to think of it, I don't really know if I am either, now that the liquor is wearing off. That has never happened to me before. Sex doesn't just happen with people I am not involved with. I am now feeling a little disheveled, and I think I need some time to digest all this." The effects of the alcohol were gone, and courage was in short supply now.

"You want time? You got it. I don't really know what to say right now. I do this, but not with girls that matter, so it's new to me as well."

"Did you really just tell me that? After I just had unprotected sex with you, you tell me you are a whore. Great. Do I need to be tested?"

"What the fuck, Rumor? Get tested if you want, but I am safe when I am with anyone except….", I stopped before I went any further.

"Except?" she asked.

If I say her then it looks like I'm desperate and grasping at straws to keep some kind of arbitrary line of communication open. But, if I say anything about Daisy or that situation, I open up a whole new can of worms.

"You. Lately, that is."

"Look, we are both adults. Let's just forget about it

and go about our night and see how things play out from here on out, yeah?"

I didn't reply. I turned and nodded, then left her there on the deck.

Back inside the party was still going on strong. Magnum had decided he was going to show off his mad dance skills. He looked like a drunk white guy trying to out-do a dancer that dances freestyle. I noticed Raige just staring in disbelief at the idiot on the table. Clearly, Mag had too much liquor. I grabbed the twitching moron and hauled him off the table and into the living room and dumped his ass on the couch. Maybe, if I caused enough of a scene with him, no one will notice that I have been gone, and perhaps no one will put together that Rumor was gone, too.

"Hey, maaan. Why you gotta go and kill my groove like that?" Magnum asked in a drunken voice.

"Mainly, because you looked like you were an epileptic up there having a seizure. You're welcome, maaan." I mocked him.

It wasn't long until he was passed out and Raige could finally have some peace and let loose for a while without Magnum trying to sway her mind to give him a chance.

Rumor quietly walked past us and yawned.

"I'm spent. I'm headed to bed. Night y'all."

All at once everyone, except Magnum, said goodnight. I watched her walk her fine self up the stairs, and fresh memories of what just happened a few minutes prior came back to me in a rush. Its awakened parts of me that I needed to stay asleep. I immediately changed my focus to Magnum and things died back down. I gave her a few minutes to get to her room, then I carried my drunken buddy from the couch to his room and plopped him down on his bed. I thought about being a good friend and at least taking his shoes off him but decided against it.

When I left his room to head to mine, I passed Rumor in the hall. We just looked at each other. No words were said, no feelings exchanged. Just blank stares. It was like she was willing me to talk to her, but what do I say? Sorry I just defiled you on the deck? Thanks for a good time? Seriously, I had no idea what to say to her. I didn't say a thing. Just looked at the door to my room, and closed the distance, leaving Rumor to be with her thoughts alone in the hall.

One thing was for sure. If I was going to keep her at arms distance, this was a sure-fire way to do it. Nothing like ignoring a girl after you sleep with her to run her off. Even for me, this is beyond cruel. She asked for it. Yes, she asked for it and I needed it. It was for the best, or that is what I tried to make myself believe.

Chapter 12

RUMOR

WHAT HAD I DONE? I was connected to him now, and no matter how I thought I wasn't, the connection was made. I'm not able to sleep with someone and not have any type of relationship with them. I am simply not wired that way. I couldn't burden him with the drama of my life. Nor do I want the drama in his life, that he won't talk about.

There were two ways the rest of my time in PCB could go. I could suck it up and be like the majority of women that are capable of casual, no strings sex. I could also ignore him, and act like none of this happened, that last night was a really awesome dream. Tomorrow was just as good of a day as any to figure that out. Tonight, the inner siren inside was basked in the glory of her escapade on the deck.

Thoughts of Creed and Crosby passed through my mind as I started trying to piece together this debacle. I had somewhat come to terms with losing Crosby. I knew I couldn't change it. Losing Creed on the other hand, that still bothered me. As much as I didn't want finality, I also needed it. I had accepted that it isn't healthy to live the way I am living, but I don't want to accept that things are really over. Not when I have zero proof of him being permanently gone. Now Fury was in the picture, and there's whatever we are. I'm caught between wanting to want him, and wanting to not ever talk to him again, for his own sake.

As thoughts of everything swirl around my head, I hear a knock on the door.

"Come in," I say with surprise in my voice. Who in the hell is knocking on my door?

I listened for the doorknob to turn and silence.

"Fury?"

Nothing.

"Well, fine. Have it your way. I'm not begging you to come in here. Remember, you're the one that knocked on my door."

"Uhhh. Rumor, I'm drunk. Really, really drunk. Even I can see there is something up with you and Fury. You should remeid... remedial...rem... you should fix it," slurred a sloshed Magnum.

"Look, Mag. I appreciate you looking out for me, but

there is nothing going on between us. If there was, would we be in separate rooms? And why are you knocking on my door?"

"Uhh, yeah. It's called de-ni-al. You both are swimming in it. See what I did there? De-ni-al. The Nile?" He said proudly.

"We all see the looks, and feel the tension. I am trying to play matchmaker. I call it. Right here, right now. You two will be together at some point. I see that even through the beer goggles."

"You're drunk, Mag. Go to bed." Oh, Magnum! How is it that the drunkest one here has the clearest vision? Shit, did he see us?

"Is this asshole bothering you?" Fury rumbled as he made his way past my door.

"He is just trying to be helpful, no worries." I lied.

Fury cut his eyes at me and tried to see what was going on in my head. I knew his look, as it was the one I shared in return. Our eyes locked, and briefly, it felt like things had settled down between us. Just as quickly as it happened, it was over.

"See? That right there! I see it. You two knockin' boots? You're acting weird and shit. I'm hungry. We got any food?" Mag changed the subject, laid down on my bed, and fell fast asleep.

Fury glared at Magnum, but didn't say anything, he just turned to leave. He stopped before he got to the door, "You sure he is okay here?"

"I think he is pretty harmless as he's plopped down on the foot of my bed passed out. Clearly he wasn't too hungry. Poor guy, drunk munchies are awful."

"Look, Rumor, do you want to talk, or does all this weirdness just have to run its course? I don't know what is going on and I damn sure don't know how to deal with it."

"Look, this is the first time I have ever done anything like that, so I have no clue how this is supposed to go. I would say that we need to figure out what it is that we want from each other in the time we have left. I am only here a couple more days, then its back to Rudy. What I do know, is that no matter how much I say, I can just let things be and not have any strings, I just don't know if it is humanly possible. Sex is supposed to mean something right?"

"Not always. Does it tonight?"

"I don't know, that's the thing. I don't want it to, but if it don't then I'm a huge slut. I don't want it to be weirder than normal between us. This can't be helping that any. Did it mean anything to you?"

"I'm not sure I have an answer to that. I will say you aren't the same as the others. You don't repulse me, and I would never call you just for a booty call. I can say that there is no love there. So take that answer for what it is."

"Truth. I can handle that."

An awkward silence passed before he said, "Since there is a passed out idiot on your bed, you can sleep in my room."

"The other girls are going to have to deal with him if I leave him here."

"So? Raige might enjoy it. She could really have some fun with this, if she wanted."

"Fury, I…"

"I won't make you, nor will I beg you. I am just trying to let you have a bed since Magnum took yours. Hell, if you don't want to, then I will load him up and drop his drunk ass back at his own room. Only this time, I will lock the door. It'll take the drunken idiot a minute to figure out why he can't open the door."

"I think that is best. I need time to wrap my head around what happened. I can't do that if I am distracted by the very thing I am trying to wrap my head around. I don't know if I am okay with everything, and clearly I can't be trusted alone with you."

He didn't say much. He looked at me with confusion and conflict in his eyes as he turned and walked away. I guess I was going to find my own sleeping arrangements tonight.

Why was this so hard? Why can't I just nail and bail like so many other people? No, not me. I have to have morals and shit.

I clearly wasn't going to sleep anytime soon, so I decided to go back downstairs and enjoy the peace and quiet. I missed Rudy in that moment. I missed the frogs croaking, crickets singing, and all the other wildlife sounds at night. Here there were only ocean sounds, and I was quickly becoming homesick. I made my way quietly down the hall and before I got to the stairs I heard Fury talking to Chief. I hurried down the stairs before I was seen, to avoid eavesdropping.

At my newfound spot of solace, which was ironically the same spot that Fury and I had sex a bit ago, my head started to clear. Was it the salty air? I realized, and came to terms with the fact that, I would see what happened. What's done is done and I couldn't change it if I tried. If we didn't speak again, that was fine. If we hooked up again, eh, there are worse things that could happen, right? He is good looking, and nice to me, most of the time. Why can't I knock the cobwebs off? We are two consenting adults. There should be no strings or weird feelings. I had to force myself to get over that.

As I came to terms with things, I felt a light touch on my shoulder. As I turned around slowly, I saw another twenty dollar bill in an outstretched hand. This time though, it wasn't Fury. It was Chief. Great, he told Chief about that comment. Oh well, seems as if these bikers have a thing for paying me for my thoughts and opinions.

"Chief? What are you doing?"

"Well, someone said that you don't like to talk unless you are getting paid for your thoughts."

"That makes me sound like a prostitute. Only patrons get my thoughts, not my body. Nonetheless, it's still sleazy. I don't want your damn money. What do you need?"

"He is all tore up and won't tell me why. Seems as if you are the cause of his discontent."

"I didn't realize I was that bad for him. I will stay away," I said sarcastically.

"Damn it, that ain't what I meant, and you know it. You two seem to have an amazing chemistry, and you don't even see it. Even Magnum noticed and he is drunk. He thought he saw you two making googoo eyes at each other before he got so trashed he started gyrating on the table."

"Gyrating?"

"Well it sure as hell wasn't dancing. I don't care how much he thinks it was. He is mistaken."

"So what do you suggest I do then, matchmaker?"

"Go talk to him."

"Yeah, because it's that easy."

"Nothing easy is worthwhile, and nothing worthwhile is easy. You have a choice to make, Rumor. I will tell you again, you are good for him. I haven't figured out yet why, but you two are something else. Don't you at least owe it to yourself to see what is there? Huh? What is it going to hurt?"

"You bikers are bossy. If I go talk to him will you leave me alone about it?"

"Yes."

"Well, that was easy enough."

"I really think it will only take this one time. I'm telling you, there is something about him now that you are here. It's weird."

"You can say that again." I whispered under my breath.

He looked at me and grinned, then shot me a wink. Not a hey-your're-sexy wink but a I-know-what-you-did wink. Shit. I can feel the color rise in my cheeks. Before I revealed everything, I went to find Fury.

A strong feeling overcame me. It hit me right in the chest. It was warm, light, and happy. Not love, God knows I wasn't ready for that, but a feeling of contentment and peace. I was finally able to accept things and possibly have a somewhat normal presence for the remainder of the time I was here. I still missed the sounds of the woods, but I wasn't as homesick as I was before.

I walked down the hall, and found the door that Fury was behind. I approached it like I had all the courage in the world. I stopped before knocking to take a deep breath and round up my courage. Just as I was about to knock, he opened the door.

"Hi," was all I could say.

"Hi. What are you doing here?"

"I came to talk, if you are up for it. If not I will go back outside and leave you alone."

Fury looked intently, his eyes slightly moving back and forth, searching for something. "It's fine, you can come in. I guess we have some stuff to deal with, don't we?"

"Yeah, its called feelings, Fury. They seem to be very confusing and contradicting, and I don't know how to deal with them. It seems as you are the root of all the feels right now."

He ushered me into his room. It was fairly bare and boring. It gave nothing away, no looks into his past, no family pictures on the walls, no warmth at all.

"Sit." he pointed to the bed.

"Okay, thanks."

"You want anything? I'll go get it right quick."

"Beer actually sounds fantastic."

"I'll be right back then."

As he left his room to go get the drinks, I couldn't help but admire the sexiness of him. He had no idea what he could do to a woman. After he was out of sight, I started gazing around the room trying to catch a glimpse into his life, maybe a hint of something, anything. Alas, there was nothing.

"Here you go. Now, what did you want to talk about?"

"Us. I mean, what happened, and if there is anything else in store, or was it just a fluke, do we tell people or do w…"

Before I could finish the random thoughts I was vomiting from my mouth, he strolled over and kissed me. It was a sweet peck on the lips, but he didn't back away. It was like he was frozen there. It turned out he was just trying to gather his thoughts and feelings and was trying to shut me up so he could think, too.

As he pulled away slowly, he looked into my eyes and said, "Do you want an us? Are you ready for a long distance relationship of any kind? You need to think about this before we go any further because it will be tough. I'm not easy to deal with on a normal basis, much less with the added distance."

"That's just it, Fury. I don't know if I do. What I do know is I like you, and I enjoy your company, when you aren't being an ass. Where are you with this?"

He thought for a minute and then shocked me with his unexpected and honest response. "I think since our little escapade on the deck a bit ago, I have realized that I am over some things and I think I can move on now. For fuck's sake, you have been in my life now for less than a week, and so much has changed for me and *in* me. I can't help but to believe it is because of you. Then I wonder how. We don't know each other so how are you, the pretty stranger, fixing me?"

"You think I am the one that is fixing you? Are you sure you want that?" I asked in a shocked, yet somewhat hopeful tone.

"I damn sure don't want to start again with someone new. These last few days have been enough to stress me out, make me rethink my life, and given me a different perspective on things. I had a wake up call of sorts, and I do think I'm ready. I would like that be with you, if you are willing to take a chance on me. You just have to realize there are things I can't talk about from my past, and you have to be okay with that. You have to trust me."

"Do you remember what I said? Your past is just that,

leave it there. You aren't that person anymore. I don't give a damn what happened in your past. I don't live there. I hope at some point you will feel comfortable enough to discuss it with me, but if it doesn't ever come to that, then that is fine, too. I would like to think you could confide in me and trust me with whatever big secret you have. I shared a pretty ugly fact about me with you, but, I don't know what kind of secret you are harboring, so I can't judge you and why you aren't able to share it."

"So…this is a thing now? You and me." He asked with a hopeful and scared tone in his voice.

"If that is what you want, we can be a thing. We can be a slow thing. We can play it by ear I suppose. I will be leaving in a few days to head home, so maybe it is only a short term thing. Who knows?"

"I don't know that I want it to be short term. Since you have been here, I have felt so much weight lifted off me. I don't want to see what it's like without you here. You have made me feel again and I'm starting to feel alive and happier and not alone."

I thought about his words and if there was a hidden question behind them, but decided not to dwell on it. There were still three or so days before I had to leave. That is, if I couldn't convince Charlie and the other girls to stay a bit longer.

"I don't know that it is possible for me to stay longer, nor do I know if I even want to. My life is back in Rudy."

"Your life there sounds like it sucks. No offense. If you want to go home, I completely understand, and we can figure something out. Let's not dwell on that yet."

I agreed. My life was a bit lackluster, boring, and sad. Here it was more exciting than it had been in a couple years. There was an ocean and excitement. I could get used to this, but I missed the trees and mountains of Rudy, too.

"Stay with me tonight," he asked in a hurried tone. Like he was trying to say it before he chickened out.

"Are you sure you're ready for that? There are sure to be questions and looks from everyone in the morning."

"I don't really care. I just want you to be with me. I will tell the guys to fuck off when they ask me questions. You ready for that with your girls?"

"Yeah, I can handle my girls."

He slowly walked over to me and stood me up. He had his big hands on my shoulders, holding me at arms length, looking at my eyes, trying to see if this was real. There was a force so strong it felt magnetic between us. "You feel it too, don't you?"

"Yes, yes I do. I just don't know what to do, or how to handle it. I say we just take it in stride and go with it. Let's see where this goes."

He dipped down and cupped my face so gently and kissed me. This kiss was different than the ones earlier. This one was not confusing, hurried, urgent, or frantic. It was the opposite of all of that. It was slow and intentional.

He's making me feel things that I don't know if I'm ready for again, or ever will be, but I'll be damned if it isn't happening anyway.

As the kiss deepened, he gently slid a hand into my hair as the other found its way to the small of my back. He pulled me tight against his hard body, and I slid my hands up his chest and along his jaw line, the stubble rough against my soft hands. I slid the other hand into the hair at the base of his neck, tugging, pulling him closer. He eased me down onto the bed, as the kisses became more urgent, yet remaining gentle. With a slight tug of my lower lip, he began his descent, moving slowly, down my neck with the occasional nip here and there. He was making me want more, all while moving at a treacherously slow pace.

The assault stopped as he sat back on his heels, pulling me up with him. His hands went to the hem of my shirt. With the slow lift, he made sure to graze my skin along the way, sending little shocks each time our skin met. Flinging my shirt to the side, he gently pushed me back onto the bed with one hand as he quickly shed his shirt with the other. I lay there in awe of his body, but before I could look too closely, he dipped down and kissed me again, his body heavy on top of mine in all the right places. He pulled away again, and began lacing kisses down my neck, where he bit down just a little, causing a moan to escape my mouth. He kept moving, across my collar bone, down across my breasts, his breath hot against my skin, causing my body to flood with heat. With one hand he massaged my breast, as he took the other breast into his warm, wet mouth, sucking, gently biting, with just enough pressure to cause a flood of heat at the apex of my thighs. I threw my head back with a moan as he moved down my stomach, his hands skimming the top of my skin leaving goosebumps in their wake. His hands slid between the fabric of my shorts and the fabric of my panties, over my hips and slowly down my legs, my skin burning where his hands touched, all the way from my head to my feet. He began slowly leaving a trail of open mouth kisses up my legs, the inside of one ankle, then the other a little further up. He kissed my calf, my knee, my inner thigh, where he bit me lightly causing me to sigh. He continued making his way to my sex, and as he began kissing his way around my panty line, he hooks his fingers in the waist line of my panties, and slowly revealed all of me.

He dipped his face down and let his nose slide up my wetness. He pulled away just enough that I could see the grin on his face as he kissed my core. Slowly he licked his way from my opening to my clit, circling it and then going back down, his tongue began a slow assault, in and out, up and around, back down, in and out, quickening his pace when my moans and pants became audible. I was breathing hard, my hand was gripping his hair, pulling him closer and holding him where I needed the pressure most, the feeling of his stubble against my thighs pushing me over the edge. An orgasm surged through me, and he quickly moved up my body and when he kissed me, I could taste my arousal on his tongue. I pushed him onto his back and straddled his hips. As I laced open mouth kisses down his neck, I let my teeth graze and was awarded with soft moans that spurred me forward. I kissed my way down his chest, sucking and applying some pressure on a nipple, his hand gripped my hips, holding me still as he ground his hips into mine. I needed him inside me.

I began working on his pants, pulling them off, placing kisses up his thighs, breathing hot heavy breaths on my way to his dick. When I reached what I wanted, I blew a hot breath from the head of his dick to the base, and I felt him shutter and moan. I ran the tip of my tongue from the base to the tip, slowly pulling it into my mouth, swirling my tongue around the tip and taking his length into my mouth, and slowly back up to the tip. I dipped back down again and again, his breathing picked up as he reached down to stop me. He hooked his arms under mine and pulled me to up his long lean body. He rolled over on top of me and kissed me as he aligned himself at my opening, and slowly he pushed inside, filling me, stretching me, as I pulsed around him. He began gently moving in and out, grinding his hips into mine thrust after thrust. My breathing quickened as I began tightening, his pace increased, getting harder and harder. He kissed me, down my neck as he kept up his pace. He gently bit down on my neck, causing me to moan as he pushed me over the edge. He slowed and started the process over again, kissing his way down my neck, moving in and out, breathing hard. As he felt my body building again, he began thrusting harder, faster, biting my shoulder as our orgasms shook through us. He gently moved to lay at my side, wrapping me in his arms and pulling me against his body. I placed my head on his chest, and as our breathing regulated, we both came down from our high, entwined our fingers, and held each other until sleep claimed us.

Chapter 13

FURY

"You seem to have taken a likin' to Rumor, and I assume she was with you seeing no one has seen her this morning. You want to tell her that they are cutting the vacation short?" Magnum said with the smell and look of a hangover dripping off him.

"Yeah, I'll tell her," I said in a reluctant hurry. I wasn't ready for her to go just yet. I had finally come to terms that it was okay for me to move on, and now her time here was being cut short. I knew I had to tell her that the cops were snooping around here and that Whiskey and Briar are taking the girls back to Rudy. I would handle Jay. I know good and well that is who instigated the prodding law enforcement. He should've waited a while before having them stop by to check on things and investigate suspicious activity. Now our whole operation is compromised. The

Rudy guys are taking their girls back before anything happens to them and they get caught up in anything.

Whiskey already had the 4Runner loaded with equipment and booze. He had the shine in water bottles in the ice chest and hidden in suit cases. Briar was chomping at the bit to get on the road, so he and Jazz took off. Whiskey was a little more relaxed about it.

I went back up stairs to wake Rumor and to my surprise she was already awake.

"Good morning."

"Same to you," I said as I walked up to her. "We need to talk."

"Here we go. You made a mistake, it's you not me, I knew ..."

"Are you 'bout done?" I cut her off. "The cops are snooping around here. I have a feeling Jay tipped them off. Y'all are leaving to go back to Rudy."

"Oh. Why are the cops coming around? I don't understand."

"Look, it really doesn't matter why, this is one of those things we don't discuss, okay? We don't want you girls in the crossfire if it should get ugly, so it is best if you go home."

Disappointment covered her face. I was sure that mine wasn't cheery.

"Where does that leave things with us? I told you I was bad luck and that you shouldn't mess with me."

"You aren't bad luck. It's because of you that I have

finally let some of my past go. It's because of you that I know now that I can move on. I will always be grateful for this time I've had with you. If you want to try to keep in touch, I would be open to that, but I won't risk you getting in the crossfire of a feud you had no part in. You have to go."

"Yeah, I guess I do."

I watched her get her clothes on and walk to the door. As she reached for the knob she turned back to look at me with hurt and disappointment and said, "It was good while it lasted though, right?" and walked out.

I couldn't even respond. I was fairly sure implied there was no working this out long distance. She made it very clear that she was hurt and was, once again, left alone. In her eyes, this was rejection and the universe saying *you are destined to be alone. You are no good for anyone.* She was good for me. I have let some shit go in the last few days that without her, I would have never done. I have let Daisy go. I still have my secrets that I can't share, and I still feel like I can't be honest with her, but she showed me how to let go and open up. However, the little *I am dead* secret will always be there to put a damper on things. It is best she go and not subject herself to my lie of a life.

I followed her to her room where she had started packing her things. I saw the disappointment and hurt on her face and knew that I was the cause.

"Rumor, this thing between us, it isn't over. I just won't

risk you or your girls getting caught in the crossfire. Jay is an idiot, an unpredictable loose cannon. You need to get out for your own saftey. I will come see you soon. I don't know how soon, but I swear, I am coming to see you."

Her sad eyes lifted up to see me and I saw hope. I walked over to embrace and show her I meant what I said. Telling her at this point would be pointless.

I tilted her head up to stare into her eyes, so she could feel what I was telling her instead of just hearing it. I kissed her softly.

"I'll help you finish packing."

A heavy silence blanketed us, making for awkward last moments together. Her bags were finally packed and loaded into the 4Runner. I hugged her goodbye and kissed her gently. I tried to reassured her, "This ain't over, Rumor. I will be down to see you soon, after some dust settles here."

She gave me a pitiful, heartbroken smile. I shut her door and patted it twice, signaling that he was good to pull away.

"Why do you look like someone kicked your puppy? You getting soft on us, huh? Can't hang because your latest piece of ass left to go home? Good. We didn't need the extra drama around here anyhow." Riddick popped off out of nowhere.

"If I want any more lip out of you, I'll bust it open."

"Annnd he's back. Good to see you again my friend," he smarted back.

I pointed at him and started walking closer to him. I remembered that he called Rumor a bitch. More anger and frustration exploded from within and I layed the bastard out. One unexpected hit. I went with it though. I wasn't about to stop now, I had a point to prove. I said I would deal with him later and that time has arrived. I picked him up by his shirt and got in his face, "That, brother, is for calling my girl a bitch. You need to know your role and treat women with a little respect. Especially if they are an old lady or with one of us. If I have to remind you again, I will make damn sure you are done here...not voted in. Do we have an understanding?" I threw him back down.

He didn't say anything, just got up and walked away as he wiped blood from his lip. But the look he shot back said all I needed to hear. He got it. He wasn't sorry for his actions, but he damn sure wouldn't do it again.

Back inside, as I was trying to recollect myself, my thoughts were interrupted.

"I assume you two were getting along well then?" Chief meddled.

"She stayed the night in my room, if you must know. So, yeah I guess we were getting along good."

He stared at me, like I should have more to say. I didn't. Not that anything was any of his business. He took the hint and moved along with his conversation.

"Good work out there with Riddick. I've been waiting on you to put that cocky punk in his place. I am surprised it took you this long."

"He was out of line and I was going to handle it when it first happened, but a certain blonde stopped me and told me she didn't care what he thought of her. Then she told me to take her looking for sand dollars. He got off then, but he should have known I was going to knock his dick in the dirt."

"Look, I need you to make sure the stills are disassembled, and that parts are hidden and all mash is dumped. Jay has alerted the cops and they are snooping hard. Take it to sea tonight and get rid of it."

"How'd you know he put the bug in the cops ear?"

"Sax."

"Sax? Oh you mean the guy with Roxxi down at Sunset Tattoo? The one that Whiskey called to confirm if Hensley was in with Sully and Jay?"

"Yeah, that's him. Turns out that Sax has some kind of beef with Jay, too. I'm not sure what it is yet, but I'm sure I will find out."

"Why don't I call him and have him over? We need to talk to him."

I went back up stairs and got my bandana and my keys. When I stopped at the bottom of the stairs, I called Sax.

"Hey, Saxton. It's Fury with the Chosen Legion. You got anything pressing going on right now?"

"No. Not that can't wait. What can I do for you?"

"Can't discuss it over the phone. Want to meet me here at the clubhouse, or you want to meet for coffee or something?"

"Let's grab some coffee. See you at Flapjacks in twenty minutes."

I got on the bike and aimlessly drove there, thoughts of my first time meeting Chief there and then, more recently, times with Rumor flashing in my head. It sucked that the girls had to go so fast, but it is probably best for her. As I tried to shake that memory and tame those thoughts, I pulled into the parking lot. I put the kickstand down, took my sunglasses off, and made my way into the resteraunt. Quickly, I spotted Sax and made my way to him.

"Long time no see. How've you been?" Saxton asked with a genuine voice.

"Same shit, different day. How are you? And Roxxi? Whiskey told me about how Charlie put a beat down on Sully the day that she went to get ink. I figured she was collateral and that she got the raw end of that deal. Is she okay?"

"Man, she is going to be, but I got a little somethin' somethin' for Jay and Sully. They belong to me, they just don't know it yet. I will own their souls."

"Why the strong feelings towards them?"

"Jay, because he is a chicken shit and is Sully's little puppet now. Whatever Sully says goes. It don't matter who it hurts. We were best friends, dude, and he stabbed me in the fucking back. I don't know for sure if it was Jay or Sully, but my garage burned down and I know one of those fuckers is behind it. They say my dad was in debt to them. I didn't owe that debt, so I told them to fuck off. Then my place burned. Why do you care?"

"I cut ties with Jay and we aren't business partners anymore. All of a sudden we have cops questioning us and telling us there have been leads of illegal activity stemming from the clubhouse. It's all bullshit. We are straight. I know he is pissed, and I bet you he is out for revenge. I just don't know how he plans on getting it yet."

We both ordered our coffee and shot the shit for a while. He finally asked me what I needed him for.

"I was thinking about seeing if you would help us with him. Sounds like you have plans for him and we want him to pay. It seems like we should work together."

"Sure man. What do I get for helping you?"

"You get to be in good with the club. You do us a favor, we do you a favor. You don't have to worry about Roxxi being alone with Jay and Sully if you don't want her to be. We will have someone go to Sunset Tattoo with her and sit until you can get there. Why don't she just move off and leave their sorry asses anyhow?"

"Sully says her dad owed him and now he is making her pay. See the trend?"

"I think this could be a very beneficial partnership if you accept. Come to the house later on." I handed him a business card with our address on it. "We can go over details with the other boys."

"See you later on then."

We got up to leave right as a policeman walked into the diner and spotted me. He pressed the button on his walkie talkie, said something that I couldn't make out, and walked over to me.

"Sir." Sax acknowledged the officer.

He looked me up and down, trying to intimidate me then said, "Legend. I hear we have a situation on our hands?"

"Enlighten me." I barked.

"Seems as if we have some illegal manufacturing and distributing of moonshine going on here in Panama City Beach and rumor has it, you and your gang are the ones running said operation."

"Well, I'm not sure who is giving you bogus info, but my *club* don't make moonshine. Where would we make it? On the back deck for all the beach goers to see? We don't sell it either. You can come see for yourself. We have nothing to hide."

"No need. We will be in touch."

After he turned to leave, Sax asked me if what he said was true. I denied the accusations again. "Look, come by the house later tonight and we will discuss things."

I paid for our coffees and we left. On the road back to the house, thoughts floated about the blonde I couldn't seem to shake. I wish I could call Rumor. I could maybe soothe the burn I didn't mean to cause. My mind raced wondering from subject to subject until I pulled into the driveway. I sat there and told myself that things worked out the way they were supposed to. I made my way inside to be greeted by Riddick's bruised face. He just let me by, without a word.

"Chief, where are you?" I bellowed through the house.

"In here," came ringing back the kitchen. I headed immediately in that general direction.

"I got news. Shitty but news nonetheless. Chances are real good that Jay is behind this mess. He's called the cops and tipped them off, and I think he may have something else up his sleeve. I'm just not sure what. Sax told me that either Sully or Jay burned down his garage. Sax is after blood and is just pretty much waiting on the right opportunity. I think we could help him and he could help us. He could do the dirty work and we could cover for him, and perhaps he could prove himself and if he wanted to prospect he could? Regardless, he is an ally now. We need to help him. Sax wants blood for the wrongs Jay and Sully have done to his family and Roxxi, and so do we. He has fucked with the wrong club.

"All of this from a cup of coffee this morning?"

"He's legit. I can tell. He didn't bullshit me. I saw the anger in his eyes when he spoke about his garage. I have a feeling that something special was lost, but I didn't ask. He is supposed to come over later to discuss more."

"Well, seeing as there is a fire bug running amuck, we should get rid of all things shine related, sooner rather than later. Get the boys on it now. Get rid of the mash in the garbage disposal. We can't wait until tonight to take it to sea. This son of a bitch has already been accused of burning down one place, so he probably already has plans in motion for us, or at least the thought. It seems as if Jay and Sully try to burn out the people that don't see eye to eye with them. If they aren't on the winning end of things then they just burn houses and rip apart lives. Regardless, we have to get all still equipment and evidence out. If the place turns to soot and ash, our name must be clear. It can't look like it was an accidental moonshine gig gone bad, which is what he is banking on. It's all got to go," Chief ordered.

I nodded my head in agreement, and left him there to find the rest of the boys.

"Shooter, I need you to take the still and its parts to an iron and metal business. Sell it after you disassemble everything. Make sure it doesn't resemble a still. Riddick, you get to take the mash and put it down the garbage disposal, one cup at a time. I hope you gag on the smell. Magnum, you are with me. Boys, if you have anything here that you don't want up in flames, I suggest you get it out. I don't know when or if it will burn, but Jay and the company he keeps seem to have a m.o. Get to it. We have to cover our asses now."

Magnum stoically sauntered up to me, "What the actual fuck is happening?"

"This is the biggest cover-our-ass production to date. I ain't kidding. If you want to keep it, you better get it out of here. I got a real bad feeling about this. I just don't know when it is going to happen."

"Where do you want to put everything?"

"I don't have much. I figure I can store it at your house."

"Sure man. That's cool."

"As far as everyone else's shit, well, they can let it burn, or they can get it out. Not my problem. Shooter has a good head on his shoulders and I figure he will take what stuff he has elsewhere. You clearly don't have much here. Riddick is a dumbass and it wouldn't hurt my feelings to see him not make it out alive, so I don't care what happens to his stuff…or him."

"Damn. Why don't you tell me how you really feel?"

"He completely disrespected Rumor with a cocky attitude right in front of me. He is on the eternal shit list."

"You know, even drunk last night, and hung over this morning, I see that girl means something to you."

"She is different from the whores around here. There's no explaining it. I don't want to either. I just want to rewind the last week or so, and not be here while Charlie and her girls were here. It's just like a woman to complicate things. I was content in my life, then a woman had to go and make me…"

I stopped before I said outloud what I knew in my heart. I felt again. I didn't want to admit it because I had spent the better part of four years trying to be numb. I was comfortable being numb. It was easy. Now, I felt things, not love, but companionship. It felt so right with Rumor. She was easy to be around. I could be as *me* as possible with her. I don't think she gave two shits about my past. In her eyes, the abyss of her mystical icy blue eyes, I didn't live there anymore and she didn't care about the person I was before. She only wanted to know me now.

"Look Fury, if you want her, go get her. It has been a real relief seeing you, dare I say, happy these last few days. It isn't like you have a nine to five job or anything. Take a week off and go see her in Rudy. Surprise her and meet her there. Show her you are serious."

"Am I contemplating taking advice from a single fuck boy? What has this world come to?" So much for trying to convince anyone that I wanted nothing more from her.

"I am just saying, the ball is in your court. You can't say you gave it your all if you don't try. If you choose not to, then you deserve to wonder what could have been."

I starred at the idiot in front of me and realized he had a point. I couldn't just leave right now though. The cops have already been tipped off and it would look suspicious if I left.

"The cops are already looking at us. I can't leave now. That would look too suspicious. I will think about it when things settle down here."

"You know, you don't have to be the only one here

for things. Chief, Shooter, Riddick, and I are more than capable of handling cops, and who is to say you don't have a family emergency? It isn't illegal to take care of family business." He hinted.

I looked at him and contemplated my options. We were being looked at, but it might actually make sense for one of us to leave. I could just call the officer that Sax and I saw at the diner and tell him that I have an emergency out of state, and if he has any questions that he is welcome to call Chief, Mag, or Shooter. That way it doesn't look like we are hiding anything, and are actually cooperating with them. If we have nothing to hide, we are less suspicious. I could say *to hell with them* and go anyway.

Chapter 14

RUMOR

WE HAD BEEN IN the car for what seemed like days. I realized it was hours, long boring hours, on the road. I missed him. How was it that a guy I didn't want to know, had me in such an emotional turmoil? He lives states and hours away, but he is the one that said he wanted this.

As we drove across the Tennessee line, into Arkansas, my ringtone started blaring. I saw it was from a blocked number, so I didn't answer it. I never do. If it was terribly important they could leave a voice message and that they did.

"I have missed you. I will explain everything soon."

I dropped my phone and starred at it in disbelief. What the actual fuck did I just hear? Charlie heard the thud and turned to see me.

"Rumor, what is it? Why are you white as a sheet? Who was that?"

I said nothing. I could only stare blankly at the phone I dropped in the floor board.

What could I say? *Oh, you know, the boyfriend that just up and disappeared with no note, no anything, just left me a fucking message on my voice mail.* That would make me sound crazy, but it is the truth. He just called and left me a message.

"Whiskey, pull over at the next gas station. Something isn't right." Charlie said.

"No. Uh. No, it's fine. Really. I am good."

"You always were shit at lying. Spill it, Rumor. What happened on that phone call?"

Instead of me sounding like a lunatic, I handed her the phone and let her listen to the voicemail. That way she was just as looney as I was if she thought the same thing I did.

"What. The. Hell?" she paused after each word.

Whiskey tuned in at that point, "What is going on? Enough with the secrets."

I could tell he meant business, and I sure as hell wasn't going to piss him off. Charlie gave me a nod and I came clean.

"That was my boyfriend, or ex-boyfriend, or whatever the hell you call someone that disappeared with no trace or any explanation."

"And?" He waited on an explanation.

Instead of repeating it, I played it for them and turned on speaker phone.

"Was that Creed?" Charlie half-asked, half-stated.

"If it wasn't, it is someone playing a sick joke. What the hell? First Fury, and now Creed? The universe hates me."

I threw myself back against my seat and shut my eyes as I tried to wrap my mind around what I had just heard. So many questions circled in my head. *Why? Why now? Is he back for good? Could I even deal with the reasoning he gave? When did he even get back?*

Just when I thought it was okay for me to move on, he calls back. It's almost like he knew. It's impossible though. It was all a huge coincidence. The universe was playing its usual evil, cruel tricks on me.

I began with my internal thoughts. Did I want him to be alive? Did I want him to come back around? Did I still love him? Had I moved on? Was this something we could over come? Was this something he would do again? Was his excuse or story going to be enough for me to forgive him? Did he even want me back? Did he have someone else? Was he with someone else the whole time we were apart? Dear God, I was with someone else. How would he handle that?

All of the questions made my head hurt. I laid my head back and shut my eyes. Hoping and praying that I would fall asleep and wake up from this nightmare.

I awoke as we were pulling into Winstead Acres, Charlie's house.

"Damn, how long did I sleep?" I sleepily asked.

"A solid four hours. You must have been wiped out." Whiskey answered quickly.

I was mentally and emotionally drained. It didn't look to get any better soon, I thought to myself, as I remembered Creed's message.

"Charlie, I have a favor to ask of you. It's kind of a big one."

"What do you need? Anything. You know that." She reassured me.

"Seeing as I haven't seen Creed in a couple of years, I don't really want to be alone with him. I have a feeling that he will case the house and I just don't want to deal with that, not after he up and left me. I honestly don't even know if I still want anything to do with him. There seemed to be something different about his voice, something I don't quite trust. If he wants to meet me, can you and Whiskey go with?"

"You didn't really think I was going to allow you to go alone did you?" Whiskey snapped.

"Umm. I didn't realize that I didn't get a say. I guess I never really thought about it."

"Look, you havent seen this numbnuts in how long now, and he just out of the blue decides to call? Something is up. If you get hurt, Charlie gets hurt. After all she has been through, I will not knowingly let her, or anyone she cares about, step into harms way. And besides that, Fury kinda has a thing for you and he would do the same thing for me," he matter-of-factly stated.

"I figure he will attempt to meet me tonight. He never did like waiting for anything. I don't really want him around here either though. Or my house, but I know that is where he is going to go."

"Guess where you ain't stayin'?"

"Bossy damn biker."

I was glad he said that because it meant I was staying here. The place was big enough, for sure, and had borders of rock wall and an electric gate so I felt safe.

"Rumor, you can stay here. Think nothing of it, it isn't like there isn't room for you." Charlie offered sweetly.

I nodded in appreciation and asked her to lead me to the room she wanted me to stay in. I unloaded my bag and hung up my clothes. I had no idea how long I was staying, and I didn't want to live out of my bag. I started processing the last and was overwhelmed by uncertainty. Uncertain of where Creed had been, uncertain of my feelings toward him now, uncertain how I was going to tell Fury. I got caught up in my thoughts about the million different things that he could have been doing. For all I know, he could be some super secret spy for the government, and had a top secret priority mission to go on. The chances of that are slim but hey, it could happen. He could have gotten in some kind of gambling trouble and had to escape or do something a little less than clean in order to save himself. He could have gotten tired of being in this little nothing town and needed to get away. The possibilities are endless and the truth is, I don't have the slightest idea why he left, or where he went. I would find out tonight. He said he would call and I truly felt he would.

After I finished hanging my clean clothes and washing the ones that were dirty, I joined Whiskey and Charlie in the kitchen.

"So, what is on the agenda for tonight?" I asked.

"Well, that kind of depends on when, and if your ex calls like he says he will. I assume we will meet him somewhere. I think it should be in a resturant though. I am hungry and there should be people around so he can't do anything real stupid," Whiskey said.

"Do you really think he would try anything? Babes, look at you. You are a little intimidating."

"True, but people are stupid."

As if on cue, my cell rang. With nervous fingers I picked up the phone and saw the caller ID. It was the same unknown number.

"Hello?"

"I was hoping you would answer."

"What do you want, Creed?"

"Well, I really expected a nicer greeting, honestly. I havent heard from you in…"

"Yeah in two fuckin' years, but guess what. That wasn't my fault. I wasn't to blame for that. I deserved an explanation, or a goodbye kiss, or a fuck-you-I-don't-love-you-anymore, but I got nothing! What was I supposed to think? Did you expect me to save myself for you until you decided you should come home again? You don't get to expect anything from me, Creed. Nothing. You can tell me now what you want or start explaining yourself," I snapped.

"You have every right to be upset."

"Damn right I do. You can't just come in here thinking everything is going to be the way it was. That ship has sailed."

"For good?"

"I don't know. I don't know anything. I don't know how I feel about you anymore and I don't know if I want anything to do with you. I don't know if I want to see you or if I want to throat punch you. What I do know is you broke me. You were the one that put me back together after Crosby and then you broke me again. I can't trust you right now. I do know that." I said as the tears came down like rain.

"I know I owe you a huge explanation, and apology. Meet me at the diner and let's talk."

"You can't just waltz back into my life like nothing happened. You left me for two years. Two fucking years I worried about you. I wondered if you were dead or alive, waited on you to call me and explain yourself, and you never did. I waited for something and day after day I got nothing."

"I'd very much like to try to explain myself over dinner."

"Fine, but I am bringing my friends. I don't want to be alone with you. I don't know you anymore and I don't trust you as far as I can throw you. Out of all of this whole shitty situation, *that* might hurt the worst. You were the one person that I trusted when

my whole world fell apart. Then you crushed me just like Crosby did."

"Whatever it takes to get you there, I can't wait to hold you in my arms again…"

"That ain't happening. I don't even know if I want you anymore, Creed. Get that through your head. I don't even know if there is an us. I don't let strangers hold me, you should know that."

"That cuts deep, Rumor."

"You cut me deeper than ever before, Creed, even deeper than Crosby and his stunt. I don't want to hear how you are upset because you can't hold me in your arms and play house again. Fuck that. Do you know how many nights I sat up crying for you? Just wishing I could hold you in my arms one more time? No, you don't, because you fucking left me. You are lucky I am meeting you at all. Do you remember what I always said? How if there wasn't trust, there was nothing. Well, we have nothing. I don't trust you anymore."

"I am the same person, Rumor. You gotta believe that."

"Wrong, Creed. I ain't got to do shit. I do what I want. If you wanted a say in that you shouldn't have bailed two years ago."

"I'm sorry, Rumor. Please meet me at the diner."

"Whiskey, Charlie, and I will be there in thirty minutes. Don't be late. I am, quite frankly, tired of waiting on you."

"I deserved that."

"I know. That's why I said it. Bye Creed."

I hung up the phone and looked at my friends. The look of anger in Whiskey's eyes was overwhelming, and the sheer loathing Charlie had at the moment was evident.

"He used to be a good guy, y'all. I just don't know what happened.

"It doesn't matter. We will go and see him and see what he has to say. If you don't like what he says, then we leave. If at any time during this meeting you feel off or awkward, just let me know and I will gladly make him leave. You are with me now and you don't have to do a damn thing if you don't want. Remember that. He is on your terms right now. Stand your ground and don't give in."

"Let's go get this chaos started." I stopped and looked at Whiskey. He towered over Charlie, he exuded protection and love at the same time. I needed that. I needed to be wanted like that, loved like that. Creed used to be that guy for me, but then he took my heart wherever the hell he went and left a gaping hole in my chest. Fury had started to fill it and I liked that feeling. I liked him. I missed him. I missed him differently than I ever missed Creed.

We got into Charlie's 4Runner and headed across town to the diner. I sat quietly in the back. I retraced my last thought of Fury. *I missed him differently than I did Creed.* How is that possible? I had know him for days. I had known Creed for years. I wanted to hear Fury's voice again and find out when he was coming to see me.

As we pulled in to the parking lot, I looked for Creed's old truck and didn't see any sign of it. I took a deep, calming breath to settle my nerves and closed my eyes and said, "Let's do this."

Upon entering, we were greeted by the waitstaff. We said we were meeting a guy and she pointed to the farthest booth in the corner. My eyes followed her finger in slow motion. My eyes traveled from her fingertip, passing over everyone else in the diner, they were just a blur of color and muddled voices, and there he was. My eyes went straight to the guy that used to hold my life in his hands, sitting in the booth in all of his sexy glory, looking just as good as he ever did. Clearly, I overlooked the truck. He gave me a sweet smile and headed to me.

Whiskey stepped in front of me and Creed stopped immediately. "No, go back to your booth and we will meet there. Don't even think about a great reunion in the middle of the diner. You have some explaining to do." Orders fell from his mouth as he crossed his big muscled up arms across his chest, sure to show his Chosen Legion patch.

Creed looked around Whiskey and expected me to correct him, which I did not. "Let's get to the table. This is weird here in the middle of the resteraunt." I said.

We walked to the table, Whiskey leading the way as Charlie held my hand for support. She squeezed my hand and said so softly, "If you want to leave just say the word and I will go get the 4Runner and meet you at the door. The ball is in your court."

"Thanks. I owe you."

"Rumor, you look, wow, you look amazing. I don't know what else to say."

"Let's start by ordering dinner." I said, totally avoiding his comment.

He patted the seat next to him. I stared in disbelief. He seriously can't think that I am going to get at arms length does he? No, I don't want him touching me. I'm afraid of what it will feel like. Would I miss it and welcome it back? I didn't want to give it a chance. Would it feel as good and warm as Fury's?

"I'll sit over here with them, thanks."

Creed's eyes sank like I had burst his bubble. I suppose he thought I was kidding and I would run hopelessly in love back to him. "Don't be delusional, Creed. I said I didn't trust you. That means I don't trust you to sit beside me. I don't trust that you will respect my space."

"Of course, I would. Why wouldn't I? I'm not a monster or some random stranger, Rumor. It's me, the same Creed you fell in love with a few years back."

"See, that's where you are wrong. My Creed wouldn't have left me without an explanation because he knew what kind of heartbreak I had been through. No, my Creed isn't here. I don't know where he is, or if he is coming back. I've wondered where he is for the last two years."

"Ouch. I guess you deserve an explanation. I just don't know that I can be as forthcoming as you wish."

"Then I don't know if there is a point to being here. I promise you one thing. I will know all about your two year hiatus. You will tell me every detail, I deserve nothing less. Even then, Creed, I don't know if there is a chance that what we had can survive this. Start talking or I walk."

"I had to leave." he paused.

"Right. I've gathered. But why? Why did you feel it was more important to leave and break my heart again? What was so important that you had to destroy me?"

"I," he paused again. "I got in with an agency that protects people."

"What in the hell are you talking about? Protects them from what?"

"People that are going to kill them. I am now a U.S. Marshall. I had to leave to help people escape certain death. I help criminals that provide damning information against other criminals live normal lives again."

"Since when are you all up in the law?"

"I have always been intrigued by witness protection. I got offered a job in Witness Protection, WITSEC, but I had to go away for training, and no one could know. I wanted to call you and let you know I was okay. I had the phone in my hands several times, but it's against the rules. I couldn't risk it."

"Rumor, are you okay?" Whiskey asked.

I nodded as I tried to think of my next move. Thoughts were whizzing around in my head like...I don't know, but something damn fast. The only thing I could say came out of my mouth as vicious as venom.

"You abandoned me for two years so you could play cops and robbers? Are you fucking kidding me right now?" The tone of my voice was getting higher pitched.

"What I do is help save people from serious situations that are sure to end terribly. These are people who are trying to turn over a new leaf, not ones that are sorry they got caught and will repeatedly offend. I'm not out to harbor snitches. I want to help legit people that realized they screwed up and are trying to right some wrongs."

All of this new information was like a punching bag coming back and smacking me in the face, and I felt disoriented and confused. I was here seeing stars and feeling light headed. I put my head in my hands and started to cry. Tears of confusion, anger, and sorrow all came from my eyes. I looked up at him and just let them fall. His face sank, and I could tell that he felt terrible. He seemed sincere when he apologized, but I could not bring myself to forgive him.

"You did this to me," I sniffled. "After all I had been through, you broke me worse than I have ever been broken before. I don't know that I can even look at you. Creed, I don't know what to say or what to think. What I do know is you should know what you've done to me. You should also know that I just, this past week, came to terms that you weren't coming back. I found a guy that I can be myself with and that really understands me. He has been through some fucked up shit, too."

"What are you saying, Rumor?"

"I'm saying there is someone else."

Confusion, anger, resentment, heartache, and sorrow all consumed his face.

"I don't understand."

"I met someone else and we are starting a relationship. Or we were, until I had to come home abruptly. Then here you come waltzing back in to my life, and now I have two men to deal with. I haven't had a man in years and now all of a sudden there are two."

"You didn't wait for me?"

"Of course, I did. Then you never showed up. I am too young to put my life on hold indefinitely. I waited for you for two years. *Two years.* I finally decided to start living again. I was lonely and I needed someone, and so did he. We were good together."

Whiskey looked at me as I revealed secrets from the last few days. I shrugged and blew him off. Clearly, he was caught off guard, but not as much as Creed.

"I...I don't know what to say. I really thought we had

something special; something that could stand the test of time."

"We did until I was left to wonder when and if you were ever coming home, how long you would be gone, and what you were doing. My Creed wouldn't have left me like that. The cops were the worst. Always blaming me for your disappearance."

"They were checking on you." He revealed.

"What? You couldn't have had someone follow me, or have them just drop in and offer to provide extra patrol so I felt safer, or hell, even say they are here if I needed them? You had them badger me repeatedly and pour salt in a wound that was so deep you could see my heart. For the record, it was broken, not that you care. Did they not tell you how I cried every single time they came and accused me of something I am incapable of?"

"That's how I knew you were okay. I had them go in and interrogate you, and then they got back to me. Hindsight, it was the wrong way to do it. I'm sorry. Who is the other guy?"

"He isn't here, so it doesn't matter. If you must know, his name is Fury. He is in Panama City Beach."

"He rides with me, he's my brother." Whiskey said with a boom.

"You are with a club now? Wait, Charlie, who is this and where is Hensley?"

"Hensley was a terrible person, and I haven't seen him for a few weeks now. This is my husband. Whiskey."

"Husband?"

"When it's right, it's right, and you just know it."

"Tell her that. It was right for so long. Now it isn't."

"Again, Creed. Not my fault. I refuse to feel guilty anymore. I did for two years. I waited and longed for you for two fucking years and you never showed up. What was I supposed to think? Was I supposed to hold on to some false hope that you were out there and would come back to me someday? I was lonely and confused. I did the waiting thing. I did it for too long. You shouldn't have asked that out of me. That isn't fair."

I took a breath before I said something that I never imagined I would say to the man who had my whole heart a couple of years ago. "If you were the one for me, you would've told me you were at least interested in the WITSEC program, or that you were interested in being a marshall. As it turns out, I knew nothing and that makes me question our whole relationship." I turned to look at Charlie and nodded that I was done. She got up and went to get the car, and left me and Whiskey there with Creed. I needed to get out of here. I couldn't handle anymore of this chaos. "Creed, I'm sorry that I can't just open my arms to you, but I am not sorry about meeting Fury. You should have came back two weeks sooner."

"Are you serious with him? Did you…"

"That is none of your business, and I'm not sure what we are. We were going to find out and try a long distance thing."

"I have a right to know. You are my fiancé, damn it."

"Was. I was your fiancé until you left me with no notice or no warning. I have nothing else to say to you Creed. Except, you caused of all this. I was so happy with you. Couldn't wait to marry you, have your children and grow old with you, and then you just weren't there."

"We can have that again, Rumor. Please, let me back in. I never really left you."

"You're wrong. You did leave me. And when you did, you killed my soul. I'm just now finding out who I am without you. I stopped living when you left. If it weren't for the Regulators, I'd have become a recluse. Goodbye, Creed. If you need a place to stay you can stay at the house. I won't be there. I can't go back," I said as I nodded at Whiskey that I was ready to leave. He got up, walked in front of me, and I followed him out the door. I turned around and looked at the man that used to be my forever. Pain and anguish of my revelations were clearly etched on his face. My heart broke for him, and for me. Seeing him again was harder than I imagined, however, it was easier, too. I never dreamed I could see him again and not go running back to him. I gave him a sad smile as a tear fell down my cheek. I lowered my head toward the door and followed Whiskey out to the 4Runner.

"Rumor?" Charlie asked.

All I could do was silently cry. The tears streaming down my face made it all too real. I hoped it was a bad dream. That my life wasn't nearly this complicated, but the tears reminded me otherwise. There were no sobs, no shoulder shuddering cries, only silent tears as I stared out the window.

"Whiskey, what do you want to do?" Charlie asked.

"I'll call Briar and have him keep an eye out for him around town. See if he hears or sees anything suspicious. I will call Fury let him know, too. He needs to be clued in on what his girl is dealing with."

I hear the beeps of keys on a phone being dialed followed by, "Fury, this is Whiskey. How are things on the beachfront? Shit. I hoped things would die down some. Damn cops sniffing around. Did you get all the equipment disassembled and disposed of? Good. Hey, I don't really know how to say this delicately, so I won't try. Rumor saw someone tonight and she needs you."

There was a brief pause in the conversation, and the air in the car stalled.

"Yeah, it was her ex, Creed. He is back and he wants her. She told him you two were trying this long distance thing for a while and that she had moved on, but she needs you. Can you get Mag or Chief to cover? You need to get here if you are going to make this work."

I wish I could hear what was being said on the other end of the phone. Curiosity was getting the best of me.

"No he wasn't threatening her, just told her there still a chance for them, he never really left her, and a bunch of other shit. Something about him being a marshall now and working for WITSEC, some witness protection organization. He left because he had to go under cover or some dumb shit. It didn't all make sense to me."

Another pause from Whiskey gave my mind time to wonder what Fury was thinking. He has to be thinking that my life is one seriously fucked up three ring circus and that he wants no part of me. That's what any sane person would do. I tuned them out at that point and mentally checked out til' we got back to Acres.

"Guys, thanks for going with me. I don't know what I would have done if I would have gone alone. Would it be too rude of me to go lay down? I need to think about this whole thing and I need to be alone."

"Sure, Rumor. Whatever you need. Make yourself at home. We will see you in the morning."

I went upstairs and changed into my night clothes. Memories of my nights on the beach came rushing back as I fell to bed, lost in my memories. Soon enough I was taken back to the warm night breezes of the ocean and nights of conversation with Fury, if only in my dreams.

Chapter 15

FURY

Her ex is now working for WITSEC. I let that rattle around in my head for a while. As I mulled it over, I began questioning everything, but mainly whether or not to go to her. He would surely be snooping around, and find me out.

"Yo, Mag." I yelled as I came into the living area. "What else is there to do as far as getting the stills disassembled and mash out? Everything out of the basement?"

"I think we are good dude. You just need to get your shit to my house," Magnum said, as if he were put out.

I had all of my things, clothes pretty much, a few knickknacks I had acquired, all loaded in a bag. I had placed my prized picture of Daisy in my cut pocket. With the threat of a fire, I couldn't afford for it to be out of my possession.

"What's wrong with you?"

"He is hangry and tired of moving shit," Shooter piped up.

"I've been doing this for what seems like days now. I'm tired and want to get the hell out of here for a while. I want food and sleep, in that order. Pronto."

"Okay, princess, let's get you some food before you go postal on us. I'll go get Chief and tell him that we are going to get some grub and see if he wants to come." Shooter said sarcastically as he curtsied to Mag for added theatrics.

"Mag, I have to get to Rudy soon. I gotta see her. There's some shit that is going down. Whiskey called me earlier. I need this shit to be handled here first though. We are done with clean up, yeah?"

"Fuck, we better be."

We went outside and waited on Shooter and Riddick.

"I guess Chief ain't coming?" I asked.

"Nah, he said he was good here. He wasn't hungry. Let's just go so we can get back."

We rode out to Flapjacks, our usual hangout. Mag ordered his food before he even sat down at the booth. The waitress jotted down our usual and left to go put it in the kitchen.

"So, I am thinking of heading to Rudy for a little while. Rumor is in a little bit of a situation and I want to go help her. Whiskey called and said that it would be a good idea for me to get there if I could."

"Everything okay, boss?" Shooter asked with a sincerity to his voice.

"I think it will be. She just needs a familiar face. Some shit has resurfaced from her past and she is in a tough spot."

The waitress brought us our food and we all ate in silence. Other than the sound of screaming sirens racing down the road, it was peaceful.

"Wonder what is going on that requires so many fire trucks?" Riddick asked outloud.

"Well, I'd assume a fire, dipshit." Shooter said with a grin.

Riddick just glared at him and then smiled and laughed, too. As we finished our meals, an officer came into the diner.

"Boys, I don't know how to say this, but your house is gone. It's a total loss. The fire fighters are there now still battling it, but it doesn't look promising."

"Shit, Chief was still there!" Magnum exclaimed.

We all threw down money on the table and got on our bikes to see what was left of the clubhouse and check on Chief. As we pulled up, the heat from the flames was almost enough that it knocked me off my bike seat. Sirens wailed, lights flashed, and people shouted orders. Chaos loomed in the air. The orders from the firemen, police officers, and paramedics all ran together. My instincts kicked in as I began to run to the blaze, but I was stopped, "Sorry fella's, can't go farther," the fire chief said.

"Our friend is still in there, or was. We have to!"

"Can't let you."

We stood there helpless as they pushed us back away from the inferno. What seemed like hours passed. It was like minutes a child counts down for Christmas morning. It had to be the longest stretch of time in my life. The flames were eventually put out and all that remained was a smoking pile of rubble. The firemen came out and paced around for a bit. Then the news I hoped I would never hear came from the police chief, "I'm sorry, but there was one casualty. That's all we have recovered." Everything went quiet as I saw the one person that gave me a fighting chance hauled out of the rubble in a body bag.

"Who is the next of kin?" The officer asked.

"Me." I said gruffly. "I'm the only one he had left."

"I'll need you to come to the station with me."

"Not yet. Not till we figure out what happened. We have a right to know. We also have a right to deal with the death of our friend and leader before we are pumped for information." Anger rolled off me in waves, and it took all I had to not bust his lip open.

"Do we know anything?" I hear Magnum ask the fire chief.

"All I can say at this time is it appears to be arson."

"Jay!" We all screamed at the same time.

"Who is this Jay?" The police asked.

"This is one of those things we will discuss at the

station. I'm not discussing anything any further with you right now. Chief was like my father and I will not hash out the details of club business with you moments after I hear that he is gone." The truth escaped from my mouth before I was able to register what was happening. I would no doubt have to do damage control over that statement.

"Look, Fury, I understand you are upset. Here's my card. Call me when you're ready to talk."

Shooter came to me, grabbed my shoulders, and turned me away from the wreckage. "Fury, let's head to the diner again, so we can call Whiskey and gather our thoughts. There isn't anything left for us to do here. It won't benefit us at all to stay and watch it smolder."

"I'll call Sax. I have a feeling he was right and Jay is behind this." Mag said in his most somber voice.

The ride back to the diner was a blur. We rode hard and fast as we had urgent business to tend to. When we walked in the door the whole resturant stopped eating and stared at us. We motioned to the waitress that we were going to our normal spot. When we sat down I wasted no time, "We have to call Whiskey. I need his input on the next steps."

"I say we hear what Whiskey has to say. He seems to have a level head on him. Mag, what did Sax say?"

"He is headed this way. Apparently, he was about to ask a favor of us. His girl was assaulted by Jay and or Sully and needs protection while he handles things. More reason for this prick to meet his maker," Magnum said, head in his hands.

I picked up my phone and called Whiskey. The rings seemed to go on for minutes, but I realized that it was just the stress of the situation.

"Whiskey, hey man. Sorry it's so late but we got business. This isn't easy for me to tell you, so I won't beat around the bush. The clubhouse is gone. It was burned to the ground. We suspect Jay. Yeah, I know. The most difficult part is that Chief didn't make it out of the house alive. Our charter's president is gone. Yeah, I will be, right after we get retribution on those pricks. Yeah, he's here now and we are going to talk to him. Seems he had a favor to ask of us anyhow. I'll call you back in a bit. Can you handle telling Briar and all the other chapters? This might get bloody. Tell them to be on standby. Thanks." I hung up the phone and met the eyes of a very empathetic Sax and a very scared and tortured Roxxi.

"I don't know which one of them hurt her, but they get to die at my hand. I need a hand though. I need somewhere to stay and keep her safe. Can we stay with you guys? Sully seems to think he can make her pay for some debt that her father owed and he's taking it out on her physically." Sax seethed.

"Brother, we would absolutley have your back, if we had a place to go of our own. The clubhouse was torched tonight and worse, Chief didn't make it out. Those two killed one of our men." I said to him with hate laced in my words.

I thought for a moment and ran an idea by the guys. "What do you say about staying at Acres in Rudy? Charlie girl told me that it was big enough to house several. No one would know where it is and we should all be safe there."

"Fury, we can't leave now. You still have to go to the cops tomorrow." Mag reminded me.

"I'll handle the cops. You don't worry about that. Just worry about you and the guys. I'll call Whiskey back and make sure its cool that we come down there indefinitely. We find a motel tonight, and I'll go to the cops shortly. Mag, Riddick, Shooter, if there is anything you need from your houses, I suggest you get it. We won't be coming back here for a while. I'll have more info in the morning. It isn't safe for you to be at your houses tonight. Text me the address of the room you get. I have a date with a cop. Tomorrow we ride out. I feel sure that Whiskey and Charlie are fine with that, but I will finalize arrangements before I talk with the law."

I left the table and went outside. I shouted at the sky and asked why. Why Chief? He was the only one that let me be me with no questions asked, ever. Not one time. Now I have to lay him down forever. I lit a smoke and gathered myself. Prepping for an interview with the cops always makes me nervous. Tonight is no different, especially knowing that I have to do damage control over the 'club business' statement I made earlier.

I dialed the cop's number and he answered rather quickly, "Officer Canon speaking."

"Uh, yeah, this is Fury. Can we meet up tonight and talk? I have business and an urgent matter to deal with out of town."

"Sure, come on down. I'm still here."

I hung up, got on the Indian, and rode hard all the way there. It was nice to hear and think of nothing. The only thing I felt and thought about was the cool air on my face. I heard the wind whizzing by my ears and at that moment, those were the only two things that mattered. It was a welcoming deafness and numbness. As I pulled into the police station, feeling started coming back and sounds filled my ears. I parked and stared at the seat. The enormity of the situation was hitting home hard now. *I am going to talk to the cops about the murder of my best friend, father figure, and my president.*

I pushed those feelings aside, and made my way in to see Canon.

"Fury, I am so sorry for your loss. It's always hard when we lose a loved one."

"Look, I appreciate the condolences, but I'm really not in a good place and I need to get out of town."

"That looks suspicious. I don't really think that's a good idea."

"Luckily I don't give two shits about what you think. I have club business and personal issues to tend to and had planned on leaving in the next few days, anyhow. Jay just expedited things for me."

"Who is this Jay you speak of?"

"He is a guy that we did business with. We all got together and had a poker game. Jay ended up talking smack to one of the girls that was there, and I put him in his place. He didn't like it, and I booted his ass out the door. I took his money playing cards. Turns out his poker face is shit."

"Well there's motive, now to find his alibi."

"Now that we have nowhere to stay, we are heading to Arkansas to be with that chapter of the club. I just didn't want you thinking we were running. This way we can still keep club business on task."

"What kind of business?"

"Not that it concerns you, but resturant."

"Now Fury, that doesn't sound like a biker gang kind of business."

"And it shouldn't. We are a club not a gang. We don't go around with dumb looking bandanas on our heads with the little corners flipped up, or go around with our pants saggin' around our knees, nor do we go around shooting up random people. Drive-by's ain't our style, they are for pussies too scared to look their targets in the eye. Look, I told you what you needed to know about Jay. When do you think we can have Chief's body sent to Arkansas? That is where we will bury him." I got straight to the point. I let him know that we were leaving and told him about Jay. Now I needed to get to the hotel so that I could try and get a couple hours sleep before our ride to Rudy tomorrow.

"Well, I don't really know. Seeing as you gave me a motive, this is now a murder investigation. He will likely be sent to the crime lab. I would say in a week or so. I can call you so you can make arrangements.""Tell you what, I have decided against a proper burial. I want him cremated and we will come back to PCB when the body is released. I'll make arrangements to have him cremated, so the crematory can get him directly from the crime lab. I never thought I would be discussing this with anyone. I was always supposed to be the one that died first. **Damn it**!" I yelled as rage took over and I slammed my fists on the desk.

"Fury, go. Leave me your number and I will call you if we need anything. You have done enough tonight. Again, I am sorry for your loss." The officer said empathetically.

I nodded my head in agreeance and headed out for the bike. I called Magnum and asked where they were staying. Once I got the name of the place, I headed there. I rode in a funky state, somewhere between pissed off and crushed. More pissed off at the fact that Chief is the one that gave this fucker a chance and said 'give him rope he will hang himself'. He did alright, and killed him in the process.

I pulled up to the Clearwater Inn and turned off the bike. I called Whiskey and updated him on the situation.

"Yeah, cops are up to speed. Thing is, now we have to discuss a resturant business at some point. I will bring it to church. Did you have a chance to ask Charlie girl if we could stay there for a while?"

"Of course you can. This place is big enough to hold us all and start up our operations again, too. Leave tomorrow and we will see you soon. Fury?"

"Yeah."

"We'll get him. The fucker will pay."

"About that, Sax and Roxxi are coming too. Apparently some shady shit happened between Sully, Jay, and Roxxi. Sax asked us for help. I hope that's okay."

"Charlie could tell that something was off with Roxxi when she was in getting her tattoo. She will be fine with it. Be careful and see you tomorrow. Hey?"

"Yeah?"

"Torch this phone. Get a prepaid. Text me with your number. I'll do the same thing after I have your new number, tell the others too."

As I thought about the events of the day, I lit a smoke. I had to pull myself together. I had revenge to get on the fucker that took my president from me, from this club. I snuffed out my cigarette and knocked on the door. Shooter opened it up for me and I made my way in.

"Sax. Roxxi." I aknowledged them as I entered the room. "Guys, tomorrow we ride out to Rudy. I want to swing by the clubhouse one more time, you know to go through the rubble and make sure there ain't anything left. We leave early. Daybreak. Let's get some rest. Tomorrow is going to be long."

Sax and Roxxi went to their room that ajoined ours. I took the couch and Mag and Shooter each took a bed. Riddick slept on the floor, prospecting sucked and I aimed to see it really sucked for him. Sleep eluded me so I laid there and thought. What would our business look like from here on? Would we be able to sustain this new location? Is there a calling for moonshine in Rudy? Would Rumor's ex be a problem that I had to deal with? Did Rumor even want anything with me now that he was back? As I asked myself these random and repetitive thoughts, minutes turned to hours. For hours now, I had been caught in a revolving door of questions. Questions with no answers.

Startled, I jumped up and had my pistol drawn. I was just at the house digging through the soot and I heard a deep voice thunder behind me, "Watch your back." Suddenly, I was back in the bedroom with my brothers and was on the couch sitting up with my heart racing and gun pointed at some imaginary male voice. I had clearly dozed off. It was about five in the morning. If I left now I could go to the house and let the others sleep a few more hours.

I got up and around in the dark. I found my boots and my cut. After slipping them on I went over to Mag and shook his shoulder.

"Hey, I'm going to run to the house. You guys just

sleep here til' I get back. I just didn't want you to flip out if you woke sooner than I got back."

"No, I'll go with you. Give me a minute. You don't need to go alone. Not now."

For someone that could be so carefree, stupid, and such a royal pain in the ass, he was also the one with the brains, at the moment.

He got his cut and boots on and nudged Shooter. "Hey man, Fury and I are heading to the clubhouse to see if anything is salvagable."

"Hang on and I'll go."

"No, you stay here with Sax and Roxxi. No one can be alone at this point."

"Riddick is here. I'm coming with you." He said with finality.

So much for not waking anyone. Now three of the six of us were awake.

We got out the door and sat on our bikes.

"What are you expecting to find?"

"I don't really know. I just don't want looters, or anyone for that matter, taking anything that might be left."

"Okay then, let's go find out what is left of our club."

We rode out and made it to the reminants of the house in just a little bit. It was about six a.m. and the morning light was just starting to shine. The first peeks of lighter blues and yellows started busting through the dark sky.

"You ready to get this over with?" I looked at Magnum.

"I think you are the one that needs to answer that. You were the closest one to Chief and you are the one that lived here."

"I don't give damn about the stuff, what I care about is that nothing that isn't supposed to be out, gets out, and if there is something salvagable of Chief's, I want to salvage it. That dude did a lot for me."

He nudged his head in the general direction of the house. All that lay before us was a big gray pile of ash and rubble, some burned two by fours, and basement walls. We walked around kicking random piles of debris. We found picture frames, televisions with busted screens, unsalvageable furniture, and other appliances. As we walked around what should have been the bedrooms, I went to where I knew Chief's would have been, or would've been above. For whatever sick reason, I felt close to him here. I kicked around ashes and soot, found the metal of his bed frame and the unsteady, torched shell of his chest of drawers. Upon closer look, there was something lighter than the soot lying about. I went over and started digging around, causing the shell to colapse on my hand.

"Fuck!" I yelled out. Partially out of pain, but mostly because it scared the shit out of me.

"Dude, you okay?" Mag asked as he ran to where I was.

"Yeah, I'm okay. Just didn't expect to have my hand smashed.

"What is that?" Mag asked out of curiousity.

"I don't know. That's what I was going after when the thing caved on me. It looks like a metal box." I reached for it.

Upon reaching it, I realized it was one of those fireproof boxes.

"Well, what is it?" Shooter asked.

"You know those fireproof boxes that your grandma used to have to keep important documents in?"

"I'll take your word for it. I wasn't particularly close to my grandparents."

"Well, mine kept her mothers wedding ring and important documents in it."

I grabbed the box and searched for the key, running my hand through ashes and broken boards. When I seemed to have sifted through all the remains of the chest of drawers I pulled back my now gray hand and tried to think like Chief.

I had to think of some place that is so obvious that it is unlikely. Would he put it in the night stand by the bed? I looked and it wasn't there, as it too had burned. I looked under his bed, or where it used to be. Now it was just the metal frame. I couldn't find this key and it was pissing me off. Just when I thought that I would give up and take a torch to it to get it open, I spotted a slightly shiny thing. It was hard to see because it was a shiny object covered in dust and ash. I saw that it is an antique trinket holder. In it were a couple of random screws, a bolt, and a washer.

Where it laid, there was a small key beside it. I knew that had to be the key to the fireproof box, so I put the key in my cut and hollered at Magnum and Shooter.

"Found it. Let's get out of here. I don't see anything else that needs saved do you?"

We made our way back out to the bikes, but as we passed where church was held, Mag stopped abruptly. He bent down and picked up the gavel, or the remnants of it.

"Here, I think this should go to you, seeing as you're next in line."

That comment hit me like a linebacker. I wasn't ready to be in control. I didn't want this yet. I wanted my pres back. He was better suited for this than I. He was calm and collected. I am not.

"Fury?" Mag asked as he held the charred gavel out for me to grab. "Fury." he said it again with more umph. "*Legend!*" he yelled finally to get me out of my deep thought. "Take the damned gavel. You are our new pres. Chief wouldn't have chosen you as VP if you weren't up for the task. Get out of your thick head and take the thing. You and you alone are the leader of this chapter now. We are under the reign of Fury now. Chief taught you all you needed to know."

I reached for the mutilated gavel and it started to crumble more, falling apart piece by piece. When I got it in my hand, I intently starred at it. After a minute of clarity, I tossed the gavel back into the ashes, "That gavel is useless.

A hammer would be better than that. We can get another one."

"What do you think is in the box?" Shooter piped up, clearly trying to shift gears.

"I don't know. I will look when I have some spare time. I want to do it alone. If it is club business I will bring it to the club."

I could tell they were disappointed that I wasn't going to open it right then, so we made our way back to our bikes. I put the box on the passenger seat and strapped it down.

"Let's go. There is nothing left for us here. We have a new headquarters in Rudy for now."

"Yay, country bumpkin, cousin lovin', outhouse usin', bumfucked nowhere. Can't wait." Sarcasm dripped from Mag's words.

"You never know, the peace from the mountains and quietness of the small town might just be what you need. You might fall in love with it."

We started our bikes and headed back to the hotel. It was time to get the others and get on the road to Rudy, our new home.

Chapter 16

RUMOR

I WIPED THE SLEEP from my eyes and stretched the night out of my muscles. It took me a second to remember that I was at Acres now. I would be until further notice. I was shaking out the unwanted thoughts beginning to enter my mind when my phone went off. I decided to leave it until I had a chance to go the bathroom and brush the funk off my teeth.

After the bathroom, I felt more refreshed and awake. Curiosity was getting the best of me, so I checked my phone and I had missed two phone calls and four texts. The calls and voicemails were from Creed.

"Hey, Rumor. I don't know what to say to fix this. You act like you don't want to fix it. I am truly sorry for hurting you, and I realize it was unfair to keep you in the dark that long. Call me back please. The number I called from should be on

your caller ID. This is the new number to reach me, the other one is no good, but you already know that."

The second voicemail was a more urgent.

"I don't know how long I can go on not having you. Physically, I am so close to you, closer than I have been such a long time, but, I'm further away then when I was gone. Rumor, I'm begging you. Please call me back."

I hit the delete button as soon as I listened to them in their entirety. Next I checked the texts to get rid of all those little red notifications. One was from Haze, one from Raige, one from Creed, and one from an unknown number.

Haze and Raige both just wanted to see if Charlie and I had made it home. I figured Charlie answered, so I deleted their messages. Creed's was more of the I-miss-you-please-call-me-back-I'm-going-crazy-without-you bullshit. The unknown number was simple. It simply said, *Hang on. I'm coming.*

My heart leapt into my throat, and there were butterflies in my belly. I knew it was Fury. After the conversation between him and Whiskey, I knew almost without a doubt it was him. I replied, *Be careful.* Then I went in search of coffee.

"Good morning," Whiskey stated.

"Morning."

"Sleep okay?"

"Actually, yeah. I did. No craziness during the night,

and no one interrupted my dreams. I'd say I'm batting a thousand for now."

He looked at me kind of funny. I decided to tell him about my phone calls and texts. When I told him about the voice mails, he interrupted me.

"Do you want him to stop contact? I can make that happen." He said in a defensive, authoritative manner.

"No, I don't. Thank you though. I am still trying to work out what is going to happen. I was engaged to him, for crying out loud. I need to give this situation more thought than one night while in shock."

I took a deep breath before I told him about the text. I got a text from an unknown number, too. His head spun towards me, "Let me see it." He totally barked an order at me. I looked at him with defiance in my eyes, and expected to hear a 'please', but I got a stern stare and a hand to receive my phone instead. He fanned his fingers up to meet his palm, motioning for me to hand it over.

"Fine, bossy ass." I plopped it in his hand. "I really think it is Fury. He mentioned to me that he wanted to come when we left Florida."

He read it and gave it back to me. "Yeah it's Fury, I was going to tell you that they are coming here for a while."

"They?"

"My brothers. All except for Chief."

None of this made sense. I looked at him and with my eyes, asked for him to continue.

"The clubhouse burned down. Arson. Everyone except Chief made it out alive. They are coming here until we figure out what to do."

"Oh my goodness. I'm so sorry. Who?"

"Won't do you any good to ask questions, Rumor. I don't have a lot of answers at this point, or any that I can go into detail about. Charlie doesn't know either, so don't bother asking her. The guys are coming here, and will be here indefinitely."

"All of them? Fury, Shooter, Magnum, and Riddick?"

"Yes. I'm going to find Charlie."

I basked in the thought of having Fury back with me, and cringed at the same time. I had to tell him about Creed. I wasn't sure how he would handle it, so I thought of several sarcastic and clever ways to share the news with him.

Hey, so, that bastard that left me two years ago suddenly came back out of nowhere.

Hey, remember that ex of mine that just up and disappeared? Well, he up and reappeared.

So, my fiance is back in the picture. Surprise!

There was no good way to tell him. This wasn't going to be easy, but I knew one thing, I couldn't wait to see Fury again.

I decided to wonder around the place and get a feel for it. It was really beautiful. I can't imagine what it would have been like to grow up here. Charlie seemed so humble about it all. It was quite possibly the biggest house I have ever been in. I had never stayed in anything that had an electric gate or a rock wall around the property. I felt safe. I walked out the back door to a beautiful outdoor oasis. I saw a gorgeous gazebo, trees of all different kinds, flowers of every color, and a koi pond that had the prettiest fish in it. Crape Myrtles lined the wall, strategically placed, alternating white and red. Hibiscus of pinks and reds and hydrangeas of blue and pink filled the flower beds. Succulents filled the window boxes, and cannas of red and yellow lined one side of the pond. Peace was easily found here. I felt calm just by being on the back porch, and I hadn't even walked the entire property yet. I hadn't explored the woods. I asked myself, *Would the overprotective biker let me out of the house and let me explore the land?* I guess time would tell. I sat in the gazeebo and thought over my situation.

The universe really did hate me. If I had ever needed proof before, I now had it. I finally found someone I was interested in and had accepted the fact that Creed wasn't coming home. Then out of no where Creed's beautiful self is messing up the life I finally have back on track. I truly was cursed. The world had proven yet again that I was destined to be alone.

"Charlie is on her way down. You want to hit the store with her? I think she is going grocery shopping." Whiskey said as he walked towards me.

"Yeah, I'll go. I need to get out." The thought of seeing Creed again snuck back in my brain and I tensed at the thought.

"You have my cell, you call me if you see him, yeah? I got you."

Charlie came down, fixed her Yeti cup full of coffee, and said, "You ready to roll? I hear we are having company and they like to eat...and drink. We need food and booze. STAT."

We loaded up in the 4Runner and set out for The Grocery Store. People always get a kick out of the name. It's original, have to give them credit.

Charlie had her long list of things to get. By the looks of it, I was going to regret agreeing to this shopping experience. There was so much meat on that list that it looked like a bunch of cave men made the list. Charlie added vegetables and different side dishes. It looked like we were cooking every night. We decided it would be faster to divide and conquer. She headed to get the massive meat list and I decided to take on veggies and home goods. Whilst wondering down the veggie isle, a voice says, "Excuse me." I didn't even bother to look away from the canned corn I was holding, "I'm sorry."

Lost in the huge dilemma of what brand choose, I heard eerie silence. I pretended I was super into the labels and was really comparing the brands.

"You didn't even realize it was me, did you?"

I snapped out of my savvy shopper mode and back to reality. It was Creed that had excused himself. Slowly, I turned around and stared at him. He really was beautiful.

"Answer me." He said softly.

"No. No, I didn't know who you were. That happens after two years of no contact."

"That stings."

"So has the last two years of my life."

We stared at each other. He looked at me like I was the very air he needed to breathe. I looked at him with a distant glare. There was no reciprocation of what he felt. Instead there was hurt and rage. I put the corn in the basket, "Now if you will excuse me, I have more shopping to do."

"Rumor," he paused. "You know we are going to run into each other right? You can't avoid me, or us, forever. Eventually, you are going to have to face me."

"Why? You didn't. Not for a long time. Instead you hid out to play cops and robbers while I pined for you. I cried myself to sleep so many nights, and I'll be damned, when I felt like it was okay to move on, is when you decided to come out of hiding. I can't forgive that."

"Forgive what exaclty?"

"Any of it. You knew you left me alone for years. You had your cop buddies come and torture me with questions that never ended that made me feel like it was *my* fault you were gone. Then out of the clear blue sky here you are. How'd you know exactly when to come back, huh?"

"I can't tell you how, but it was finally legal and I knew I had to come back for you. I wasn't going to lose you for good."

"So, I am to suffer immeasurable loneliness and guilt for two years while you play with handcuffs and police batons, and you expect me to just wait on you to come back? You magically know that I am seeing a guy, because I finally accepted that you aren't coming home, and I am supposed to welcome you back with open arms and just erase the last two years? Was that your plan?"

"Well, Rumor, when you put it like that it makes me sound like a dick."

"You are a dick! I have *not* forgiven you, nor do I know if I will be able to. You hurt me badly, broke my heart, and shredded any trust I had in you. You are no more to me right now than an ex. You just happen to be the ex that I was going to marry and spend my life with. If you think this easy for me, it isn't. It's damned hard. It's so hard to walk away from someone that you loved more than anything, because it turns out you didn't know them at all. If you really loved me, you would have known what losing you would do to me. After all, you picked up the pieces of me after the fiasco with Crosby. What happened to that guy, huh?" Tears were flowing like streams now. How dare he approach me like this in public and expect me to just fall back into his arms.

"Look, I always wanted to work for the marshalls and in WITSEC."

"Bullshit! Why didn't you ever tell me?"

"Because I knew I would have to leave you at some point, and I didn't want you to talk me out of it."

"That. That right there is one reason we will never be together again. I don't do secrets. You were extremely selfish with that decision, and if you didn't trust me to support you, you should've never proposed. You were going to be my husband." I said with a hushed whimper as I closed my eyes and turned my head. I said all I could and I needed for this to end. I needed to be away from him.

"Rumor, don't go. Talk to me, please." He begged.

"Goodbye, Creed. For the record, I did love you, wholeheartedly. I hate that this is how we ended, but that wasn't a decision I made. You made it for me when you left and didn't return."

Nothing else was said at that point. I dried my eyes, straightened myself, left the veggie isle, and headed to the other end of the store. Vegetables be damned. Charlie could come back with me. I walked over to the soap and shampoo isle. I aimlessly looked at all the different masculine soaps. I didn't know what they wanted, so I got the economy pack of Irish Spring. I bought the cheapest shampoo I could find and picked up a conditioner. Fury's hair was long, so he might actually need some. I picked up a few more odds and ends and set out to find Charlie.

Much to my surprise, she was right in the middle of the main isle giving a man absolute hell. That man was Creed.

As I approached them, humiliation, pride, gratefulness, and other unwelcome feelings emerged.

"Charlie, come on. Stop it. People are staring at us. Just let it go. I already talked to him. He should get it by now. He knows he fucked up. We still need to stop and get liquor, let's go." I tugged on her arm and pushed the cart with the other hand.

"Leave her alone, you jackass. You were so good at it for two years, why can't you be good at it now?"

Of course, he didn't answer. He just stood there crushed and shocked. My tiny friend was vicious. I finally got her to the check out line, turned to her and said, "What the hell was that?"

"That was me telling him you are trying to move on with the life that he doesn't get to be a part of because he did what he did. Rumor, I saw you two. I saw you from across the aisle. I was standing at the end cap listening to every thing."

"*And you didn't come rescue me?*" I said louder than I intended.

"You handled him well on your own. I wasn't going to let it get too bad, you know that. I wanted to give you space to handle your shit. I damn sure planned on giving him an ear full when you were done."

"Well, thanks, but you didn't have to do that."

"I know, I did it because I wanted to."

It was much easier loading the 4Runner with the food than it was getting the food in the first place.

"So, we're going to Lucky's for lunch right?" I asked.

"That's the plan."

We chatted back and forth on the way across the county line. Our county was dry which meant no liquor was sold within the county, but the smart Walkin family bought land just across the county line and built a liquor store.

"Havin' a party are ya?" The cashier asked.

"Something like that, I suppose." Charlie replied.

"Here you go hun. Y'all be careful and have fun."

"Will do ma'am." I replied.

As we were loading the back seats with liquor, I looked down and saw that we had a flat tire.

"Uhhh, Charlie girl?"

"Yeah, what's up?"

"I hate to be the bearer of bad news, but you have a flat on the back. It's on my side."

"Well shit. Okay, I'll get the jack and spare out."

"You could just call Whiskey. I'm sure he would do it for you."

"Oh Rumor, I don't need a man to change my tire."

She wrestled getting the spare down for about fifteen minutes before a man interrupted her string of four letter words.

"Seems like I just keep bumping into you. This doesn't just happen, you know."

Creed. Again.

"Well Creed, it isn't some sick twist of fate that we ran into each other again. This is you using your newly found cop skills, and listening to what I said in The Grocery Store. You know damned good and well that our county is dry, and you knew that we were coming to get beer. What do you need?"

"Other than you? I see you have a flat. Let me help you change it."

"No thanks. I have it under control." Charlie spat.

"Yeah, it looks like you do. Let me guess, you've had it all this time, you weren't cussing at your spare, right? Why don't you just let me help you?" He said, slightly annoyed.

"Mainly because I have a point to prove. Now, kindly walk away before I cause another scene. We appreciate the offer, but your service isn't needed. Good day." She said forcefully.

"As you wish."

He turned to walk away and immediatley spun back to us. He stared like he wanted to say something, but thought better of it. He curtly nodded and turned away.

"I would let him help us, over my dead body." Charlie piped up.

"What do you want me to do?"

"Start loosening the lug nuts. I will jack it up in a second. I almost have the damn spare down. Once that is done, it will be gravy. Then we can grab a bite before we go home."

Chapter 17

FURY

AFTER ABOUT TWELVE hours on the road, we finally arrived at a huge rock wall and fancy electric gate. The enormity of it and the way it seemed to protect whatever was behind the wall was comforting. I didn't realize how much I needed to know that Rumor was safe, until now. Most of the time I was on the road, I was thinking about her, wondering if she still wanted to give us a go, wondering if she was safe, or if that psychopath had gotten to her and made her go with him against her will. Realistically, I knew that Whiskey wouldn't have let that happen but the thought still crossed my mind.

"Hey, glad you made it. I'll let you in." I heard Charlie say as the gates slowly opened. We roared through and arrived at a massive house. We parked our bikes and stretched. Whiskey, Charlie, and Rumor all met us outside the house.

I lit a cigarette and looked at her. She looked different. Sad. Confused. Almost like the world was on her shoulders and she was struggling to figure out how to handle it. But damn, she was just as beautiful as she was the last day I saw her. These feelings that I knew I had to confront eventually, made their way into my chest. I walked over to her, threw my half-smoked cigarette down, stomped it out, and picked her up and hugged her. She welcomed me with open arms, and a wave of relief seemed to wash over her. It was as if my presence took some of the load she appeared to be carrying away. I would gladly carry it for her. I bent down and kissed her quickly, only she didn't let me go. She deepened the kiss which was a subtle hint that she needed me, that she wanted me. I put her down on her feet and looked to the boys. They stared in disbelief that I was capable of this type of affection. Rumor took off back to the house. I didn't see where she went but knew that it wouldn't be long until I was holding her again.

The mood was heavy, everyone was unsure of what to say or how to act. None of us had ever been through this. Losing Chief had turned our worlds upside down.

"Well, no sense in standing out in the heat. Let's go inside, and I will show everyone to their rooms. There is food and beer inside, too."

"Beer sounds amazing," Magnum said.

When I entered the house, I was taken aback. It was massive and grand, but rustic, like a log cabin. It had huge wooden beams and vintage chandeliers. The stairs were a combination of wrought iron and cedar.

"Yall's rooms are this way." Charlie stated as she led us up the stairs, and showed us to different rooms.

"Fury, you can stay here." She pointed to a room adjacent to another room that had women's clothes laid on the bed and bags on the floor.

"Yes, that is where Rumor is staying," she said as she winked and walked away to show the others their rooms. Clearly, it was written all over my face.

Once we were all downstairs, we all had a few beers and began to settle in from the trip.

"How was the ride?" Whiskey asked.

"Fuckin' long." Magnum stated in a less than pleased tone. "My ass hurts from sitting so long. This douche wouldn't let us stop very often." He said as he pointed at me.

"Look, I needed to be here yesterday. I didn't have time to stop so you could powder your nose and stretch your legs, princess. I've got shit to deal with and Whiskey told me to hurry because Rumor might need me."

About that time, Rumor appeared from the kitchen holding two beers.

"Yeah I remember, alright. You have to open pandora's secret box that you won't open in front of anyone."

"Mag, drop it. I said if it had to deal with the club I would bring it to the club. Do you trust me?"

"Yeah, but he was our pres, too. I think we all have a right to know what he kept in that box."

"Well, you thought wrong. Leave it."

Magnum sulled up and pouted like a toddler. He would have to get over it. I meant what I said. If it pertained to the club, I would bring it to the club's attention.

"Rumor, do you want to come outside with me?" I asked her.

"Uh, Yeah. I'd like that."

I followed her out to the gazebo. We silently stared at the woods that surrounded us.

"Fury, I have something to tell you. It's bizarre and insane and throws a huge wrench in my plans, but you have a right to know."

"Go on."

"My ex, the one that disappeared is back. He is here and wanting to pick up right where we left off."

"Is that what you want?"

"No, of course not." She replied in a snap.

"What do you want?" I asked.

"You."

I looked at her and let the words sink in. She wanted me. She is choosing me over the love of her life. None of this made sense. She waited for this for two years and now he's at her feet and she is stepping away from it?

"Are you sure?" I asked. I needed the confirmation.

"Yeah, what do you want?"

"I told you in PCB that I wanted to give us a chance. I meant it. I will stop at nothing to make sure that you are happy and safe. Is this guy a threat to you?"

"Not that I am aware of, but that doesn't mean anything. I clearly don't know him anymore."

"Come here."

I opened my arms and she quickly closed the gap between us. I reached down and cupped her face with my hands and stared in her clear blue eyes and said, "If you don't want him around, then he wont be around. If you want me here, then that's what you will have. This is entirely up to you. Either way I am stuck here at Acres indefinitely. I hope that you'll make my stay a little easier and better, but I do understand that you had a life before I came along."

"Fury, you need to know that we were engaged. I was going to marry him."

"Do you still want to marry him?"

"No, not even a little. I wonder what might have been, but that is all. He has broken my trust, and that can't be gotten back. I need to start over. You haven't given me any reason to distrust you. I know that you have something you aren't comfortable confiding in me, and that is okay. I hope that you will feel comfortable to at some point, but even with your secret between us, I at least know that you have one. That is more trust than I have with Creed , engaged or not. He forefited his right to be in my life when he went off to training and left me in the dust."

"If he does't matter to you, why did you tell me that you were engaged?"

"I don't want secrets between us. I know you aren't comfortable telling me whatever it is you aren't telling me, but you were honest with me from the beginning. I don't like it, but I respect it. It doesn't change who you are or what I think of you."

Oh but it should, Rumor. Oh but it should. I thought to myself.

"Why the look?"

I hadn't realized that I had a look, but my facial expression had to be one of uncertainty.

"Mainly I am wondering, how he left you, and I have figured out why. You are too good for your own good. You are too trusting and good hearted. People take advantage of you. You really should be more distrusting of people."

I could tell she was thinking about my statement, because her face shifted to a very puzzled look.

"I think you are right. I trusted Crosby, then I trusted Creed." She chuckled and shook her head.

"What is the laugh for?" I asked.

"Maybe the third time is a charm? Maybe you will be the one that doesn't break my heart. Here's to hoping."

"Rumor, I would never purposely hurt you. I can't change what those others did, but I can promise that I won't let you down. I'm not going to disappear for long periods of time and not tell you why. If I was going to kill myself...Well," I paused.

"Well what?"

"I'd have done it a long time ago. Before I found the club. Those fuckers get on my nerves and piss me off something fierce, but they are the most loyal people I have ever met, and without them, I wouldn't be here."

"How are you doing, you know, since Chief is gone?"

"It's hard, ya know? He is the one that got me in the club life, and the one that helped me in one of my hardest times. He was the dad I didn't have. It was only four years, but in those years, he made me a man. I owe him my fuckin' life. Retaliation is coming and it's going to be bloody. You need to know that. Can you handle this?"

"It looks like I don't have a choice."

I cut her off, "Yes, you do. You always do."

"I mean, if I want to give us a go, then I have no choice. I would want justice for my loved ones, too. The way I figure it, you went out of your comfort zone for us, I can get out of mine for you. I need a life change anyway. My life has been boring for so long. You do you, and I will be right here. Just promise me you will come back."

"If I don't come back its because I'm in a body bag. Either way, you will know what is up with me. I won't leave you like those other dopes left you."

She smiled her sweet smile and hugged me tight. It felt nice, and I needed the comfort she brought to my life. I bent down to kiss her and was interrupted by Charlie.

"There you two are. I think we are going to eat. Y'all

going to join us? It's nothing fancy tonight. Either pizza or sandwhiches. I'll get Rumor to cook for us tomorrow night," she said with a wink.

"Looks like we have been summoned. To be continued?"

"Yes."

"Yeah we're coming, be right there."

We walked into the house and a different feeling came over me. Home. It felt like home. How though? I had just gotten here. Rumor was smiling and carrying on conversations with everyone. She seemed happy.

I have to figure out if there is a way that her ex could find out I am not actually Legend Morrow. I thought about it for a while and became more pissed off by the minute. Surely, the WITSEC people were legit and didn't leave any gaps in covering me.

We were all in the living room talking and catching up when I stood and said, "I'm beat. I'm going to hit the sack. Catch you all tomorrow." I bent down and gave Rumor a kiss on the head and before I headed to my room I whispered, "You can come too, if you want."

I stripped down to my boxers, and got into bed. I wanted to sleep, but I laid there awake. I stayed awake for what seemed like ages, thinking about everything from retaliation on Jay and Sully, to the lock box I had yet to open. I would talk to the guys tomorrow about how to handle those two bastards. I know Sax gets dibs on Jay, but

I am going to tell him that I'm getting a beating in on him first. I want to feel his bones crack under the force of my fists. I want to make it slow and painful for him.

Rumor knocked on the door and said simultaneously, "You still want company?"

"You don't have to knock.   Come in. I'm just laying here in bed thinking."

"She walked over to the bed and sat down. She turned to me and those clear eyes looked deep into mine and asked, "Are you sure you are okay? It's okay to not be okay, you know?"

"I'm honestly better now that you're in here with me."

She walked to me and bent down close to my face, "That's real good to hear, Fury, because I feel better knowing you're here." She put her lips on mine. A sense of urgency took over for her and her hands were quickly in my hair. She was pulling me closer to her, like she was trying to wear me. It was like she needed me to cover her. She had control of the situation and I gladly let her have it, I needed the distraction. She stopped after a long kiss. She was short of breath and frazzled as she pulled away.

"Sorry. I don't know what came over me."

"I don't mind. You can finish if you want."

"Let's think about things."

"I don't need to think about anything. I want you to come here and be with me. I want you to take my mind off the shit that has gone down over the last 72 hours. I want you, Rumor. I want you."

She bent back down and kissed me again, only this time I didn't let her have control. I deepened the kiss to suit me. I gripped her hair and pulled her face as close to mine as I could get. I kissed her like she was never going to be kissed again. She pulled away and gasped for air. I let her catch her breath and then I pulled her down to me. I needed her closer.

"Take your clothes off and stay a while. I want to feel you next to me. I've decided I like it better when you are beside me."

She nodded in agreement. I undressed her in a frenzy as lips clashed, tounges dueled, and our bodies connected.

"Rumor. Are you ready?"

"Yes." She said to me with desire in her eyes.

"I can't wait any longer. I have to have you."

I lowered her onto my length and felt my eyes roll back in my head. The feel of her around me was almost more than I could stand. Almost. She started moving at her own fast pace. As she chased her pleasure, mine was coming like a freight train that couldn't be derailed.

"Rumor, hold on." I grabbed her hips and worked her up and down, and backward and forward until she was lost in the moment. I never slowed my pace. I kept going, chasing away all the bad that happened, until I it was gone. I pushed down on her hips and held her down on me, clearly hitting a nerve with her as she lost herself again. That's all it took to send me over the edge. She bent down and kissed me, and I kissed her back and held her. It felt good just to hold her, to have her back in my arms.

"Rumor, I'm so glad you crashed at my house for a week. As shitty as this week has been, you have made it bearable. Thank you for just being here."

At some point I fell asleep, because the next thing I knew, I heard birds chirping and felt the light shining bright in my eyes. I guess my physical and mental fatigue had gotten the best of me. It's not like I had been put through the mental wringer or anything.

I got up and went outside to smoke. It was seven thirty. Surely I wasn't the only one up. Whiskey was always up early in PCB, so I hoped he was an early riser here, too. I walked through threshold of the sliding door to the backyard and lit my cigarette. I looked around and saw Whiskey starring out into the woods from the gazebo.

"Hey, I am taking your man card if you tell me you are into peace and quiet in the woods, surrounded by beautiful trees and colorful flowers." I kidded with him. "You okay?"

"Yeah, why?" He asked.

"This ain't like you."

I blew smoke out and let that sink in. He was kind of right. I had never cut up like this with him.

"It was just funny to see you in your cut out here in the *Country Living* gazebo. Imagine the cover of a magazine with a big flowery gazebo that is so nice, light, and pretty. Now put a biker in a cut in the middle. That mental image is why I was kidding around with you."

"Just thinkin'. That's all." Whiskey said, not engaging in my banter.

Sucking in on my smoke, I took in a lung full and exhaled slowly.

"We've got some thinking to do. I say we call church today and discuss what happens from here." I said in a serious tone.

"What do you want to happen?"

"I thought about seeing if your Rudy charter wants to merge. We would eventually get our shine business going around here. You can't tell me some of these redneck people in the woods don't want some good shine. Also, we need to open a resturant."

"Why the hell do we need to do that? That's the most random thing you've said."

"I know it will be voted on, but when I was giving my statement to Officer Canon, I told him that we were coming here to handle some club business and he asked what kind. This isn't going to go away anytime soon so we need to at least get some plans drawn up or something to make it look like we are trying to get into the restaurant business. If nothing ever comes of it, we can say it fell through and we decided against it."

"Damn dude, you've thought this through, yeah?"

"Yes. I have. I am up for the merge of the two charters. Yours is little, anyhow. Let's bring it to the table to discuss later. I'm sure there will be more to talk about."

"You're probably right, Fury. Shit is going to be busy around here for a bit with the fire, Chief, the merger, Rumor and her situation. This is liable to be a chaotic nightmare for us for a while."

"That's fine. We have no choice but to handle it."

"There you are." A sleepy sweet voice said.

"Babes. What are you doing up so early? It isn't nine yet." Whiskey said.

"Magnum is snoring so loud it woke me up. I opened the door to see who was running a damned chainsaw at eight in the morning, and saw sleeping beauty."

"He was hitting the liquor pretty hard last night Charlie girl. Let him sleep it off. It's been a rough few days for him."

"Its been rough for all of you, not just him. It's okay to say you are struggling. If you need anything you can just ask. I will help in any way I can. Chances are, if I can't, I know someone who can. I'll leave you two to finish your discussion. Would you like coffee?" She asked us both.

"Yes." I accepted.

"Sure, babes. He will want his black as well."

"Be back in a bit." She went inside. Whiskey's eyes followed her every move.

"If anything ever happened to her I don't know what I would do. She is to be protected at all times."

"Man, Hensley is dead. There isn't anything else to worry about."

"Sully, Jay, anyone else that we might have pissed off, there is always something to worry about. I know it sounds insane. Since we have been together, I have a primal need to keep her away from any other shitty or unsafe situations. I just think of all the ways I can protect her," he admitted.

"You're right. You sound insane," I blurted. He really did sound like a psychopath. "There isn't going to be anything else that goes wrong. No one knows we are here, and the security here is like Fort Knox."

"Fuck you. One day you will feel the way I do. Speaking of, how are things with you and Rumor?"

"New. Weird. She says she wants nothing to do with Creed. How do you just get over a fiance?"

"Well, that is something you have to ask her. I can assure you that she wants nothing to do with him. You should've seen the way she shut him down."

"Oh, I can imagine. She put me in my place and called me out when I acted like an ass to her. I know she can stand her ground."

"Rumor left no room for him to misunderstand her intent. If he didn't understand, then it's because he's a dumbass. That isn't to say he won't try again. By the look on his face, I would say he isn't quite over her."

"He has to come through me to get her."

"Whiskey, Fury, coffee's ready." Charlie yelled.

"We better go before she wakes up the whole house."

After everyone finished the breakfast that Rumor

fixed, I called the guys into the living room. We needed to discuss things and see where everyone stood.

"We need to vote on some things. Meet in the shed in the back. Charlie has agreed to let us use that for club business. I've called in the others." Whiskey instructed as plates were cleared from the table.

I walked to Rumor and slid my hands around her waist. I pulled her to me and kissed the top of her head.

"Thank you. You didn't have to do that."

"I'm a guest here and feel like I need to help, too. Cooking breakfast and doing dishes is nothing. Go, go do your thing."

I begrudgingly walked away from her. I could have stayed right there and held her for a while longer. She was right, I did have business to handle.

"Sax, stay close. As soon as we get done with the club business we are going to need you to come and discuss some business," I sternly said. My tone was a command, not a question.

I walked out the door to be with the rest of my club.

"We have some big things we need to vote on, and the vote has to be unanimous. If one *nay* is said, then it's off. Since the clubhouse burned in Panama City and Chief isn't here with us anymore, Fury and I discussed the possibility of merging the two charters." Whiskey announced.

He went around the table and got head nods *and yeas* from everyone.

"Good, that is solved. With Chief being gone, that put Fury as acting pres. We need to vote on that and a VP."

"I vote Fury for president and Whiskey for VP," Magnum was the first to speak.

I looked at him inquisitively. He could have been in the running for it.

"Dude, Whiskey is better suited for the position than I am. You know it and I know it." Mag said as he read the confusion on my face.

Once again yeas all the way around. Briar was named secretary. Shooter was deemed sargeant at arms. Magnum was appointed treasurer.

"I told the cops we were coming here to do club business. When questioned, I told him it wasn't his business, but, with the way shit went down, I didn't want anymore attention our way. I told him we were talking about opening up a restaurant."

Quiet consumed the shed. A room of eyes stared at me. Without words, I knew they were asking what the hell was wrong with me and expected an explanation.

"I was put on the spot. I thought about it on the ride to Rudy. What if we opened a resturant and moved our shine that way? We would be able to run a catering business and distribute the shine. It would work as a cover and a legit business, too."

"Yea," Shooter piped up.

Slowly but surely the remaining guys said yea too.

"That is the least of our worries. We need to discuss retaliation. Sully and Jay will pay. However, Sax has agreed to help us, but Jay dies at his hands. That understood?"

Heads nodded all the way around. "Shooter, go get Sax." I ordered.

Once Sax had taken his seat at the makeshift table, I asked him how he wanted to go about this.

"I don't care how it happens, as long as I am the one that puts him out. You guys can handle Sully, but Jay is mine. We can go back and take care of business there."

"That will give me a chance to pick up Chief's ashes, too."

"I am not leaving our girls alone. Who goes and who stays?"

"Riddick can stay." Mag stated.

"No. He made moves on Rumor, and she doesn't like or trust him. I'll kill him if he fucks up like that again."

Whiskey reminded the group that Briar was from the area, and would be perfect for the job.

"Look, I know how protective he is of his girls. You guys didn't see the shit I went through when Charlie and I first started talking. Dude, tell them."

"I'll stay here and keep Riddick in check, too. Nothing will happen to our girls while I am on guard. If the dumbshit shows up here, then I will kill him. I made no bones about putting Whiskey in his place and I like him. It won't be any problem for me to put Jay in the dirt, if he shows his face. Your women are safe with me," Briar reinforced what Whiskey said.

"Fine. It's settled. Briar and Riddick stay at Acres while the rest of us are on stand-by. We will wait to ride out to PCB, as soon as I get word from officer Canon that Chief is ready for pick up." I shook my head in disbelief. A somber mood blanketed the room.

"Fury? We will get him brother," Magnum promised.

"I never thought I would be bringing Chief to bumfucked nowhere, especially in an urn via my saddle bags. He is supposed to be here damn it."

No one spoke, they just nodded in agreement. No one said anything as we all let the somber thought sink in.

"Who knows a good architect? We need to get some plans drawn up for back up. We can decide who will run the resturant when and if we go through with this." I tried to change the subject.

"I'll ask Charlie if she knows anyone. Her dad was friends with some pretty big people from around here." Briar stated.

"Seriously, is there anything she can't do or help us do? Dear God, she is perfect." Whiskey gloated.

I rolled my eyes at the love stricken fool, "If there's nothing else, you are free to go. Just stay close. We ride out as soon as I hear from Canon."

Everyone filed out and headed back to the house. Briar and Whiskey stayed back.

"You realize shit is about to get heavy, right? You are new to the position and I want you to know that whatever you need, I'm here for you." Briar slapped my shoulder.

"Thanks brother. It's going to be tough. Honestly, it's going to take all I have to not shoot Jay as soon as I see him. I know Sax gets him, but fuck he needs to at least feel just an ounce of the rage that I have inside of me. If he knew what I had…", I stopped myself.

"We get it, Fury. We get it. Just know that we are here for whatever you need. Once in, Always First." Whiskey piped up.

I lit a cigarette and asked if this was going to be our new place for club business. Whiskey said he would talk to Charlie girl and see what she thought. He didn't expect it to be an issue, and neither did I. The space only housed a folding table and folding chairs, a weed-eater, and an empty gas can. I figured she doesn't have much need for the space, at least until we could have a shop built.

"Guys, I have a thought. Say we did build a resturant. We can have our ladies work and manage it. The profit off it and the shine could be astronomical. We need to seriously discuss this with them before we bring this into the club. We need to have all our ducks in a row. I'll get estimates together for constructing the building, getting permits, and all that legal bullshit. We can discuss this with our ladies to see if they would be willing to manage it." Whiskey stated.

"Charlie already knows we run shine, Jazz ain't stupid, so between the two of them they could keep it on the hush hush. They could run the catering vans," Briar thought out loud.

"That sounds good. Later on, the three of us, with our girls, can nail this down, then take it to the club," I ordered. "For now let's get in there with the rest of them and figure out our plan for the day. What is there to do here anyway?" I asked.

Laughter rang out from both of them.

"Dude, Rudy is so small that there are a few churches, a ball field, one gas station, and a creek. That's it. This is part of the reason I really think that we could do good here. We would be the only resturant in town, and we'd have a place to store our shine. We need to figure out what we are going to serve. We are for sure getting our private club license so we can serve booze. No one in town does. We will strike gold right there."

Mid-morning turned to early afternoon. Some of us decided to go to the creek and swim and wet a line. Charlie loaded up her 4Runner with poles, tackle, ice chests of beer and water, and tanning lotion. Whiskey, Briar, myself, and our ladies headed for a quiet spot on the creek. The country side here was beautiful with the hills and mountains. It was very different from the beaches of Panama City.

We pulled up to a side road that was blocked by a gate.

It reminded me of the ones back home in Austin. I hadn't seen dirt roads since I left Texas. Whiskey got out and unlocked it and held it open as Charlie pulled through. Whiskey pulled the gate to again, and Briar looked back to Jazz and asked if she was okay being in the back with the stuff. We had stuffed her back in the third row seat so we could haul the poles and ice chests. Charlie had her back window down so that the poles had room and didn't break.

"Oh honey, you act like this is the first time I have done this," She grinned at him.

Whiskey got in and we preceded to the Honey Hole, as Charlie called it.

"How do you have a key to a place like this, Charlie girl?" I asked curiously.

"I was kind of wondering the same thing, babes."

Charlie looked to the very back where Jazz sat and glanced back at the road. Jazz nudged Briar and he finally said, "Charlie's family owned it. It was left to her when her parents died."

Whiskey put his hand lovingly on her thigh and squeezed, "Thank you for sharing it with us."

"It's yours now, too." She held up her finger that had her ring on it.

"It isn't legal yet. We still have to get a marriage license."

"I know, but all that is keeping it from being legal is a piece of paper. What really matters is that I know it. I don't really care about the legal bullshit, you know that."

"Well, I want you to have my last name…on paper." He replied.

"Here we are." She said as she pulled to a stop.

I looked around and took in the most serene place I have seen in a long time. It was clear water with a rock bar that seemed to go on for miles. The water so clear I could see the bottom, even out in the deepest parts. The trees were so big and green, and provided shade to most places. Charlie, Jazz, and Briar started taking the stuff to the dock.

Whiskey, Rumor, and I looked around and tried to take everything in.

"Charlie, how did I not know of this place?" Rumor asked in awe.

"I don't bring many people here. I am the only one with a key to that gate."

We got to the wooden dock built over part of the creek. After our lines were baited and our drinks were cracked open, Whiskey threw in the first line.

We all followed suit shortly thereafter.

"Rumor, did you want me to do that for you?" I asked her as I watched her try, then successfully bait her hook.

"No. I got it." She went and got a towel from the bag. She looked to me and said, "I just don't like to leave the worm slime on my hands."

She and Charlie giggled because Charlie was doing the same thing. Briar had baited Jazz's for her.

After a few casts and a couple of beers in, Briar said to Charlie, "Charlie girl, you and the other two women come here a sec."

"What about our poles? I was just starting to get bites?"

"It can wait. This is important." Whiskey said to her.

I saw Rumor reeling in her line, so I went over and helped her.

"Thank you, but I really do know how to fish. My step-dad taught me years ago."

"Come on, this involves you, too." I put my hand on the small of her back and ushered her to the group.

"Girls, we have an idea, a pretty lucrative one. It can only happen if you are on board."

"Go on," Jazz urged.

"We're wanting to open a restaurant and catering service. We could sell liquor if granted the license and have a good business that the club could have ownership of."

"How would you make your…" Charlie started.

"We will see how it goes," Briar cut her off.

"Oh Jesus, I ain't stupid, and Rumor is going to find out anyhow. Rumor, the boys make moonshine and sell it." Jazz said as she rolled her eyes.

All eyes focused on Rumor. Everyone expected her to ask questions, but when she didn't, I simply said, "Since the other two are privy to the operation, I was hoping you would be okay to help us, too."

"Go on, I'm listening."

"In a nutshell, we were hoping the three of you would manage the place. Rumor since you are an experienced waitress, you could be a huge asset to us," Briar pointed out.

"What if I don't want to leave my job now?"

"What if I told you the pay would definitely be worth your time?" I asked.

"I'm interested, but I need more details first."

"Well, Charlie and I are in. Does that help you make up your mind?"

She sat there quietly and listened as we continued the conversation and discussed all the possiblities. We talked about what we would serve, possible décor options, and locations available.

"So, are you on board yet, Rumor?" Charlie asked with a wink.

"I suppose. I've been at my job for so long. It's secure, you know. I suppose it will be nice to not drive thirty minutes to get to work.

"Rumor, I promise, you have nothing to worry about. I won't let you fail," Whiskey reassured her.

"You know, we are taking a risk, too. The likelihood of us failing isn't likely. We don't fail," Briar proudly stated.

I should have been the one to reassure her, but honestly, how was I supposed to do that? I only know moonshine. I know nothing about running a legit business.

"Rumor, we wouldn't ask you if we thought this was a potential failure. We will get all the details worked out and let y'all know when to report to work."

Jazz stopped him before he continued, "I know you don't discuss club business with anyone outside the club. I get that and respect that. I wouldn't ask anything about your shine business, but this is different. This puts us in the middle of it, and if you want us to manage things for you then we should get a say in business side of things."

"What exactly are you referring to Jazz?" I barked at her.

"Look, you ain't got to be a horse's ass to me because I asked questions and voiced my opinion."

"Baby, just let it go." Briar pleaded.

"No, I won't. He can talk to you like that but he isn't going to talk like that to me. I ain't his bitch. I'll not be talked to like one."

I glared at her and Rumor butted in, "You were kind of a douche just then." She said as she slid a little closer to me.

"Fine, sorry. Are you happy?"

"Well, it's a start. I was referring to the theme, décor, menu, and name. Things like that. Things that you guys probably don't really give two shits about. Those very things are likely to be what keeps customers coming back."

I looked at Briar and Whiskey and they both nodded in agreement.

"Have it your way. You girls can design it however you

see fit, but try to stick to some kind of reasonable budget. I will get with you girls as soon as I get the bank accounts transferred from Panama City. We should have plenty to get up and running."

"Babes, what are you thinking?" Whiskey asked Charlie.

"I was thinking of serving home cooked meals. Having a set menu and changing it weekly. Like having themes. For instance, nacho week, barbecue week, seafood week, and so on."

"This all of the sudden came to you? That's pretty in depth for an on a whim thought," I blurted.

"Fury, I get you are stressed out, but seriously, you're an ass. If you must know, no it wasn't just an on a whim thought. Since I was a little girl, I wanted to own a restaurant. I wanted a cool place that I could have as my escape and be something to be proud of. The problem is I suck at cooking."

"You never told me you wanted to have a resturant," Jazz said in shock.

"Surprise! When I would talk about it with Hensley, he would shoot it down and say how stupid it was because I wasn't a good cook, so I gave up on it."

"Well, that's all I needed to hear. I'll make it happen for you, babes."

"Rumor, are you good? We could really use you in the kitchen, and to wait tables. Jazz can help you in the kitchen."

"I think so. I guess it wouldn't hurt to give it a shot. Do we know when this is going to take place? I need to give my current job some notice."

"It'll still be a little bit. I have to transfer funds, and we have to purchase land, an…"

"No you don't. I will donate the land." Charlie said.

"Is there anything else you want to just throw out there, Charlie? Where might this land be that you are donating?" Briar asked, as if it made a difference. I could tell by the look on her face that she dared him to tell her no.

"Well, *dad*, it's the land that is right beside The Gas Station."

"I forgot you owned that, but why don't you sell it to us?"

"What the hell am I going to do with it? The profit will benefit me anyhow. My husband's business effects me too. I would be glad to help, so consider this an investment."

"You are sure about this, babes?"

"Yes, under one condition."

"And that would be?" I asked. I was still shocked that she was going to hand over the land for us to put a business on.

"The name of the restaurant has to be, Wish You Were Beer or Let's Just Wine About It."

Everyone started laughing. I wasn't amused.

"Seriously? Charlie those are genius." Briar finally said.

"Or She Ain't Here. Or He Ain't Here."

"Oh no. I like Wish You Were Beer." Jazz said to Charlie, amazed at Charlie's wit.

"Fury, Briar, Whiskey, do you all like it?" Charlie asked.

"Babes, it is perfect. It's catchy, and says that we will have booze. It's awesome."

"Charlie girl, it's genius. Just like you."

"Well, seems as if everyone has spoken." I replied dryly.

As chatter over the restaurant consumed the group, I walked away to smoke. As I inhaled, the burn of the smoke soothed my frazzled nerves.

"What is the matter, Fury?" I hear from the voice that I have grown very fond of.

"Everything. This is happening and there isn't a damn thing I can do to stop it. That fucker, Jay, made that decision for me, for us. Now I am left to start over again in a town I don't know, and some chick that I don't know is giving us land that should rightly be bought. I clearly have no say in that either." I snapped.

"Sounds like you are just on a power trip." She hurriedly replied back, hitting me with a truth bomb.

Her honesty didn't sit well and instantly pissed me off. I didn't say anything, just let the anger stew in my head. She doesn't know what I've been through in the last few days. I'd like to think I had control over something.

"Look, Charlie is just trying to help you. She is right you know, this is going to benefit her, too. She wouldn't just give over prime land if it didn't. She isn't stupid. If she didn't believe in the cause, she would've made you buy it. She clearly believes in the restaurant, and she has the rest of us to help her make her newly realized dream come true.."

I blew out the white smoke and nodded my head.

"I know she means well. I appreciate it, but I have to think of how that looks for taxes, with the state board of health, and all the legal shit. I can't have people snooping around and finding out shit."

"Look, Fury. I don't know much about moonshine, but I know there are stills. I would think that she isn't going to build stills in the resturant. That would be stupid. I would imagine that she will have you build them at Acres and we can distribute the goods from the restaurant. You need to relax and have some faith. Charlie is a smart and tough cookie. Now that she is married to Whiskey, you guys are pretty set up. Her parents clearly left her more than I knew. All I knew about was the insurance policies, Acres, her mustang, and the house that she and Hensley lived in. I didn't have any idea that she had land and the hook up with the higher ups in the surrounding communities. I suppose she is a very valuable asset. I know whatever you need, she would make happen for you, especially since you guys helped free her, and she has her happily ever after. Don't look a gift horse in the mouth, Fury. Accept it and move on. If it is that big of a deal, make it on terms," Rumor said.

"Such as?"

"Well, if you don't want it to look like she gave you the land, then put it in her name since it is her land. Her hubby is the VP of the club, so he will have interest in it. It will look legit, you are just over thinking things. Drink a beer. Chill out. It's all going to work out and be okay. Just believe."

Just believe. That sounded so nice. I wanted to believe, but so much is hanging in the balance of uncertainty right now. There is the fact that I am me, or Fury I should say. Rumor must never find out who I really am. Now we have all these new plans, we still have to go get Chief's remains, and find and deal with Jay and Sully."

"Look, leave it with Charlie while you are gone. Sounds like she has a plan anyhow. She is a very business driven person, and will not steer you wrong. She won't do anything to sabotage your operation. You are going to have to trust her and your brothers. They trust her."

"For someone that knows nothing about the situation, you sure nailed everything on the head. I have a hard time letting people take over. I really don't trust people. I know that Whiskey and Briar wouldn't do anything to hurt the club, it's just that..." I stopped.

"Just what?"

"I am used to having to do everything, so that it is the way it's supposed to be. I'm the one responsible for the well-being of the club now. If something goes wrong it's on me."

"Relax. No one here is going to let that happen." She hugged me.

I let my arms wrap around her and allowed her to comfort me. As her words sunk in, a peace came over me. I wasn't at ease completely, but enough that I could enjoy my time away. I pinched the cherry off my cigarette and put the butt in my pocket. I bent down for a kiss and was surprised when I was met halfway. There she was, again, soothing me when I needed it most.

"Thank you. I needed to hear that."

"Welcome. I had to do something, because if you acted like an ass much longer, I couldn't have saved you. Jazz is quiet most of the time, but when you piss her off, it's no holds barred. She is vicious. Charlie is a package of dynamite, too."

I nodded and agreed that I had been an ass. "It's part of my charm."

"Let's go back over there and fish some more, or swim. I need to relax some."

Chapter 18

RUMOR

Back at Acres, Roxxi cooked dinner. Her and Sax were talking about plans for building a tattoo shop here, if they decided to stay around. She left everything she knew in Panama City. She was starting over, too.

We all gathered around the massive table with our beer and dinner.

Magnum asked, "So, you guys have a good outing? Fish biting?"

"Yeah we caught some, but mostly just swam and shot the shit. You know, took some time to unwind." Charlie said.

"When is Raige coming over?"

"Mag, dude, she don't want anything to do with you, give it up." Briar said, shaking his head.

"I can't forget her. She is fine as hell, and I can not get her off my mind. I need more beer."

"Yeah, like a hole in the head." Whiskey said.

RING RING RING

"What?" Fury answered the phone, clearly pissed off again. It must be miserable to be that unhappy. I wish I could help him be more pleasant, to show him that life isn't as gloomy as he makes it.

"I see. We'll be there tomorrow. We will leave at day break. Have us a hotel ready." He smashed the end button on the phone.

"Men, meeting now. Sax, you too."

They all went to the living room to meet, they weren't concerned with privacy, as we all heard what was being discussed.

"That was Canon. Chief is ready. I will pick him up tomorrow, and we can stop and see if he has any other leads on Jay. We will also go, under the radar, to find him and Sully. If you know anything, or anywhere they might be, it'd come in real handy about now, Sax."

"I can get in touch with someone that can hook us up with intel on their whereabouts."

"Make your call, do what you got to do, and find Sully. I'm sure when you find him, we will also find Jay. The puppet isn't going to get too far from his master."

"You got it."

Sax came back in the kitchen and sat down. He made

some calls, texted a few people frantically, like he was on a mission and he was running against the clock.

"Done." He said, walking back into the living room.

"Damnation, that was fast." Briar said in amazement.

"They are staying at Sully's. He has a pretty sweet and expensive car collection and they are there guarding them. Apparently, the word on the street is that The Chosen Legion is after blood and they are hiding at the only place they think I don't know about. They underestimate me."

"Good work."

"Men, we ride out at daylight. Have fun with your ladies tonight, we don't return until we have one or both of these fuckers. Preferably both of them."

Sounds of yeas and clanking beer bottles filled my ears. Over the noise and ruckus, my sights were set on Fury. Even with the scowl on his face and the worry etched in his features, he was simply gorgeous. Perpetually pissed off never looked so good. His long, tall frame was leaned against the wall, and his arms were crossed over his muscular chest. His reddish brown hair was disheveled, but looked perfectly messy. His hazel eyes glanced the room over until they met mine. Even though he always looked mad at the world, when his eyes met mine there was a sense of peace about him. He even gave me a half grin. I could tell something was eating at him.

At the risk of being yelled at, I made my way to him. When I got in front of all six feet ridiculous inches of him,

I looked into his eyes and inquired, "So, you going to be okay?"

"Don't have a choice but to be." He was short.

"You know it is okay to show some kind of emotion. You don't have to be the tough guy all the time."

"I am showing emotion. Can't you see? I'm pissed off."

"Touché. Look, I don't know, nor do I care, what is about to happen. From the look of rage on your face, I can only assume the worst. Just know that I am waiting here for you when you get home, yeah?"

"I don't know when that will be, Rumor. It isn't fair for me to ask you to wait."

"Then don't."

"Huh?"

"You aren't asking. I'm telling you that I'll be here when you get home. Besides, I have this waiting game down like a motherfucking champ." I said as I shot him a wink.

"I guess you do. Let's go out to the gazebo where it is quiet. We need to talk."

We made our way hand in hand through the crowd of people in the living room, which earned us some looks and comments from the guys.

"Briar, he is touching someone, *and it ain't holding them by the throat!*" Magnum screeched.

Once we were outside, he let go of my hand and lit a cigarette.

"Rumor, this is your chance to walk away. I am telling

you this is going to get rough, and if your ex is in with the WITSEC program, then I don't want you involved with me."

"What does that have to do with the price of tea in China?"

He thought for a second, shut his eyes, and hung his head. I could tell there was something he wanted to share.

"The less you know, the safer you are. I won't purposely put you in a shitty position, but I'm telling you to leave me alone, for your own good."

Sadness tore through me. Memories of the short time we had been together flooded my mind and tears formed in the corner of my eyes.

"No, no sir. You, Fury, don't get that luxury. You don't get to tell me what is best for me. Remember? We've had this argument before. I get to make that call. I want you, and I am choosing to stay with you knowing that you aren't exactly flying on the right side of the law. I don't give a hot damn about any of that. I care about you. You are the one that made me see that I was wasting my life waiting on something that might not have ever returned. Granted, he did, but I don't want my old life. I want to see where this goes. Lawful or not. I don't care."

Those words sank deep into his hard head, because it took him a while to reply. He cupped my face with his cigarette between his fingers, "I want to look into these eyes of yours more, I want to kiss you more, I want *more* and I haven't wanted *anything* in a long time. You changed that, but what I want doesn't matter. I can't commit to this. It isn't fair to you. Rumor, this has to end, it has to stop. You are too good for me and this life. Go live your life and don't get caught up in my web. I'm not the one for you." He look me in the eyes, smoke swirled in front of his face, and he said, "I am sorry Rumor. I'm sorry I ever got involved with you. If it weren't for me you would be back with your fiancé now. Go back to him, he can give you stability. I can't. I have nothing to offer you except what you see now."

"Jazz and Charlie do it. Why am I any different? What did I do to make you change your mind? I thought we had an agreement." I said as tears started to well in my eyes.

"It's for the best. I said it's done. You are safer and better off without me in your life." He said with finality in his voice.

He walked back into the house, taking my crushed feelings with him. He managed to break me again. For the third time.

I walked back into the house after I dried my tears some and made sure my face wasn't beat red. As I went to my room, I felt everyone's eyes on me. They had to know something was off.

I got to my room and shut the door. I cried. I cried because here I was again. I was being robbed of something that I wanted so desperately. Fury *is* good. Why can't he see that? He wants me to run back to the arms of Creed?

Creed is the reason I'm in this position to begin with. I couldn't let him go with out saying one last thing to him. I wanted him to feel bad and needed him to see and feel the pain he caused me. I sauntered to Fury's room, and threw the door open. I caught him off guard. He dropped something, but didn't immediately bend over to retrieve it, he just stared at me with a look of surprise.

"You are good, Fury. I see it. I see your heart. You don't want me to see it, hell, you don't want anyone to, but guess what, I see you. I see through that rough and tough exterior. I see that you are a good person, one capable and deserving. If you weren't, you wouldn't be warning me to stay away. You wouldn't be trying to push me back into the arms of the very one that broke me. Just know before you go, that you are sabotaging what we have. You could've made, no, *we* could have made this work. This is on you. Congratulations! You're number three. The third one to break my heart. You promised you wouldn't and you did." I turned and walked back to my room. I fell to the floor and cried silent tears so no one else would hear me.

Daylight came and the only reason I was awake was I heard the bikes pipes rumble as they pulled out of Acres. Thoughts of yesterday flooded my mind. I thought about the resturant. Did he, or they, still need me? I would have to talk to Briar and Whiskey. I wasn't giving my notice at work until I had something definitive.

I laid there in bed thinking of what was going to

happen to us, to the guys. My thoughts raced as to what they could possibly be doing when they got back to PCB. I decided that I couldn't lay there anymore, I needed coffee. I made my way downstairs, and Briar caught my eye. I tried to avoid eye contact, so I slid right by him and made my way to the coffee pot.

"Don't listen to him." He said as he walked out of the kitchen.

I snapped my head around, "What? How did you know?"

He came back to the kitchen island. He put down his coffee and said, "Shooter and I heard you guys last night in the gazebo. He thinks he is saving or protecting you from something, when in reality, he is just sabotaging the situation. He is going to be fine. Nothing is going to happen to him. He wants to kill Sully and Jay, but that won't happen because the rest of the boys won't let him do anything stupid. He is going to come back and be who he was before he got the call to return to Panama City. Just hang in there."

I was unable to say anything, so I turned around and finished making my coffee. My head was a jumbled mess. Leave him alone. Don't give up on him. If I listen to what everyone was telling me, I will never figure out what I need to do. I was feeling as confused as a chameleon in a bag of Skittles.

"What? Wait! Briar, hold on." I chased him. I caught

up to him on the back deck. I asked, "What the heck? I don't know what to do. You're saying don't give up. He is saying don't wait on him, and I deserve better. I need answers."

He took a drink of his coffee and looked at me for a long time, too long for comfort, before he said, "Look, I can't tell you that it will be easy. I can just tell you that since you have been around, he is happy-ish, and he is trying to save you from him. He has a good heart, but also he knows that we don't always abide by the rules, as you have learned. Just don't listen to him. If you want to keep this thing going, then do it. He will want it, too. He just doesn't want you getting caught up in any kind of blow back from this."

"So you are saying to wait it out and basically, don't listen to him. You men are irritating, you know that?" I said as I left him alone on the deck. I went inside and headed to my room. I didn't end up in my room, I ended up in Fury's. I looked around and sat on his unmade bed. Thoughts of everything that happened and everything that was said in the last week were flying around my head. I have lived so much more in the short time that I have known him than I have in years. Did I really want to give up on that? Did I really want to move on, again, and go back to Creed? These thought gave me chills and a feeling of uneasiness.

I hung my head in my hands and looked down to the floor as I continued warring with myself about everything.

Just thinking about everything that had transpired exhausted me. I closed my eyes and took in a deep breath, trying to force myself to relax. When I opened my eyes, I saw something on the floor. I picked it up and stared. It was a picture of a gorgeous Native American woman. She had the most gorgeous green eyes and long dark hair. Who was she? I flipped over the picture and read the back. *I will always love you, Eric.* Who was Eric? Why did Fury have his picture, and why did he look so sad when I busted in here last night?

I held on to the picture. I would give it back when he returned, and let him know that I was, in fact, not giving up on him. I had to know where this was going. All of a sudden, I felt deep in the pit of my stomach, a wrectching, nauseous feeling at the very thought of not having him in my life. I thought of Creed and knew I was not supposed to be with him. He didn't do anything for me anymore. I felt nothing except anger and resentment for him. I knew then, while sitting on his messy bed, holding some guy named Eric's picture, that I was meant to see what was in store for us. I had the feeling it wouldn't be easy. I even felt like he was going to balk at the idea, but I knew that I had to stick it out.

I went back down stairs and refilled my cup. When I ran into Briar again, I insisted, "I listened. I won't give up on us. I can't go back to Creed like he told me to do." He looked at me and smiled a soft smile. "Do you know who Eric is?"

"No, why?"

"I went in his room and sat on his bed for a bit. I had my head down, trying to wrap it around this whole situation, and saw a picture. The inscription on the back was written to a guy named Eric. Just weird. When I busted through his door to talk to him last night, he was looking at something and dropped it," I explained.

"There's no telling. It might be a picture that belonged to his parents. Maybe a picture that his grandma gave to his grandpa or something like that. I don't know anything about him before he was in the club. No one does. He made sure we all knew that it was off limits to talk about when he patched in. It's understood that we don't discuss his life prior to The Chosen Legion. Magnum made that mistake once and he ended up with a black eye and a jacked jaw over it."

"No one stopped him?"

"I wasn't there. This was in Panama City, four years ago. I was an eighteen year old punk kid. Still trying to figure out what I wanted out of life."

"How did you end up in the club? Weren't you and Jazz together then?"

"Yeah, I went with some friends, Whiskey and a couple of other guys, to Panama City Beach for vacation. While we were there we encountered The Chosen Legion. We were all intrigued by Chief, Magnum, and Fury. We happened upon the beach in front of the clubhouse and were not so kindly told that we were trespassing. Fury, was actually the one to let us know. Long story short, Whiskey and I were the only ones that were cut out for it. We stayed in touch and ended up patching in down the road. When Chief decided that he couldn't convince us to stay in Panama City, he said we could start a charter here in Rudy. Whiskey took off to Texas shortly after that."

"Why haven't I seen many of y'all around?"

"We are fairly little. Our bigger charters have most of the members. Here the only ones you will know are me and Whiskey. We have a few other members, but they don't come around a lot outside of club business. You will likely get to meet them soon though, seeing as Acres is our home now."

"So you have known Fury was an ass for some time then, right?"

He laughed, "I guess I have."

"Thanks. I think I am going to run home. I need to grab some more clothes and things from my house."

"Not alone you aren't. I ain't taking that ass chewin'. I can go with you."

I was going to argue, but then remembered that I really didn't want to possibility see Creed alone.

"Fine, I just need to grab some things."

We took Jazz's car to my house. When we got there, we saw something we didn't expect to see. An empty driveway.

"Well, this makes things a bit easier. I'll be right back." I said.

"I'll go with you, he might be inside. I don't need Fury coming down on me because I let you go in alone. No thanks."

"Fine, you can help me carry things out, too." I hastily replied.

I got the keys out and unlocked the door, but it wasn't locked. I looked at Briar and let him go in first, hand firmly on his pistol. He looked around and didn't see anything suspicious, so he motioned me to come inside.

I went to my room, found my bed unmade and both male and female clothes on the floor. Only problem was, the female clothing wasn't mine. I was disgusted and a little hurt. I went through my drawers and grabbed enough clothes to last me for a while, then grabbed my shoes and work shirts and jeans.

I wouldn't be returning here. I would let him take over the payments, or I would have him refinance it in his name.

I handed the clothes to Briar. He went to put them in the car, while I started packing up my pictures. As I put a frame in a box, I jumped when I heard, "I didn't think you were coming back."

I snapped my head around, and there he was. Creed was in a towel, still wet from the shower.

"I didn't think you could fuck another girl in our home... I never brought anyone else here after you disappeared. You're still trying to mend things between us. I guess it's different with men. You can't wait a week, but you damn sure expected me to wait years."

"You said there was nothing for us."

"Clearly I was right. If you were really still trying to get me back, you wouldn't be screwing someone else. You can refinance the house, I will sign anything you need. I am not staying here and you confirmed what I already knew. We are done, there is nothing between us anymore, and once again, this is your fault." I grabbed my pictures, looked around and got the rest of the things I wanted to keep, little nick knacks that people had given me. Most importantly though I grabbed my pictures. They meant everything to me.

"Rumor, I…"

"I believe she has spoken. Just leave it." Briar rumbled.

"You don't travel alone anymore do you Rumor? What is it with these guys in cuts?"

"They belong to the MC The Chosen Legion, and they have done more for me in the last two or three weeks than you have in the past two years. I hope you are happy with your choice. We could've had it all. I had intentions…" I said as I walked past him and back out to the car.

We got into the car and headed back to Acres. The ride back was quiet and I welcomed the silence. Seeing her clothes on the floor, not knowing who *her* was, stung a bit. more than I expected it to. How was I that easy to get over? Especially after he came back here and begged me to take him back? There is no way he happened upon someone that quickly. That meant that there must have been someone else for a while. He hadn't been in town long enough to find some side fling. Where ever he came from, he must have had someone else the whole time.

Chapter 19

FURY

IN TYPICAL RUMOR fashion, she interrupted my moment by storming through the doorway like a hurricane. I was staring and studying my picture of Daisy, but Rumor startled me and caused me to drop the picture. I had made an attempt to shut her out and save her, but she wasn't having any part of it. She was giving me every reason to give us a chance, and I kept shutting her down. I couldn't have her. waiting at home on me not knowing how everything was going to pan out. I didn't know if I was going to come home alive, or end up in a Florida jail. She didn't need to be in the middle of that. Her ice blue, clear eyes were swollen and red. I knew I had made her cry, and it hurt, but it was for the best. If I didn't push her away she would end up like Daisy, and I could not mentally handle hurting another woman.

After she left, I decided it was time to unlock the fire proof box. I grabbed the key and turned the lock. I shook from anticipation of seeing what was inside. **CLICK**. The top slightly bounced as it unlocked, its hinges a bit squeaky from the soot and ash.

Several dusty folders were stacked inside. In typical Chief fashion, he had it completely organized. The box was labeled, except for one section. I started rummaging through and found a folder labeled *Important Club Info*. I took a deep breath, and cautiously opened it. I found a lot of notes about different members, numbers of business allies and customers, and history of the club.

There was a file on each of us. Magnum, Shooter, Chief, Whiskey, Briar, Riddick, and me. I glanced through them all, not seeing anything interesting, until I came to mine.

The first page was like everyone else's. It included date of birth, hometowns, parent names, high school information, prior job, phone numbers, and addresses. The typical demographic stuff. However, it didn't make sense, these things were my real information, not Legends. This was Eric's.

I fumbled through my file and found a hand written letter addressed to me.

Fury,

If you are reading this, you now have the gavel. You will do well by the club. I know you can't afford to let anything go wrong. I know what you have riding on this. I know what you're thinking right now, and yes, I have known all along. I found out about you and knew you were a perfect fit for this club and business. I saw how loyal you were to a couple of loser buddies, and I knew you were a safe bet, especially once you found out that we were legit. I have a friend in law enforcement that called in a favor. He sent you to Panama City and I watched you for a while. You know the rest. Your secret has always been safe with me and I have never uttered a word to anyone. Just in case you needed further affirmation…It's nice to meet you, Eric Martin. I hate to hear about your tragic death in that fiery car crash. It's a shame that your beautiful fiancé and that precious unborn baby will never know you. I did my research. Now, put Eric Martin to rest. He doesn't exist anymore. Don't look back, kid.

The next part was in a different colored ink and I could tell he had recently updated it. *And don't let go of the girl. I saw how you looked at her. She is yours, if you don't fuck it up. Do what you gotta do, but don't let that one go. She is good for you. Now burn this file. You won't need it anymore. -Chief*

I sat with my mouth open and wondered how all of this was even possible. How could he have known and not tell me? I felt honored that he kept my secret, but at the same time, I was pissed off. He left me one final order, so I complied. I took my file outside and burned it. I couldn't risk it getting into the hands of anyone. Watching the last traces of Eric Martin go up in smoke was oddly calming. I could breathe freely now, knowing no one would ever know my true identity. Even in death, that bastard had a way of keeping me calm. I lit a smoke and watched the rest of my past fly into the night.

I fumbled through the rest of the folders and found one that said BANK DOCS. I opened it and saw account information and ABA numbers ready for me. There were also instructions on sticky notes. Damn, Chief was always thinking ahead.

I checked the last statement balance and there was over four hundred thousand in the account, and on top was a sticky note.

If you've found this, move the account to wherever you are. Use the ABA numbers to help you. -Chief

I made sure the ashes from my file were out, so I wouldn't cause a forest fire, and I headed inside. I grabbed a beer and went upstairs to go through the rest of the box. There weren't many things left in there. There were little trinkets such as a money clip, pocket watch, a worry stone, and an old rusty pocket knife. I decided to share the stuff with the club when I told them about the finances. I was also going to let them know that Charlie wasn't going to have to give us the land if she didn't want to. Although, I feared the stubborn little shit wouldn't take our money easily.

I was going to keep his engraved pocket watch. The inside of the lid said *Don't look back, love Pawpaw.* He told me that very thing, even after he died, I felt like I needed it as a regular reminder that I am not who I used to be. Magnum would get the money clip. It was engraved as well with the saying, *Money ain't everything, but it helps everything.* That was something Magnum would say. The pocket knife would be Shooter's. He had a way with fixing things, and I knew he would be able to bring life back to it. Whiskey was going to get the worry stone. He was so wrapped up in his girl and keeping her safe, that I felt like he needed it more than anyone else. He's going to end up giving himself an ulcer over Charlie. It sure is nice to see him happy.

After I made my way through the box and the memories of Chief, I decided to go outside and smoke again. My nerves couldn't take much more, and I needed a breather. This fucker had successfully given me a headache from the grave. I knew he was laughing his ass off because he had me feeling things. He knows how to get to me like no one else.

I let my mind wonder, and it immediately drifted to how I had treated Rumor. I needed her, but more importantly, I needed her to be safe. I couldn't risk her getting hurt over this. I had no doubt she was physically going to be fine, I was worried about her being emotionally damaged. She doesn't deserve to have to wait again. She deserves to be happy now, she has waited long enough. I hate that I told her to move on, and deep down I hope she ignored me. I would love for nothing more than to come home to her, and to show her that I am trying for her. I needed her to hang on, but since I told her to go back to Creed, I deserved what I got. I hope she is stubborn and didn't listen to me.

I went upstairs and went to bed. I set my alarm for the ass crack of dawn. I more tossing and turning than I did sleeping. Rumor was on my mind and I wanted nothing more than to go in and crawl in bed with her, but this distance is what is best for her. Then Jay and Sully were infiltrating my thoughts. I couldn't wait to have them in my possession. Oh, the fun we would have with those two jokers. They don't realize they have met their demise. Sax is going to have a blast with this, and we have his back.

DAWN ARRIVED, I got up, and packed up the bank papers that Whiskey got from Charlie from the Bank of Rudy. She had all the information ready. She was going to be a great old lady. She does what is best for the club, no questions asked. I wondered how Rumor would be as… I cut off my thoughts and didn't let myself entertain that notion. Not when I just told her she needed to move on.

Bike pipes rumbled to life and Whiskey, Mag, and Sax rode out. We decided it would look rather suspicious to bring back two hostages on the back of bikes, so I drove Whiskey's truck, with Shooter in the passenger seat. It was equipped with a locking bed cover, which would be beneficial.

The two of us rode in silence for a while. I lit a cigarette and enjoyed the burn of the smoke, as it calmed the thoughts in my head. As I blew out, Shooter looked at me.

"What?" I asked.

"You might have just fucked up and we might not be able to fix it."

My mind was clearly not thinking the same as his, "Whiskey will get over the smoke smell. There's no way he expected me to go hours without a smoke. He had to see this coming."

"You really are a clueless asshole, aren't you?"

I looked at him, obviously irritated.

"Would you quit accusing me of something, then leaving me hanging? What the actual fuck are you talking about?"

"Rumor, you dumb shit. You are going to royally sour her to anything that has to do with you. You didn't even go tell her goodbye. She ain't the only one that heard you talking last night. You need your fool head examined, and your ass whipped. Maybe that would help you find a fucking clue. Hell, I'm not involved at all, and I'm pissed off at you." He was lighting into me and it completely caught me off guard. Shooter never voices his opinion.

"What do you mean? I did her a favor, and why did you stay and listen if you heard us talking?"

"You didn't do her any favors. That's a cop out. You hurt her and made her feel inferior. You made it seem like she is not as important to you as you are to her. She is a grown ass woman and has a mind of her own. You are screwing with it and took away her choice. You are no better than her ex. One and the same, cut from the same cloth. If she takes you back, you better kiss the ground she walks on, and thank her daily. If she does take you back and give you a second chance, she is more forgiving than you deserve."

That pissed me off. It stung to heard that from someone that is normally reserved and quiet. I wouldn't let him see that I was affected though. I was now the president of this club and I had a reputation to uphold.

"Fuck off, Shooter. Mind your business. I didn't ask you to hang around and listen to my conversation. Only then, would your opinion be warranted. Unless it's club related, don't fucking lecture me."

He didn't know what I was protecting her from. I was trying to save her from becoming the next Daisy. There was no way for me to convey that to him. He was right though, she did deserve better than me.

The rest of the ride was quiet and long. Shooter

started snoring and that pissed me off. I didn't get any sleep and he was sawing logs. Luckily for me, his chainsaw breathing kept me from thinking about Rumor. He had me contemplating his murder, but I wasn't thinking about Rumor.

Once we arrived in Panama City, we pulled into the same hotel we were in the last time. I went in and paid for our rooms, cash of course, and under the fake name, Elton James. No one would have any idea that we were here. When we got in the room, I called Canon and told him I was back.

"Canon, I am back in town to pick up Chief. Is there a time you want to meet me? Tomorrow is fine. Thanks man, I appreciate it."

"Tomorrow we get Chief's ashes…" I cut Shooter off.

"Ahhh! Fuck, did you have to say it out loud? Yeah, I know why we are here." The finality and heaviness of it sank in.

"Look, I know you are hurting. We all are, but don't be a dick to us. Save that shit for Jay and Sully. Enough is enough, dude," Whiskey said. He stood and walked over toward me, with his fists balled up like he was about to put me in my place.

I had successfully pissed him off. This day was going to shit really fuckin' quick. I stormed outside, so I didn't fight with my VP. I knew he was right, and. He isn't known for backing down or losing. I would certainly have my tired ass put in my place if I didn't walk away. Between Rumor and Chief, I didn't know how much more my head could take. I felt like I did when I left Daisy, confused, and full of doubt and anger. Now I had to go pick up the ashes of my president, friend, and the one who saved me. I lit a smoke when I got outside and to help calm the hell down. Something about the smoke filling my lungs gave my head the break I clearly needed. Sometimes the cloudy cigarette smoke gave me clarity. I needed just enough to gather myself, so I wasn't a total jerk to everyone, especially my brothers.

I got on the bike and headed somewhere, I needed to be anywhere but here. My ass hurt from riding all day, I was hungry, and I needed a drink. I couldn't stay here with them. I had to ride somewhere. I started heading down the road and aimlessly ended up at Flap Jacks. This was a natural end point, because this is where Chief brought me and introduced me to the world I now know. I might as well eat the same thing I had during our first meeting, so that's what I ordered. Life had come full circle.

I watched out the window as the world went by one slow moving car at a time. I was brought out of my trance when I heard, "I knew I would find you here."

Magnum came to find me.

"What are you doing here? I left for a reason, and I don't feel like company."

"You're right, but a brother knows when to step away

and when to man the fuck up. You are going to be a royal pain in my ass and be a major dick. I knew that going in, but I would be a shitty person and brother if I let you be alone. You are rough and tough but you still grieve. That is exactly what this is. Grief. You don't get to do it alone when you are a potentially hazard to yourself and the club. You are a ticking time bomb and I won't let you self-destruct." He said as he scolded me like a step child.

I sat there in my own head while I stared at him. I willed him to say one more thing. Magnum didn't disappoint, "You act like you are the only one that lost someone close to them. Wake the hell up. Let me tell you something. You aren't the only damsel in distress that has ever needed saving, okay, princess? When I was first introduced to Chief, I was living on the streets, hungry, beaten, and…" He paused, closed his eyes, and took a deep breath. "The rest isn't important, but Chief saved my life. I have no doubt that I would've been dead years ago had he not come around when he did. He took me in and hid me out. There was a missing person report on me. Chief hid me away until I was old enough to fend for myself and tell my shit-for-brains parents to fuck right off and enjoy their trip to hell clothed in their gasoline panties. He could have been thrown into jail for harboring a minor, a runaway minor at that. Get out of your feels and quit feeling sorry for yourself. You ain't the only fucking one that misses him."

A look of shock took over my face. Magnum had just shared with me something I never knew, and I was speechless. All I could do was stare at him and see if more words came out of his mouth.

"See? You aren't the only one that has a fucked-up past. Get over yourself, stop being a dick, and let's focus on getting Chief, picking up dumb and dumber, and getting the fuck back to those hillbilly sticks that we are going to call home for a while, yeah?"

I didn't say anything, I just attempted to eat the food on my plate. Food didn't interest me. I took a few more bites and pushed the plate away.

"Look, we will get revenge on them, okay? The rest of us want it, too. You're going to have to learn to move on. You have the gavel now, heavy as it may be. You are the one making the calls and leading us to good and prosperous avenues, but you can't do that if you are hellbent on being pissed off. For the time being, you need to put aside your anger and buck up. We need you. This has to be a team effort, and you are the leader of the pack now. The time has come to show us what you are made of."

Those three words hit me hard. *We need you.* I haven't been needed since I was with Daisy. As it turns out, she didn't need me, and is just fine without me. The club was different. They needed me, I knew that now.

"Look, I get it okay. You were in a tough spot and you can't talk about what happened. There isn't a whole lot of difference in us man. The only difference is I can talk about mine and you can't for whatever reason."

"You're right. Chief found me when I least expected it, but when I needed to be saved the most. I can't go into details, and probably wouldn't if I could. It's too much. I do have a new-found respect for your goofy ass though. I had no idea you were in a shitty situation like that."

He slowly closed his eyes and hung his head, "It's tough to talk about, but I felt like you needed to know that you were being a rude asshole and that you aren't the only one feeling the pain of losing him. If I pissed you off, sorry not sorry. You needed to hear it."

I nodded and closed my eyes because he was right. I was being a selfish prick. I was able to eat about half my food and looked up at Mag who was staring out the window.

"Mag let's go. Let's get back to the hotel, drink a few beers, and put this day in the books. We need to make tomorrow an early one."

I paid the ticket and headed out the door. Before I threw my leg over the seat, I was wrapped in an ambush bear hug. I didn't have the heart to push the emotional jack ass off me. He had just revealed a huge part of his shitty past to me. I know he meant well and right now wasn't a time to be a jerk, so I awkwardly clapped him on the back and said, "We got this, bro. We got this. We will get Chief the justice he deserves. We just have to listen to Sax and trust that he knows what he is doing. You and your feelings can get the fuck off me." I was hoping to lighten the mood. It worked because Magnum backed off with a shitty grin on his face.

"Fucker." I replied. He knew what he was doing, and it worked. I was in a better place than I was a little bit ago because of that goofy bastard. He irritated me and made me wonder how he tied his shoes most days, but today he was there for me in a way that I didn't realize I needed.

Back at the hotel, the other guys were drinking beer and shooting the shit.

"You think you can play nice now, Fury?" Asked a slightly irritated Whiskey.

"Yeah." I wasn't going to share what Magnum had just told me about Chief's generosity. If he wanted Whiskey to know, he could damn well tell him, that isn't my place.

"Glad to see your mental break made you more tolerable and happier," He replied sarcastically. I supposed I deserved it and since I was walking on thin ice with him, I remained quiet.

Sax began to tell us about Sully's prized possession, his car collection. We would devise a plan to torch them. We still had to figure out the details of how we would get Jay and Sully together.

"You guys don't worry about getting them together. Let's get to Jay and he will lead us to Sully. I promise, he will squeal when tortured even the smallest amount. He is a pansy. I'll worry about getting him then the rest will fall into place. If it's okay with y'all, while y'all are getting Chief tomorrow, I will locate Jay. We can play the rest by ear once we have Jay in our possession," Sax stated.

"Sounds fine to me. Boys?" I asked everyone else.

Everyone nodded in agreement that tomorrow was the day. We all drank a few beers and went to bed. The next twelve hours would be challenging to pull off. Grabbing Jay without being caught would be risky, but a risk all involved were more than willing to make.

My head hit the pillow but once again, sleep evaded me. I laid there and stared at the ceiling for what seemed like hours and thought of absolutely nothing. As thoughts of nothingness were abundant in my head, sleep should have easily claimed me. I got up and went outside to smoke a cigarette and try to figure out a way to fall asleep. While I was smoking, I had a vision. I saw Chief as plain as if he were standing there in person. He walked up to me and said, *"Kid, you're on a path of self-destruction. Stop wanting revenge so badly that you don't sleep. You have come all this way for something, don't fuck it up now."*

"Chief?" I said as I fanned the smoke from my face. I was for sure that I had obviously lost my mind. I was delusional from the lack of rest.

"You ain't imagining anything, so stop flailing your arms like a fool. I'm here, but only to tell you to stop being so hellbent on getting revenge that you sacrifice the club or yourself. You

will have more responsibilities coming soon enough, and everyone involved will need you around. We don't need your grumpy ass in the slammer or dead. Pull your head out."

"More responsibilities? What the hell?"

"You will find out soon enough. Don't be afraid, and don't run away. Don't push the people away that are going to need you the most."

"You are being very vague, ya know? Now my mind is going to wonder all over the place."

"All good things in time. Just use your head, and trust your instincts, especially where your girl is concerned. She's a good one. Don't let her go." He said as he faded away just like the smoke from my cigarette.

I couldn't even ask what in the fresh hell he was talking about, because he evaporated so rapidly. He was gone before I got my wits about me and could fully put together a full cohesive thought. I was left to wonder what the hell he was talking about. I finished my smoke and went in to put my too-tired-to-function self to bed.

Chapter 20

FURY

MORNING CAME, AND SAX WAS on the ball. He found Jay's location and was figuring out where and when to get him. Shooter had picked up breakfast for us. I attempted to eat but was only able to get a few bites down. My nerves were taking over, knowing I had to pick up Chief's ashes. I went out and smoked again as if the nicotine would somehow stop the pain, halt all the emotions that attempted to creep back in, or stop the nausea from crawling up in my throat.

"I've called Jay. He's meeting us at Sunset Tattoo. Let's ride." Sax said in a serious tone, as if this is was the final mission in life. I can see where he would be okay if it was.

The guys mounted their bikes while Shooter and I loaded up in the truck. We drove to Sunset and waited on

Jay. The idiot thought that Sax was going to travel alone. Upon arrival at the dilapidated building, he unlocked the door to the space that used to be Roxxi's haven. The paint was peeling, and the stench of the stale air hit us in the face as we entered. We all went to the back, except for Sax. He was waiting out front for Jay.

Jay arrived at the old building and sauntered in. He made an ass out of himself by trying to intimidate Sax, but Sax immediately grabbed him by the throat and mades him talk. In order to stay alive, Jay did exactly what Sax said. He took out his cell and called Sully. He shared that Sax was back in town and took the order from him to take Sax to him. He didn't know that he had fallen right into our web. Jay was loaded in the truck with Shooter and I, and Sax looked to Magnum and said something. We sat and watched what was unfolding in front of us. Sax walked over to Sunset, and Mag followed him in. It was only a few minutes, then we hear gun shots and an explosion. Flames made their way out of the building, as Sax and Magnum ran out the doors. They motioned that everything was okay and yelled to load up and hit the road to Sully's. Jay was in the front of the truck, with his hands behind his back, and we barked orders at him to give us directions.

Hours later we arrived, but we waited til' dark to make our appearance. We all eyeballed his massive fucking estate. Shooter got out to discuss his next move with Sax, "How do you want to start this?"

Sax points his finger to the back of the truck, "Put Jay in the back, and lock the bed cover. If he gets out, he will blow this."

Shooter had an evil grin on his face as he walked to the truck and grabbed Jay by the hair and drugs him out. He walked towards to the bed and Jay began to fight him, "I'll suffocate in there!"

"It'll be painless, and it won't be remotely close to the pain you caused Roxxi and the others you hurt."

"I'm sorry Sax, come on man," He begged.

He gave up the fight, got in, and Shooter locked the cover. Mag and Sax took off to the house while Shooter and stayed back and awaited the show. It wasn't long until I saw the yellow glow of an explosion and heard the boom of the roof being blown off his precious car garage where his expensive car collection was housed. His precious cars that were worth hundreds of thousands of dollars were scorched and turned to black piles of smoking steel.

In a few minutes, Shooter and I see Mag and Sax appear out of the darkness with guns pointed at the slimy looking bastard, that I presumed was Sully. As they got closer, Shooter got out and waited for them at the bed of the truck. When they arrived, he opened the bed cover and Jay scrambled out and leapt to his feet. He dive bombed Magnum, who hit the ground. The hit took him completely off guard. He cussed out loud as he lost his balance and his gun scattered to the ground away from him. Jay took advantage of Magnum being down and escaped into the night. I headed to chase him down, but Sax motioned that Sully was the one we really needed right now. "He is nothing without his puppet master. Let him go. I will worry about him later."

"He gave me up?" Sully asks jerking his head into the direction Jay headed in.

"He chose to save his own ass, and with any luck he will get eaten by a wild animal or fall and smash his head in on some rocks." Sax said in a non-sarcastic tone. Sully hesitated but gave up and got in the back of the truck. We wanted to make sure he stayed asleep and quiet, so we drugged and knocked him out.

"We heading home now?" Whiskey asks.

"The real fun begins now," Sax said. "Let's go try and get some sleep. He is locked in there with no way out. Tomorrow we get ready to ride home.

Back at the hotel, we chilled out and had a few drinks. I took a deep breath and said, "Tomorrow morning I am going to get Chief and then we head home."

The events of the day had been exhausting. Tonight hit us hard and we all seemed to need sleep. It wasn't as good of sleep as it could have been if we had been with our better halves, but it would keep us between the lines tomorrow for the ride home.

I laid there in a place of half sleep and thought of home. I was in Panama City and I was calling another town home. The enormity of that thought and feeling weighed heavily on my chest. Sleep finally took over, and I didn't wake till morning.

I called Canon and arranged to meet him but seeing as there was a captive in the bed of the truck, I asked Magnum if I could take his bike. I met Canon at the funeral home and when I walked in, he handed me a black, matte urn.

"I hate that we are seeing each other under these circumstances. I hope you don't mind, but I didn't want to bother you, so I went ahead and chose what I thought you would appreciate for the urn. It seemed to be the best match for you."

I wrapped my head around what he said. Was I mad that a decision was taken away from me about the last place Chief would rest? Or was I thankful I wasn't burdened by this decision? I stared at the urn, looked back to Canon, and was silent for what felt like several minutes.

When I found my words again, I said, "Thank you. I'm not entirely sure I would have handled that decision well. Turns out, over the last few days, I have lost my cool when it comes to Chief. This is a nice urn. It's simple and not flashy just like Chief would have wanted. I will take him, and we will decide as a club what to do with is ashes."

"I truly am sorry for this, Fury. Did you get a new bike?"

"Uh, mine is getting an oil change and a new set of tires. I borrowed one from a brother. This one's saddle bags are slightly bigger than mine, so there is more room for the urn." I lied. I didn't think he would notice that the bike was different, but there was no way I could tell him that there was a hostage in the back of the truck I drove.

"Tell your friend he has a nice ride. Take care, Fury. If we find out anything about the arsonist, we will let you know. We are still looking for Jay. He is our prime suspect."

"It is appreciated." I nodded, put Chief in the saddlebag, started up the bike, and took off to the bank. I had to transfer the funds from the bank here in Florida to the bank back in Rudy. I went in prepared with the appropriate documents and my business attitude.

"Can I help you sir?" The cashier asked.

"I need to transfer funds from this account." I slid her the account information for the club account here in Florida, "To this account. Here is the ABA number and the routing number to the Bank of Rudy."

"I hate to lose your business. May I ask if it was something we did?"

"No, we are moving." I didn't elaborate or give anything away.

She looked at me with questioning eyes but did what I asked. She handed me the documents and I signed them. "There you go. Everything has been transferred over just as you wish. I wish you luck in your new endeavors and in your new town."

I simply nodded, got the documents and headed out

the door. I was leaving behind the only life I had ever known since Austin. The familiarity of PCB was soon to be a thing of the past, to be replaced with another new hometown. I was leaving with my memories, our money, and our president with no intention to ever return. We could settle with the insurance company via phone and email. If not, I would come back, but only on business. I wouldn't, hell, I couldn't, stay here without Chief. I knew that my time here on the beach was done.

BACK AT THE HOTEL, the guys were up and getting around. I brought Chief inside and sat him on the table beside the tv. "Boys, there he is. That fucker in the back of the truck is going to end up to just like him, without the pretty urn. Sax, I promised that you could have him, but if you need help or decide you don't want this on your hands, I will do it with pleasure. Because of him and that pussy Jay," I pointed to the urn, "My president is dead and all we have left is his remains. Sully doesn't get to live. He dies by your hands or mine. Up to you."

"We are ready to head home, if you are, Fury. Let's get this over with, it's time to move on." Whiskey was offering his support. "We have Sully to deal with and we need to collectively figure out what to do with Chief's ashes. So much death but part of it feels good."

I put Chief in the front of the truck, and the boys rode behind us back to Rudy.

BACK AT WINSTEAD Acres, hours after we started the trek back, we were greeted by our ladies and the rest of our members. Briar and Riddick were the first out the door to meet us at the truck.

"Y'all need any help? Where is he?" Riddick asked.

"He's in the back of the truck. Take him to the garage and tie him up. I don't think he'll get away, he's hardly conscious." I ordered. "Also, out here in the middle of bumfucked Egypt there has to be hog farms. Find one. That is what we will do with the body. Mag, if you and Sax want, you can yank teeth. Hogs can't digest them. We will bury them somewhere else."

Briar chimed in, "Ol' man Cluck has a hog farm. He doesn't feed them properly, so I bet they would tear up fresh meat."

I left the boys to their tasks and searched for Rumor, hoping that she didn't take our last conversation seriously.

I ran into Charlie, who simply stated, "She doesn't really want to talk to you yet. You fucked up. You fucked up big time."

"It was for her own good. She didn't need to be linked to me in any way while I was on that trip, because had something gone wrong, I wasn't going to be the downfall of another woman," I said before I realized what escaped my mouth.

"Look, I don't know, nor do I care, who you hurt in your past. That don't affect me now, and it doesn't affect Rumor

294   *Harlow Brown*

either. You need to fix this, if she lets you. You might have good intentions, but you hurt her. I hope she listened to Briar, but I know she is done with the confusion." She scolded me like I was an errant child.

I deserved it though. It needed to be done. I wouldn't feel bad for protecting her. I wish Eric would have had the balls that Fury does. Perhaps, he would know his kid if that was the case.

Magnum went in and tried to find a drink as Sax went to find Roxxi. I knew they were headed to the garage to do whatever they needed to do to Sully. I was fine with it as long as they cleaned it up. I knew that Roxxi needed closure, too.

I went in search of the one person I hoped had ignored the orders I gave her. I went aimlessly looking through the house. I went upstairs and knocked on her bedroom door. Nothing. I went down stairs and to the gazebo. Amongst the flowers I saw nothing, and I kept wondering where the hell she could've gone. I gave up, sat down, and lit a smoke.

"I bet she doesn't want to talk to you, but I also bet that she doesn't want anything to do with her ex. If I were you, I'd do some serious kissing up to make shit right between y'all. Her ex screwed up bigger than you, and that's your saving grace. That's the only reason you even still have a snowballs chance in hell of fixing this." Briar said as he headed inside. I guess he came out here and told me to make sure I knew I fucked up, and that there was still a chance, if I played my cards right. Chief even said something along those same lines.

I sent her a text

Me: I'm home. Where are you? Can you talk?

I waited for an answer and nothing came in the time I found appropriate.

Me: Rumor, I'm sorry you were hurt, but I'm not sorry I did it. You've come to mean an awful lot to me and I wasn't going to put you in harm's way, or subject you to any situation that could have gone south. The less you knew, the better.

I waited longer, and nothing.

Me: It was good while it lasted, yeah?

I put my cigarette out and looked up to the sky as if answers were going to fall on my head. I took a deep breath and headed back inside.

Mag and Sax dealt with Sully and were out disposing of him at ol' man Cluck's farm. I went back to the truck and got Chief's urn. When Charlie girl saw it, her look took me by surprise. She is usually is so collected, but this was just out of the ordinary for her.

"Fury, is that what I think it is?"

"If you think it is a cremated body, then yes."

"Oh boy. This is more difficult than I thought."

"I can put him in my room, that way you don't have to see it. As soon as the guys get back, we'll decide what we are going to do with him. I don't want to make it awkward for you. You're being so generous to let us crash here til' we figure out our next move."

"It's not a big deal. I just didn't expect to get hit in the feels as hard as I did. It's like seeing the urn made it final, ya know?"

I get it. I understood all too well. She wouldn't understand the bond that we had and how things are never going to be the same again.

"Don't, don't look at me like that. Remember, I lost my parents on the same day. I do get how hard this is. Don't give me that patronizing look. I might not know your story, but you sure as shit know mine. I know it's not easy, so don't think I can't empathize with you."

"I didn't say anything," I said, shocked.

"You didn't have to. Your face said it all. I understand loss and pain, okay. I could probably give you a lesson or twelve. You need to realize that you aren't the only one that loved him. Everyone else did, too. I hadn't known him long at all, but you know what? Because of him, and you too, I got to put an end to a very dark and sad chapter in my life. I will always be grateful and thankful to Chief. He didn't have to help me out, but he did because of who I was with."

"I will put him somewhere, so you don't have to see him." I said as if the urn was Chief in his physical form. I knew I owed her an apology, but I wasn't ready to admit that I was being a selfish asshat.

"Thanks. If you want, you can put him in the garage. I'm

not using it, so you can have it as a make shift clubhouse. I won't go out there, so you all can have him with you there. Just a thought." She said and turned away. She stopped on a dime, turned back and said to me, "Go find her," and she left.

Like I haven't been trying to find her since I have been back?

Chapter 21

RUMOR

HE WAS BACK. I heard the truck and the bikes as they pulled through the gates of Acres. I wandered out into the vastness of the estate, because I needed to be away from all the drama. I thought about the mystery woman who had been in my house, I wondered who the hell Eric was, and why Fury had this picture of a beautiful girl? Furthermore, why was he eyeballing it as if he lost a friend? *Oh, the mysterious Fury.* If there was another woman involved, I don't think my heart could take it. I knew deep down it wasn't Fury's fault that I was suddenly jealous, but something about seeing the person who you were planning to spend the rest of your life with have another woman's clothes at the feet of the bed you shared, made one's mind wonder. If Fury was hiding something, he had to come clean. I couldn't take anymore secrets or drama. I needed normalcy. I needed stability. I needed truth.

I got the text messages he sent but didn't have a clue how to respond. How was I supposed to just say, *oh by the way, that whole I don't care who you were before I met you thing, yeah well it matters now.* I understood how it sounded , and I knew he wasn't ready to tell me anything. I wish I didn't want to know, but all the shit with Creed, the disappearance and the surprise woman, spurred my curiosity. I had to know. I have the right to know so I can protect my heart from any further heartbreak. I would be totally broken if I found out something that was detrimental later on in the relationship after I had fallen in love.

Fury: I'm not giving up. Reply.

I chuckled because I know in his mind, he thought that was sweet. He wanted me to know he wasn't giving up, and I admired him for that. It gave me a sense of false hope. I knew for sure that he wanted to see where this went, but what if he couldn't tell me what I needed to know? Then what happened?

Me: I'm hiding in the woods. I don't want to talk to anyone. I am wrapping my head around some things.

Fury: Too bad. I'm coming to find you. The place is fenced in, it won't be difficult. You can either come out here, or I'm coming in after you.

So much for being alone. I headed back because I

knew that he would do just that, and I might as well face him now. When I entered the cleared part of the yard, I saw him standing there, all six-foot-ridiculous of him, his back to me. He was wearing his cut and white tee shirt, his arm muscles bulged in the sleeves, and his reddish-brown hair hung down. It was a sight to see.

"What was so important that you had to see me this instant?" I startled him.

He turned around and stopped dead in his tracks.

"What?", I ask.

"You look…"

"I look what? Pretty, upset, confused, hurt, angry, or is it just exhausted?"

"All of it, but mostly beautiful."

"No. Uh-uh. No flattery here buddy. I have been more than nice and patient with you, and now I have some things to say. You wanted me, you got me. You might want to sit for this." I walked past him and made my way to the gazebo.

He followed me at vampire like speed, and when we got to the gazebo, he kissed me like he was trying to tell me how sorry he was. I pulled away and tried to catch my breath. My mind was total mush.

"Ahem." I cleared my throat and straightened my hair. "It's good to see you, too. Now listen."

"Can I…"

"No. It's my turn. First, I don't care who you are. You

don't get to decide if I stick things out with you. I knew good and well what the complications were. I knew you could go to jail. That you weren't exactly on the up and up with this trip. Relationships take work. They are two-sided. The way you left me was lopsided. You took away my voice, and that isn't fair."

"I didn't want you in the crosshairs if something went south. I was protecting you."

"What happens when you make a shine run? Huh? Are we going to break up every time you have to do that? This is not going to work. If you're in, you're all in, or you're all out." I stopped and took a deep breath because I was scared of how this was going to end. "Which brings me to my next topic. I thought I could live without knowing things about your past. I overlooked things and thought your past was just that. Then Creed happened, and I found out much more than I ever knew about him. He was my best friend, Fury, the one I wanted to marry. I didn't know him at all. Then he brought some other girl into the home that we shared shortly after he pledged his love for me."

"Rumor..."

"When we last spoke, you dropped something." I reached in my pocket and handed him Eric's picture. His face became long and ghostly white. His eyes widened, and he stared at it.

"Fury, I have to know. There are so many secrets already that I am not comfortable moving forward with you, until some things are out. It's not fair. It's no fault of yours. I know I said it didn't matter, but my sucky life happened and now I need answers. I'm so sorry. I know you weren't ready, and I will probably lose you over this, however, I have to know. With everything that happened to me in the last two years, and specifically in the last two weeks. Who is the girl in this picture? Who is Eric?"

I took a deep breath and felt like a weight had been lifted. Then I saw his face. He was tormented, torn, battling something I couldn't help him with.

"Rumor, it isn't that easy. I want to tell you. I *can't* tell you."

"Okay. Why can't you tell me?"

"I can't say that either." He scrubbed his hands up and down his face and started to breathe heavy.

"I can't be kept in the dark anymore. I deserve to know the whole story, to know all of you. You get all of me. Do you not trust me enough? What else do I have to do to prove myself? Tell me, damn it." I said as I felt the unwelcome tears start to form.

"It's not you. This is why I didn't want to get involved. I'm a secret. My whole life is a goddamned secret that I can't tell. I have too much at stake and some important people depending on me. There, are you happy?"

I stared at him as the tears flowed freely down my face, leaving stained cheeks in their wakes. Why couldn't he trust me? What had I done that I didn't deserve his trust?

"Why did I have to fall in love with you?" I said in a quiet voice, as I shook my head and walked away. I wanted him to stop me, to tell me not to go. I wanted him to pour his heart out to me. I kept wanting. He let me walk. If I couldn't have all of him, I didn't want any of him. I knew that was a lie. I wanted what I could get, but I knew I deserved the whole package. I longed for a relationship with no secrets. I wasn't settling this time. I was honest with him, and it wasn't too much to ask for the same in return.

I quickly made it to my room and shut the door. The floodgates opened before I could prepare for them. Pained sobs escaped my lungs, and I fell to the floor clutching my chest. Why did it hurt so bad? We weren't even together. Perhaps I was finally grieving the secrets of my past. Why did Crosby kill himself? Why did Creed not tell me he wanted to be a U.S. Marshall? Why did he leave me with no explanation? Why couldn't Fury trust me with his secret? What was so big and bad that he wouldn't share it? It didn't matter. He couldn't share his story and I wouldn't settle anymore.

I managed to get off the floor after a good cry, sat in the window sill and stared down at him. He didn't move for a long time. He stared at the photo. The photo held secrets to his past, perhaps the one that held the answers to all of my questions. I swore I could hear him talking, but there wasn't anyone around. I couldn't bear to look at the sad sight below me. I wanted to help him, but he had to let me. It was all up to him from this point. I was going to see if I was worth the risk, which posed another question, what was the risk? I got in my pajamas and crawled into bed where I continued to weep. The sobs had subsided, but there was a steady stream of silent tears. I cried until it all went black.

Chapter 22

FURY

IT HAPPENED. IT FINALLY HAPPENED, the day I knew would come from the minute I first saw her. I knew it wasn't fair to her, but she said it didn't matter. I knew better. It always matters.

This was the confirmation that I was serving a life sentence for being stupid. I wasn't worthy of Rumor. I wasn't worthy of anyone. I gave that up when I got involved with the Ray brothers. If only I knew then what I know now. I'd have left that shit alone.

I lit a cigarette to try and soothe my nerves, while I stared at Daisy.

"I'm so sorry. I have caused so many lives to be affected from my fuck up. I didn't mean to hurt you. I was making some quick money selling some shit that I had no business messing with. Then the Ray brothers intervened and screwed me over. God, Daisy, I'm so sorry." I said out loud. No one was around, and I didn't care at this point. I needed a drink, something stronger than beer.

I went to the kitchen and found some Crown Royal. I didn't even bother with a chaser. I turned it up and watched the bubbles rise from the fast pace I guzzled it. I welcomed the burn, it was distracting, and I temporarily forgot about the shit storm that was my life. I took another large swig of the whiskey to help drown the memories. It wasn't helping. The memories of everyone I had loved and lost were swirling in my head. All the reminders of the mistakes I made were running rampant, and the hurt of everything was clawing its way into my throat and had a death grip. I felt like I was suffocating. No matter how hard I tried to forget, no matter how far away I was from the origin of these problems, no matter how deep I got into the bottle, the memories were stronger than the whiskey.

With my head a perfect, fuzzy place of chaos, I made my way, bottle in hand, back to the gazebo. I needed to be where I could smoke myself stupid and drink til' I could purge everything that had haunted me for the last few years. I put a cigarette to my lips and clicked the lighter until the yellow flame shot up. I stuck the cigarette into the flame and inhaled the heat and smoke from it. It burned but felt so good. I exhaled the warmth and took another swallow of the alcohol.

I leaned my head back and shut my eyes. Everything was starting to spin.

"You still don't listen I see," I heard a familiar voice.

"What the"

"Yeah, numb nuts, it's me. Seems as if you are going to fuck up royally if I don't come to you once more. I told your stupid ass not to let her go. How much clearer do I have to be?"

"Goood to know the booze is-uh workin'." I stuttered.

"It ain't the booze, Fury. It's your president, your friend, your mother fucking brain, apparently. There is no amount of booze that will make this go away. You see, you have nowhere else to go. You are stuck here, and so is she. Fix it. She deserves to know you, and you deserve to have her. She would give you everything you thought you couldn't have if you would just tell her. What have you got to lose, huh? A past? Don't even say you are protecting Daisy and Eric. Wake up. I was the president of an outlaw MC for God's sakes. You really think those Ray brothers are still a problem? After you proved your loyalty, I handled that. You're welcome. You have nothing to lose except Rumor. I hope she has mercy on your dumb, drunk ass. You won't get another chance with her if you don't make it right, now. I'm telling you to trust your gut, or if you are too chickenshit to do that, at least trust me. I never lied to you or steered you wrong."

"You took care of them…like forever? Daisy is going to be okay no matter what?"

"Yes. So, you can tell her everything and it won't matter.

She won't tell anyone and even if she did, there is a paper trail that says you are Legend. Eric is dead, remember? So even if she did, which she won't, she would look like the crazy one. Face it, Eric is gone, forever. It's time you buried him just like the whole damn town did when you left."

I stared at the bottle in my hand and hung my head.

"That's going to hurt in the morning. I'd watch how you let your head hang and bobble tonight. Man up. You know what you need to do. Trust me."

The voice was gone. I looked around, turned my head, and the world took a second to catch up. Everything was tilted and moving, only I was sitting still. I tried to get up and walk, but I had no legs. Well, I did, but they were worthless. I manually lifted my foot with my hand and watched it fall to the wooden floor of the gazebo. I felt nothing. After Chief left, I achieved what I set out to do. I drowned the memories. It took a fifth of Crown, but those bastards were under water now. I sat outside with the empty bottle and watched the sun come up over the tree line.

It seemed like just a few seconds then I heard, "Is he dead?" followed by a poke to the arm with a thick finger.

"Fury? Dude wake up. Did you party all alone?"

"Why are you yelling, damn it." I looked around and tried to blink the fuzzy away.

"I'm not yelling, but I oughta." Whiskey said.

"Why you gotta be a dick?" I asked as I stood or tried to stand. I fell right back down.

"I went to see what was wrong with Rumor. She woke me crying this morning. I came to find you. By the looks of things, you are the cause of her tears, and she is the cause of your all-night bender. By the way, from the smell of things, you're going to need a Gatorade. Trust me."

"Why do I keep hearing that?"

"What are you talking about?"

I found a moment of clarity in my head full of fog. If I told him I had talked to Chief, he would have me committed.

"Nothing."

"Come on. Let's get you inside. You need to sleep this off, but first you need a couple of ibuprofen and a Gatorade. I'm not sure how long you were passed out, but it wasn't long enough. You're still fucked up. Up ya go." He helped me to my feet.

I stood and pushed him away. I walked to the door and pulled it open. Coffee and breakfast filled my nose, and I had an overwhelming urge to puke. I stumbled my way up the stairs and fumbled to the bathroom where I purged the things that needed to be purged last night. Mission accomplished, it just took longer than expected.

Once I was done calling the dinosaurs, I looked in the mirror. Staring back was a decent looking dude, that was slightly wobbly, but it was so clear. I knew what I had to do. I would talk to Rumor. If nothing else came from that epic meltdown, I did remember Chief telling me that

I needed to not let her go. It was going to have to wait til' I got some sleep, because a heavy wave of exhaustion blanketed me, and I had to find my bed. I felt like I was carrying the world on my shoulders.

Chapter 23

RUMOR

I HOPED I WOULD FEEL DIFFERENT this morning, but no such luck. I woke with pain in my chest and sad thoughts on replay in my mind. I missed what could have been. We had to pretend like everything was as normal. I would find an apartment or another place to rent so I didn't have to stay here with Fury. My heart couldn't handle being near him.

I went downstairs for coffee. I stopped in the bathroom, and as soon as I opened the door, I instantly shut it. My nose was consumed with the stench of alcohol and vomit. I think the smell had burned in my nostrils. Who the hell was so drunk they threw up? I thought for a second and then it hit me. Fury. Was he upset, too? Did he want to tell me about his past? It didn't matter. He didn't and that spoke volumes.

I decided to find another bathroom to use. There were several to choose from. I went to the powder room downstairs off the living room, then made my way to the pot of morning gold.

No one was here, but there were plates and coffee cups in the sink. I looked outside and tried to see who or if anyone was out there. I saw Whiskey and Briar.

As I walked their way with my coffee in hand, they stopped talking.

"Morning."

"Same to you."

"Hey, since Creed is getting the house, I'm going to look for a place to rent. Would y'all know of anywhere?"

"Why wouldn't you stay here until you are on your feet?" Briar asked.

"Things would be a bit awkward, I imagine. Fury made it crystal clear last night that he didn't want anything between us."

"He did what? You realize he is shitty drunk and probably didn't mean anything he said or did last night, right?" Briar continued.

"He was stone cold sober when he and I talked. He made it clear that he isn't willing to give me what I need in order to proceed with a relationship. It's best if I just move. I wouldn't ask him to. Hell, he isn't even from here, so he needs to get adjusted and settled first."

"You're seriously trying to put him first when he has

made it clear, in your opinion, that he isn't willing to do whatever that you asked of him? Is that right?" Whiskey asked.

"It's the nice thing to do. I'd do it for anyone."

"Look. I see the look on your face. You don't want this to be over. You're tired, and those red rimmed eyes say it all. You wouldn't have woken me up crying if you were done. I don't know what happened between you two, but I know that it ain't over."

"I didn't mean to wake you. I'm sorry."

"No one ever does. It's fine. Just don't be hasty. Remember that whatever you need might come a little slower for Fury. He doesn't do emotions well."

"Clearly." I said and rolled my eyes.

"If you want to look for somewhere to rent, I will keep an eye out." Briar said.

"I think that would be best. Thanks guys."

I walked on, coffee in hand, and allowed my thoughts to run wild. Did I want to give him more time? If he didn't trust me enough last night, how would he trust me enough when he finally decided to open up? What would change? Why wasn't it enough then? Who was he? What was he hiding that was so bad that no one could know? All the questions flooded, and I still had no answers. I couldn't do it again. I had to know about his past. I knew he was honest about everything, except that. If I let him slide and not tell me, then how do I know he wouldn't up and leave me, too?

I began thinking about Crosby again. Had he been open and honest with me, I would have known he needed help. I would have known he was clearly depressed, and his depression was the reason for the drinking. I would have known why he thought he wasn't good enough for me, and why he thought my life was better without him.

Had Creed been honest with me, I wouldn't have wondered what happened to him for two years. I put my life on hold for him. He could have told me he wanted to be a marshal, and I wouldn't have stopped him from fulfilling his dream. I would have encouraged it, and let's face it, if he were really that upset about me, he wouldn't have had another woman in the house so soon. He would still be trying to win me back.

I couldn't risk it. Fury had to tell me. My life couldn't handle being that shaken up again. I couldn't handle being that messed up again. Mentally, that was rough.

As I sipped the warm blonde liquid, I stopped and leaned up against a tree. I leaned my head back and shut my eyes. My life really was cursed, and I was convinced that I had done something to piss off the gods that aligned the planets and stars.

Work would distract me. I decided to clean up and get ready for my shift. While showering, I heard the door open.

"Umm, showering here. It'll be a sec."

"You can't run if you are soaking wet and locked in the

shower. I choose now to talk to you. It seems as if drinking myself stupid turned out to be an awakening of sorts. Look, I want to tell you everything, but I can't no..."

"Yeah, you've made that clear. Weren't you sleeping? Could you go back to it? It'd be so much easier if you would just leave me alone. We could both move on." I said in a hateful tone.

"I wasn't done. I would rather be sleeping. I feel hammered as hell and this headache is a reminder of what I need to get off my chest. So, listen. As I was saying, I can't tell you *here*. It has to be just you and me. No one else can know. I am trusting you with literally everything I have worked for. Call in. Let's go on a ride. We can go back to the creek if Charlie will let us take the key." He pleaded.

"Fury, I can't just skip work. They depend on me, and I need to think about this. Why is it okay for you to talk to me today, but yesterday you couldn't? This isn't making sense. It's really hard to believe you right now. I want to, but I just don't."

"Let's just say I drank until I figured out that whiskey doesn't fix anything. I drank until an old friend reminded me of what was important. It took getting so fucked up that I could hardly move to realize that I had pushed away the best thing to ever happen to me. Dare I say, even better than what I'm protecting. Rumor, I need you. Just work with me."

I wanted to. Honestly, I did, but I needed time to

think, time to digest all of this. As the hot water continued to beat down on me, I told him, "I'm going to work. You can pick me up at two o'clock. Be there or we don't have a chance. This has to be it for me." I stepped out of the shower and grabbed a towel. His eyes skimmed over my body. He looked at me in a way that I have never been looked at before. He wanted me. Not for my body. He genuinely wanted *me*. I walked over to him with the towel draped around my chest, put a hand on his face and looked up into those hazel eyes.

"Don't hurt me, Fury. I don't think I can take it again. Third time is a charm, yeah?" I said sincerely as I walked to get dressed. Before I got all the way out the door, I turned to him, "Brush your teeth, shower, and for the love of all things good and holy, take a nap. You look like hell." I winked at him, found my work clothes, and when I looked back at him, he was staring at me with a stupid half grin on his face.

"What are you looking at?"

"You."

"Why?"

"Here I am trying to be sweet to keep you from doing what I originally said to do and instead convince you to stay, and you gotta go and make light of the situation."

"Fury, I'd like to talk. Honestly, but the deal is, you smell like a distillery and vomit. You look like you haven't slept in days. I don't want to be around you hung over like this. Find yourself some Gatorade, a couple of ibuprofen, and go to sleep. I'll give you the chance you asked for."

"I have already taken some and drank a Gatorade, but this headache is legit keeping me awake. I tried to sleep. Epic fail."

"Next time just come to me. That'll teach you," I walked off. Before I got out of the door I turned and said, "I mean it, do those things. It will make you feel better. See you around two." I went down the stairs, out the door, and headed to wait tables. This had been a very interesting morning.

Work dragged by. The hours were slow, and the customers were few. Thoughts of my afternoon plans kept me in a trance. I heard the door ding and saw a man walk in, walk to a table and sit down. As I approached the table, I realized that the last customer of the day was none other than Creed.

"Creed. What are you doing?" I rolled my eyes at his presence.

"Eating. How about you?"

"Oh, ya know, herding elephants." I stared at him like he was a moron. "What the hell does it look like I'm doing?"

He stared at me for too long, then leaned in and got too close. "You know we aren't over right? You can't seriously just throw away what we had. I told you I had to leave. I didn't have a choice. Why can't we make this work?"

"Creed." I sighed and sat opposite him. "After I saw the mystery woman's clothes on our floor when I came to get some things, I was done. If you seriously wanted me, you wouldn't have had someone in our bed so quickly. The truth is, things worked out just as they were supposed to. It is what it is. I'm not going to force it, and, again, you didn't have to up and leave me. You could've talked to me, or at the very least broke things off with me so I would have some kind of inkling of what happened, and I could have moved on with my life. Oh, but wait. You were selfish and wanted me to wait on you to return."

He didn't say anything. I continued, "You took away something from me that no one can give back. You took my time. I can't get back all the hours I sat and cried or worried about you. I can't get back all the times I stayed at home while friends went out, hoping you would call. I can't get back the piece of me that you broke forever. I used to be a trusting person, but I'm a skeptic now. Because of you, I feel like people are always hiding something from me, just waiting on the other shoe to drop. That is no way to live. This is why I'm not coming back. I won't have this discussion again. Enjoy your meal. I will have someone else come wait on you."

I got up and went to the back and I found the owner. I needed a breather.

"Hey, would you do me a favor? My ex is out there, and I am not comfortable waiting on him. Would you mind?"

"Sure, honey. It's two anyhow. I'll see you later. Go enjoy your day! If the hunk of a man on the motorcycle at your car is any indication of how it's going to go, I envy you!"

Fury. There he was. Commanding the space while not even trying. He looked tremendously better than when I left this morning. Sleep and a shower did wonders. Now I had to find out if I was about to lose two men in one day.

Chapter 24

FURY

THERE SHE WAS. RIGHT at 2 o'clock, she walked out of the restaurant to me as she promised. I had a hard time believing my eyes, as I didn't deserve the chance, I was given. I had to pull out all of the stops this go around. She made it clear to me that she wasn't accepting anything less than what she deserved.

"Hey."

"Hey back."

I looked back and saw whom I assumed was Creed sitting in the restaurant.

"Is there something you want to tell me?" I asked, my tone was a little harsh.

"No, that isn't how this is going to work. You're the one that has things to tell me, remember?"

"What's he doing here?"

"Trying to get me back."

I looked at her and appreciated her honesty.

"I'm here with you, not inside with him, so chill out. Let's go to the creek or wherever you want to go."

"Hop on." I pointed to my bike.

"Let me get my suit." She grabbed her bathing suit out of the front seat and stuck it in the saddlebag.

I looked at the sad guy in the window and waved as I took off with the one thing that I was going to avoid giving back to him. He shouldn't have left her.

With the wind in my face and her arms around me, I had a sense of peace and a calmness that I didn't realize I needed. I hadn't realized I was so tense. My bike was my sanctuary. Nothing much got to me here. Except Rumor. I welcomed her touch and hoped she could see the me she already knows, which is the only one that matters. The person I was about to tell her about died, and she needed to know that.

We pulled up to the creek where we all had the big idea for the restaurant operation. Charlie was kind enough to lend me the key. I held out my hand and offered to help her down. She touched my hand and I felt electric currents shoot through my chest. I needed her to be okay with my story. Our eyes closed in on each other and for a moment, we stared at one another. I hesitated, made an effort to kiss her, but backed off. I didn't want to push myself on her.

"You should've kissed me." She said, which caught me by surprise.

So, I did. I held her head in my hands and kissed her like I hadn't seen her in a month.

"Why did that feel like a goodbye kiss?" She asked, as she searched my eyes for any answers.

"It might be. You might not be able to handle what I'm about to tell you. I'm trusting you here, Rumor. Turns out, the only other person that knows this secret is dead. I didn't even know he knew. It has to stay between us. Charlie, Raige, Hazel, none of them can know. So much depends on this. I'm only telling you because I can't be without you. I have to fight for you, step out of my comfort zone, and show you that I am serious. After all you have been through, you deserve the truth. Brace yourself. You're going to need to, trust me." We went over to the dock and she sat Indian style in front of me. We were both obviously nervous.

"Let's get this started, I can't take the suspense anymore. Did you kill someone? Are you wanted? My mind is all over the place and I need answers." She shook her head. "I need the truth. Why is it so hard to have that?"

"Rumor, my story isn't pretty. It's not easy to talk about. I left my entire life behind to better the life of someone else."

"Well that doesn't sound so bad."

"Just promise me that when I'm done, you'll remember

that I'm not that person anymore, and the guy you know, is the only person I am now."

"I can't. I don't know what I am promising. I promise to keep an open mind and not to judge you."

I took in a deep breath and shut my eyes. I decided I needed a smoke. I couldn't do this without one. As I inhaled the tobacco, I felt my nerves start to loosen. When I opened my eyes, I saw Rumor and her clear, blue eyes begging for information. Begging to know me. I started at the beginning and spilled my deepest secret, the one that I was sworn to never repeat. The one I would only repeat to her, because I couldn't lose her, and this is what it was going to take to keep her.

"The police banged on the front door to my house. That's what I saw as I stood in the distance, hidden in the bushes across the road. I watched them beat on the door to the house where my girl and my unborn baby were sleeping. She wiped the sleep from her eyes as she answered the door. The reflection of the police car lights cast red then blue hues on her beautiful face. I could see her shaking her head and I read her lips as she said, "No, no, no you're wrong. There is a mistake, Eric is alive." As the officer spoke to her, I watched her crumple into a weeping pile of tears, wrecked with emotion and sorrow as they told her that I was dead. I watched the fire burn out of her eyes. I watched her cry as the flames that burned inside of me died, too. When the officer handed her my hat, she screamed my name, and cradled the hat as she rocked back and forth. I would have given anything to run up and hold her. To tell her that everything was going to be okay, to let her know this was a misunderstanding and I wasn't leaving her. It wasn't an option, not if I wanted them to have a fighting chance.

I did what I had to do. I saved Daisy and our son. This life wasn't for them. She didn't know what I was involved in. She trusted that I would make all of the right choices and I didn't. I got into bed with the wrong people, and they turned on me. They told a bunch of lies and kept the money and dope for themselves, and to my suppliers, it looked like I stabbed them in the back and tried to rip them off. We'd had run-in's before and I was already on thin ice with them. The Ray brothers were out for blood, and when they sent word, that was something they never went back on. I had no choice but to turn to the law. In return, I had to leave and be put under witness protection. I needed them safe. I promised her I would do what it took, and I delivered. I had to leave them and never look back…or not get caught anyhow. I loved her so much that I let her go that night. I knew she would be okay without me. She was strong, probably the most emotionally strong person I know. Truthfully, she is better off. However, it doesn't take the soul-crushing hurt and sternum-splitting ache away. I honestly felt my heart breaking as I watched her crumble apart. Since I knew I was the cause of her anguish and I wasn't able to do anything to comfort her, I tried to give her the best gift I could that night, a new life and a clean slate. The rest of the night was a blur. I sat hunkered down in those bushes until the front door shut and the rotating red and blue lights ceased to spin. My world as I knew it was over. I needed to move on and not come back because if I did, they would kill Daisy and the baby. That wasn't an option. I was off to find my way in a town I didn't know. I had to make a new life for myself in Panama City Beach, Florida. That's where the witness protection program sent me, all set with a new identity as Legend Morrow."

I tried to gauge her reaction for a minute. She was still, wide-eyed, and her mouth was wide open.

"Rumor, say something."

She moved her eyes to mine and closed her mouth.

"Not what you thought, huh? Do you see why I have been so closed off now? Why I couldn't open up to you? It isn't like I didn't want to, because trust me, I did. My life would have been so much easier. I have a son and an ex-fiancé to protect."

"Are you clean now?"

"Yes. I haven't touched it since."

"You are Eric from the picture." She paused. "*You are Eric!*"

"Shhh. Yes. I am Eric Martin. I died in a horrific fiery crash and they identified my remains through dental records. I was cremated. I got here and was given a new name, Legend Morrow. The club dubbed me Fury. I know it's a lot to take in but understand that I couldn't tell anyone. Chief had a friend that was a lawman in PCB and he called in a favor. Chief agreed to watch over me. After Chief and I talked during our first meeting, the ball started rolling and I eventually came to be a Chosen One."

"Have you seen them? Do you still want to? Are you over her?"

"Slow down. I have seen them a handful of times, but I haven't been back since…us. I will always love her. She is the mother of my son. I don't want her, I know I can never have her. I have moved on, as has she, but it took years. Of course, I want to see them. What father doesn't want to see his son? I have come to terms with the fact that I am simply a sperm donor to that kid. End of the story is, I did what I had to do to protect them. If I didn't leave, the Ray brothers would have come after Daisy and in the end she and Eric would have both been dead."

"Your son's name is Eric?"

"One of the times I went to see them, I saw a stork sign in the yard. That's the only reason I know his name."

"The girl in the picture, that was her?"

"Yes. That's Daisy."

"She's beautiful."

I know she didn't really want to talk about how pretty my ex was.

"What's going on in that gorgeous head of yours?"

"What's not going on is the better question. Mainly I am wondering, why now? You couldn't tell me this until now? What changed?"

"I wanted to keep you. It's that simple. However, I felt safe telling you. I was given some unexpected intel of sorts and know now that the Ray brothers won't be an issue, but most importantly, I trust you."

"And this is why you shouldn't even entertain the idea of being with him. I'm the man for you." A man's voice boomed.

Rumor audibly gasped and shrieked, "Creed? How did you find us?"

"Darlin' I'm a marshal. I could have figured it out, but I followed you. I left shortly after you. Now do you see why I'm the one you should be with. This guy isn't even real. He has been playing you for the short time that you have known him. I'm here, in real life, a real person, with a legit identity. Did you hear why he was here instead of at home with his girl and son?"

"Yeah. I did, and we were sorting through everything when you appeared. You're getting really good at showing up when you aren't wanted. Too bad you had to lose me for good to start coming around again." She stood up and walked to him. "You had your chance. You blew it. That's not on him, and damn sure not on me. This is on you, big boy. Own it. Accept it and go on. If you would give me half a second to think for myself, I will come to my own conclusions about Fury and the mess he just shared with me. No, it isn't ideal, but it is what it is. At least he told me his secret, unlike you, and he has a whole hell of a lot more to lose than you ever did. I don't know what the future holds for Fury and me, but I can tell you that our future is none of your concern nor are you included. Leave me alone. I wish you would go back to wherever the hell you came from."

He took us both by surprise and lunged at her and had her in a headlock with a pistol aimed at her head.

"I guess we are going to do this the hard way. I tried to give you the chance to return to me, but you wouldn't. You're better than this fraud. We have things to work out." He said through gritted teeth.

"*Fury!*"

Creed practically dragged Rumor away. I started following him when I saw his back was turned and that he wasn't going to turn the gun on either of us.

The sound of a truck was rumbling down the lane and gravel was thrown as he gassed it as he tried to get away.

I ran to my bike, hopped on, with all intentions to chase him down and save my girl. Even over the rumble of my pipes I heard my tires grabbing hold of the dirt on the road and the gravel slipping under them. Then I heard the sound that vehicles make in the movies when the getaway truck starts to fishtail and lose control. The worst thought ran through my mind. I knew he was going to crash head first into a tree and hurt Rumor. The rage was pumping through my veins and I was hot and ready to kill. I would stop at nothing to save her.

Eeerrrrck! Clash! The sound of metal bending flooded my ears and I drove faster to get to her.

When I got to the truck, it was in the ditch on the side of the road and was only damaged minimally. The bumper was bent, and the headlight was broken, but it was still drivable.

"*Ouch!*" A manly voice screeched.

I got to the truck and saw my girl defending herself. She elbowed him in the nose and banged the back of his head off the back glass. I stepped in.

"Rumor, get out. Go to the bike."

She did as I told her. I got the bleeding idiot by the throat and squeezed until he was a pretty shade of purple.

"Did they not teach you to drive better in your special training? I hope you said all you needed to say to her because you are done speaking…forever." I squeezed his neck until he was gasping for air. I heard a pop and knew that I had silenced him forever. I had crushed, or severely damaged, his larynx.

I heard footsteps but dropped the gasping fool on the ground.

"Rumor, I need to know that you are okay with me. All of me. This is how it is. People that can hurt me or the people I have loved in the past get hurt. It's violent at times and there is usually no remorse. If you can't handle that, now is the time for you to go." I remind her again, with the hope that she won't listen.

"I'll help you get him back to the club. I'll drive the truck. Meet me back at Acres."

"Does this mean you and me…we're still giving this a go?"

"No. This means I have a whole hell of a lot to digest, and I am pissed off and fucking done with this asshole. I'll help you get him back, so y'all can talk to him. As for us, we aren't over, but we aren't together."

"That's better than I expected. I'll take it."

"Well, that's good seeing as I didn't give you any other option." She smarted off. Only, she wasn't kidding. I'm not sure if she was just stressed because of the last few minutes or what but she wasn't cutting either of us any slack.

I loaded him up in the truck and Rumor went to the driver's side. She opened the door and out fell pictures. Pictures of her. So many pictures that there was no way he could have taken them because he was gone during the time stamps on the pictures. She flipped through them. There she was sitting on the porch of the house they lived in, there was one of her and Raige bundled up around a fire at a party last fall, there was another one of Charlie and her on the practice field, and it looked like Charlie was running for a bunt and throwing the out to Rumor on first base. The next one was the one that hit her the hardest. I knew because of the tear that slowly fell down her cheek. It was just a few weeks ago. It was when the Regulators won the World Series. How? Who did he have watching her and taking photos? Did he really keep an eye on her? He was keeping tabs on her and making sure he knew what she was up to and where she was. Question is, how? Who did he know that would have done that but not tell her?

"He must have hired a private investigator. None of our mutual friends would have kept this a secret from me." She looked at me.

For a moment, I thought I lost her. The look of excitement on her face when she realized he had been watching her, cut me like a knife. The look quickly shifted to one of sheer anger and hurt, so did my thoughts.

"So, he stalked me, kept an eye on me, and knew pretty much where I was at all times, but he couldn't even let me know he was okay? Nah. Bad idea, bro." She said as she cut her eyes to him and took a breath before she continued, "He should've hid these. Now I just feel dirty, like a peeping Tom was watching me for years." She confessed.

"Let's not worry about this now. We have limited time till sleeping beauty wakes and he will likely have a headache and be really pissed. We need to get him back to Acres PDQ."

"PDQ?"

"Pretty damn quick. Let's roll." I bent down and kissed her, and I let our lips stay connected as we both took in a deep breath. "Let's go." I turned and walked back to my bike.

I straddled the seat and before I started it. I called Whiskey and gave him a half- truth story. I told him that Rumor's ex followed us and threatened her and attempted to kidnap her. He said he would have Shooter and the rest of the guys ready in thirty minutes when we got back home.

I PULLED UP to the gate at Acres and pressed the code Charlie had given me and the gate opened with ease. I pulled through and parked my bike so I could help the boys get Creed out of the truck.

"Church. Now. Riddick, help us get him to the shed. Tie him up. Make it good. He can't get away." I snapped my fingers and vigorously walked around to the side of the truck.

In a few minutes, we were all in the shed and had Creed tied up, still out cold.

"Boys, this joker is pig food, too. You don't just waltz up and threaten and kidnap my girl and expect to live through it. He even held a gun to her head. Mag, you and Sax yanked teeth last night, right?"

"Yeah."

"Good. Do it again. Riddick, you help."

I patted my cut to ensure that my pistol was in there, I pulled it out and double checked that the silencer was on it. I aimed straight for his heart. Slowly I pulled the trigger and a small *pew pew* escaped the end of the barrel. With that I knew that Daisy and Eric were safe. He couldn't hurt them or put them in danger now, and Rumor didn't have to worry about this jerk coming around anymore either. This was a win-win for everyone.

"Riddick, you and Magnum find Saxton and have him help. Go feed the livestock and stop somewhere along the way home and bury the teeth in a deep hole and cover it with rocks and dirt. Make it look natural. See you in a bit."

I walked out of the building and the summer air hit me in the face. I felt oddly at ease. I just killed a marshal and was okay with it. I was certainly going to hell, but I was fine with it. I justified it. I did what I had to do, period.

I went straight to the fridge for beer. Before I had the chance to open the door, a certain blonde had her hand outstretched with a beer for me. I reached and got it from her.

"We need to talk."

"Yeah, I guess we have shit to sort out."

"Come with me. I'll drive you. I packed an ice chest." She led the way.

I followed because what else do you do when the girl of your dreams, the one that holds all the secrets of your past in her hands, tells you to come for a ride and that she has beer? You go and don't ask questions.

We got into her car and she headed northbound. I had no idea where she was taking me, and I didn't care. I was with her, she was giving me a chance, and I would go anywhere she wanted.

Chapter 25

RUMOR

A<small>LL OF A SUDDEN</small>, I <small>WAS</small> consumed with nerves and the full range of emotions. I glanced at him and he was staring at me. To make things even more awkward, I knew he wanted to smoke, but I ignored that thought. I didn't want him smoking in my car.

"So, where are we going?"

"Some where there aren't any distractions."

"More specific?"

"I'm taking you to my favorite place in the world, other than the ball field. It's just out of town and it's a bluff that overlooks the interstate. The cars and trucks go by and life just goes on. You get to see everything, and no one ever notices you. It's like you're on top of the world."

"Oh."

"Look, it's not the beach, or the creek, but so far bodies of water haven't exactly been good luck for us. Bad shit happens around water."

He didn't say anything. He nodded his head because he knew I was right. We pulled up to the spot and got out. I led the way with the flashlight while Fury grabbed the ice chest and followed behind me.

We made it to the open spot where you can see the cars zooming by underneath. I sat and let my legs dangle off the edge of the bluff. Fury plopped down beside me and cracked open a beer.

"So…" Fury started.

"So." I answered.

We stared at the traffic below.

"So, you are ready for an honest relationship? Fury, I can't have anything less. Not with how my life has been the last few years. I simply can't live with the what if's and the secrets. My mind will go a hundred different directions. It's time for me to have normalcy and sanity like everyone else."

"I just told you something that I was sworn to keep to myself for life. Something that could ultimately kill my son and his mother. Short of telling you the last time I took a shit, you know everything about me."

"You…you're okay? I promise that I won't say anything to anyone. I know what you have riding on this. You can trust me. Always. Even if things don't work out, I will never betray you."

"So, we're going to see this through?" He perked up and turned to face me.

"I think that you get me. You understand me like no one else. You didn't lie to me. Well, you didn't lie to me on purpose, and you risked the lives of your son and his mom to make me happy, and to hopefully keep me. If you can do that, I can give you a chance. Just know, there are no secrets from here on. That's a deal breaker."

"I can handle that. I promise I have nothing else to hide."

"Well, shit, I hope not!" I exclaimed. "Fury?"

"Yeah?"

"Is Creed going to be an issue for us?"

"Not anymore. We need to get his truck back to the house or sink it in the river or something. We can't have his truck just floating around."

"About that…" I trailed off leaving something for his imagination.

"No secrets remember."

"It's actually my truck. The title is in my name. He put it in my name to help me establish my credit. It looks as if Creed pulled his vanishing act again, only this time he left the truck." I smirked, hoping he read in between the lines.

"Are you serious? We don't have to dispose of a truck? You have two vehicles?" He asked, shock evident in his voice.

"As a heart attack. And yes. When he took off with the truck, I got my car. Not having a ride is for the birds. Before you even ask, I did report it stolen. Nothing ever came of it. It all makes sense now. Being a marshal would surely keep him from any kind of legal trouble."

I clearly lifted a huge load off him and the club. He tipped his beer and drank it down.

"So, are sure you are okay with this? Me, the club, our businesses, our lifestyle? We're not your average people."

Could I be involved with a criminal? Could I give my heart to someone who blatantly said he was violent? What kind of life would this be for me? All of a sudden, all the questions started to overwhelm me, and I could feel the doubt creeping up and I tried to keep it from showing on my face.

"Here come the doubts, right?" He asked on cue.

"Yes. No. I don't know. I want the things we talked about with Charlie and Jazz. You know, the restaurant and the business. I want the relationship with you. I worry about the bad things like, oh you know, jail and the thought that you aren't afraid to do what is necessary for me." I stopped to gauge his reaction.

"Rumor, I told you it wasn't pretty, and you should've walked. I will be ruthless where you are concerned. If someone threatens you, they die. If someone pisses you off, they bleed. If someone crosses you, they deal with me. I've fought many demons, buried many more, and bared to you the one thing I was sworn to never reveal to anyone. I wanted to prove that you are what I want, what I need. I have come alive since you entered my life. You will never take place of Daisy, and I don't want you to. I want something new with you. Something I have never been able to do. I want a real relationship. One that doesn't have secrets. This is me, the person I had to become and the person that has finally found his place and his reason. Don't take that away from me. Let me prove that I am the man you want, the man you need. Don't let your fear of the unknown stop you from having this. You're my second chance, Rumor. Don't take this away from me, damn it."

He spilled his guts and made broke my heart break a little. Not because I wasn't giving him a chance, because after a confession like that he deserved it, but because he told me more than he has told anyone. He has that level of trust in me.

"Fury, I'm willing to give this a chance. I've never been with someone on the wrong side of the law, and that scares me. What happens if you get caught? How long are your runs? Are there people that want you dead? What am I in for?"

"All of the above. Rumor, I wouldn't have entertained the idea of any of this had I not thought you were strong enough mentally and physically to handle me and all that I am. I'd have taken off on my bike while you and the others were at the club house if I thought you weren't up for this, and you would have never known how I felt. For fucks sake, I know it's scary and I get that. I expect you to have some reservations, but that's why you have to trust me. You can come talk to me any time about anything." He explained.

I believed him. There was a calmness and reassurance that he exuded at that moment and I knew he wasn't lying. This unexpected stranger has successfully put me back together and made my life make sense again.

I must have been smiling from ear to ear because he asked, "What seems to have you so happy?"

"You. Us. Here. Everything. You have just made my life whole again and you did it in my favorite spot in the world." I stopped and took in a breath before I finished my thought. "You know, I would come here so many times and watch the traffic below and wonder if that car or that truck was Creed. I thought he would come back for me at any time. I came here to remember, escape, and forget at the same time. I hope that I don't have to visit this place as often now."

He came closer to me and kissed me. It was just a simple peck, but it was immediately followed by, "Promise me."

"Promise you what?" I asked.

"Promise me you will tell me if you feel you need to come here. I'll do everything in my power to see that you don't end up here. You need a new favorite place, Rumor. This one is tainted."

"I think I can handle that." I agreed, sheepishly.

We turned back to the traffic under us and watched the world go by. Thoughts ran through my head at speeds I couldn't fathom. Random thoughts from business endeavors to hiding bodies were like bright flashes of light behind my eyes.

"What now?" He asked with worry in his voice.

"You. You're a lot to take on. The big picture just hit me. Specifically, your ability to hide a body and your moonshine operation. I am going to be in this now. This is going to take some time to sink in. I'm okay with it…I think, but I don't want to let you down. Have patience with me, yeah?"

"First, you won't always know about the ugly side of business. That's something that isn't discussed outside of the members. Secondly, I owe you all the time in the world. You were good enough to wait on me. Even after Creed made you wait for years, you chose to be patient with me. If you need some time to adjust, then you get all of it you need. I really think you are over thinking everything. We'll take it in stride. Let's just figure us out first, the rest will all work out. Stop worrying."

I smiled, tucked myself under his arm, and he pulled me in for a hug. I let the moment soak in. This was real. This was happening. I was going to be happy. I was going to be normal. Well, as normal as dating an outlaw can be.

"Let's go home, yeah?" I suggested.

"Home as in your home that you shared with Creed or home as in Charlie's place?"

"We should probably stay at Charlie's until we're sure the cops aren't coming snooping. I get to tell them that I saw him, but he wanted to reconcile our relationship, but I caught him with another woman and when confronted about it he disappeared again. I say we wait until the investigation dies down before we move in my house."

"Wait. What? We move in?" Fury asked in surprise.

"Um, eventually. That was too soon, huh? I didn't mean I was asking you to move in. I was saying it needed to be a while til' I moved back in there and I assume you will be over there some, too. I mean that's what normal people do." I shot him a smile.

"We can and will cross that bridge when we get there. That isn't something we need to focus on just yet. But Rumor, just for the record, I would do it in a heartbeat. Let's go." He was good at leaving me in some state of shock.

We traveled home in silence, the both of us absorbing the events of the evening. Upon arriving at Acres, before I could reach for the handle, a big, strong hand reached across my face and turned my head. There were those big hazel eyes I've grown to adore.

"Rumor, thank you. Thank you for taking a chance on me when you didn't have to. I don't know what I did to deserve this, but I'm glad the stars finally aligned for me, for us." He said and kissed me again. It was sweet. It was urgent. It was needy. It was perfection. Our tongues tangled for what seemed like forever before we broke apart.

As he gasped for oxygen, he put his forehead on mine and sweetly said, "This is right."

"Yes. It does feel different for sure."

"I wouldn't trade Daisy and our relationship for anything, but even as much as I loved her, what we had doesn't compare to this. I have never felt so…"

"So what, Fury."

"Free. It's like the truth finally set me free. Mind you, you're the only one that knows that truth, but I feel like a weight has been lifted off me. Lying to my brothers has been hard, but not as hard as it was lying to you. I feel like I can be the best president possible with that weight lifted. I can take on more club shit because the weight of that secret is gone. Because of you, I get to move on and put my past to bed forever."

Tears stung my eyes. My big, scary, moody biker was feeling things. I'm sure he would only show this sweet side to me and I was okay with that. I knew the real Fury. He would likely still be an asshole because that is what he had to become. He was just like any of the other guys, well, except for the thing we don't speak of. As far as I was concerned, Eric died. I wasn't falling in love with a dead person, I was falling hopelessly for Legend Morrow, aka Fury, and he was full of life.

"Fury, you bring me peace. I know how you feel."

A harsh look covered his face.

"What's the matter? Why are you so irritated?"

"I'm not, but I have a reputation to uphold." He smiled and winked at me as his face turned cold again.

The End

Epilogue

A FEW MONTHS HAD PASSED, and we were in the middle of fall. The leaves were vibrant shades of red, yellow, orange, and brown. As they fell to the ground in the front yard of Acres, I heard Fury discussing what I could only assume was a business deal. He was talking in code, a habit of his I had grown to live with.

"Yes, Dirt, I understand. I know shit happens and that's part of the business. It will get fixed and it will be right, I have no doubt. Yes, that's fine. We plan on coming to visit real soon. Yes, tell Dane and Kat and the rest of the Savage Angel's that we said hello. See ya."

"Fury, who was that?" I asked.

"No one you have met yet. It's business, don't worry." He pulled me close and kissed my lips.

"Is this business going to involve the restaurant?"

"Probably."

"Then tell me, please." I got irritated.

"I can't just yet. I will tell you when the time is right." He leaned in for a kiss and I dodged.

"No way, Jose." If you won't give me what I want, then two can play at that game. "I'm going to be late for work."

"Rumor, damn it. I said I would tell you when I could. Don't be mad."

"Oh, I'm not." I stomped off.

"Of course, you're not." I could practically hear his eyes roll.

I left Acres and headed to Wish You Were Beer. We were down to the inside now and needed to decorate. There were a few items for the kitchen that hadn't been delivered, but we were down to the fun stuff now. Charlie pulled up and came in to assist.

"Mornin' Glory." She announced as she be-bopped her way inside.

"Yeah," I snapped as I grabbed the paint and brush. I painted the walls in the women's bathroom. Charlie was so hellbent on colorful, so the walls were a turquoise color and were going to have song lyrics written on the walls in black. We decided on *I got that boom boom that all the boys chase and all the right junk in all the right places~ Meghan Trainor, Body like a backroad, drive it with my eyes closed~Sam Hunt, When all your mascara is going to waste, when things get ugly you just got to face that you can't cry pretty~Carrie Underwood,* and *Fat bottom girls you make the rockin' world go 'round~ Queen.*

We were going for a positive environment that the ladies would love. Jazz had pretty handwriting, so we had her draw on the wall and I painted over her handwriting.

The men's was all about beer. We went with songs about beer and broken hearts. *Don't think for a second I'm out to drown your memory baby you ain't worth the whiskey~ Cole Swindell, Ask any ol' barstool in this town that's my newfound party crowd~Jason Aldean, It's beer time~Justin Moore, There's only two things in the world I need to get close to and that's a big ole brew and little ole you~Mel McDaniels.*

The dining room had a plethora of song lyrics, movie quotes, and a few television quotes. Jazz was dead set on *He's her lobster~Phoebe* and *Joey doesn't share food~ Joey, PIVOT~Ross, How you doin'?~ Joey, We were on a break ~Ross, Whoop-ah!~Chandler, I got off the plane~ Rachael, SEVEN! Seven, seven seven seven seven! ~Monica, I'm full and yet I know if I stop eating this, I'll regret it~Chandler, I'll be there for you when the rain starts to fall, I'll be there for you 'cause you're there for me too. ~ The Rembrandts.* Her favorite show was *Friends,* clearly.

Charlie chose Aerosmith for her music lyrics and Sweet Home Alabama for her movie quotes. *I'm back. I'm back in the saddle again~ Aerosmith, You're my angel come and save me tonight~ Aerosmith, I don't want to close my eyes I don't want to fall asleep 'cause I'd miss you baby and I don't want to miss a thing~ Aerosmith, Dream on dream on dream on dream until your dreams come true~Aerosmith. What do you want to be married to me for anyhow? So I can kiss you anytime I want~ Sweet Home Alabama, You can't ride two horses with one ass sugar bean~ Sweet Home Alabama, The truth is I gave my heart away a long time ago, my whole heart, and I never really got it back. ~Sweet Home Alabama.*

I chose *Sons of Anarchy* quotes. *I accept that. ~Chucky, There's an old saying,'That what doesn't kill you, makes you stronger.' I don't believe that. I think the things that try to kill you make you angry and sad. Strength comes from the good things-your family, your friends, the satisfaction of hard work. Those are the things that'll keep you whole. Those are the things to hold on to when you're broken~Jax Teller, We don't know who we are until we are connected with someone else. We're just better human beings when we're with the person we're supposed to be with. ~Tara Knowles, I killed a fed for you. Nothing says endless love like capital murder~Jax Teller.* I chose one lyric.

Bury me in my boots and don't forget the whiskey light a cigarette girl lean on in and kiss me send me on my way with some black roses this is the path I've chosen and you can't go with me my hourglass was always half empty it was bound to be the bottle or the bullet that bit me So when I go baby you know just what to do…bury me in my boots~The Cadillac Three

"Hey, Charlie, what do you say we let the first week

of customers leave a quote they would like to see on the wall?" I asked, trying to get in a better mood.

"I think that's a great idea. It will make them feel like they are a part of the business. Good thinking. I think the guys need to give us some input. It is their business, too."

"Yeah, I guess."

"What's wrong?"

"Fury wouldn't tell me something this morning, and it pissed me off. I know it's club business or whatever, but I don't like it. It had to do with the restaurant, so since I quit my job to come help out here, I should get to know about things that happen in this business. Am I wrong?"

"Yes and no. Yes, because the club does business and they don't discuss it with anyone outside of members. That is just how it is. You eventually get past it. No because this is your business, and you did quit a reliable job to work here."

I went back to paining the quotes on the wall and got lost in my own thoughts. I know he wouldn't keep something from me on purpose. Perhaps I did jump the gun. I snapped out of my painting trance by the voice that had the power to melt me.

"Are you done being pissed yet?" Fury asked timidly, well, as timid as Fury could be.

"Maybe."

"So, no. Okay then. That means you won't interrupt when I say there is going to be a change of scenery for a bit."

My world stopped, and I knew he meant that he was leaving me.

"I knew it was too good to be true, and that you would hurt me just like they did."

"Rumor, stop…"

"Why? Why did you start this?"

"Rumor, are you done flipping out? I'm trying to tell you we are going to Australia to see the Grinders on tour. I've been talking to Dirt with the Savage Angels. He mentioned that the Grinders were on tour and it'd be a while before he could run a business endeavor by Dane. Then he said that he could get us backstage passes and the full VIP package. Damn, woman."

"Wait, what? You're coming back?"

"Yes. We are coming back."

He looked at me, "We're coming back and we'll have one a hell of a vacation while we are there."

"Whoa. We as in the club or we as in you and me?"

"Certain club members but most importantly, you and me."

I dropped my paint brush and stared at him for a minute with my mouth wide open.

"Pick your chin up, Rumor." He chided. "I had to make sure the deal was still going through before I got your hopes up. I had to make sure that Whiskey and Charlie and Briar and Jazz were good to come along."

"Who'll take care of things here? When do we leave? Is it hot there? I have to get a passport!" I started rambling.

"Rumor, chill out. We have time for all of this. We won't leave for a month or so. I wanted to get this place going good first. Magnum, Sax, and Riddick won't mind watching this place for us."

"Is Sax a member now?"

"All I can say is, things are in the works."

"Fury, I'm sorry I acted a fool earlier. I just hate secrets. I felt like I had a right to know since it involved the restaurant. I get that you wanted things finalized though."

"You suck at lying by the way. I could tell you were pissed by your stomp."

I giggled because I knew it was true.

"You think it's safe to move back to the house yet?"

"Well that was a swift change of subject." He caught me off guard.

"I need to talk to you about that. I have decided that I don't want to live there. I don't want any part of my old life. I want to sell it and build a new house. Charlie won't care if I stay at Acres until it's built."

"You're sure? I can rent it from you."

"Why? You'd be giving me money and staying with me. How many nights have you slept in your room at Acres since we became official? Hmm?"

"Fine, fair point. We can see if one of the boys wants to buy it, if you're okay with that."

"Sure. I'm not going back, so I don't care who has it. They can rent it or buy it. Whatever they want."

"I can't wait to show you Oz."

"I've always wanted to go there."

"Well, look at me making dreams come true."

Dedications

I dedicated this book to a special person. He was taken from us too soon and this is what I *wish* were the case for him. Unfortunately, it isn't. He really is gone and really did leave behind a child and girlfriend. Those of you that know this real story, will get how hard this book was for me to write and why I had to have it just so-so.

Special thanks to Bo. There are certain scenes in this book that I just couldn't write. Thank you for making that happen. Thank you for being an ear to listen and a brain to bounce ideas off of. I love you, Tonto.

Karessa, you have been a ride or die for so long now that I can't remember. I appreciate you and your feedback more than you know. Your beta reading is so beyond helpful. You, Bo, and April get the really rough versions and help me make them what they are now. Love you, mean it.

April, I don't really know where to start with you. Since high school you and I have been close. You get me.

Without your input in this book, I really feel like Fury would have been weak. Your opinion toughened him up some and made him rougher around the edges. He needed that. Thank you. I love you. Life might keep us from seeing each other or talking on a regular basis, but you are still my best friend.

You three girls are my biggest support and my closest friends. I am blessed beyond measure with your friendship. Thanks for putting up with me. I realize I am a handful.

Gale, your enthusiasm for my words blows my mind. Your input on the new scene solidified it for me. Thank you for everything…even not related to books.

C.G. Lee, thank you for answering question after question because I'm a forgetful soul and can't remember anything for more than a minute! I'd have had things real screwed up if not for you. Thank you.

Aaron, you are my rock and my biggest supporter. I couldn't do this without you. Your faith in me blows my mind. Thank you for supporting my dream. I do not deserve you.

Belinda, Debb, Samantha, and Robyn, you girls are the bees knees. I am so grateful that I was introduced to you. Thank you for agreeing to beta read for me and helping make this book the best it can be. I can't wait to see you in Oz again in March 2019.

Kathleen, I don't even have words for you. Your friendship leaves me speechless. You are always there for me, even across the ocean. Can't wait to see you again as well. It's been too long.

MariaLisa, thank you for just being you. I love the planner and it's been a huge help in my lack of organization. Thank you.

Emily, you bailed me out BIG TIME. I know now why my sister loves you so much. Thank you. That's all I can say. I'm proud to have you edit this book in a pinch and in such little time when things didn't pan out with my original editor. You are a lifesaver.

Readers, thanks for giving book two a chance. I hope you enjoyed Fury's story and get why it's so personal and took me so long to write. Without each and everyone of you this wouldn't be possible for me to do. Thank you.

Follow me at the following social media outlets:
Instagram: @harlowbrownauthor and you can enter #dontlookback as well.
Facebook: www.facebook.com/dontlookback16
Twitter: @Harlowbrown1
Email: harlowbrownauthor@gmail.com

~Don't Look Back~

Made in the USA
Coppell, TX
30 December 2021

70429754R00197